THE STONES SPEAK

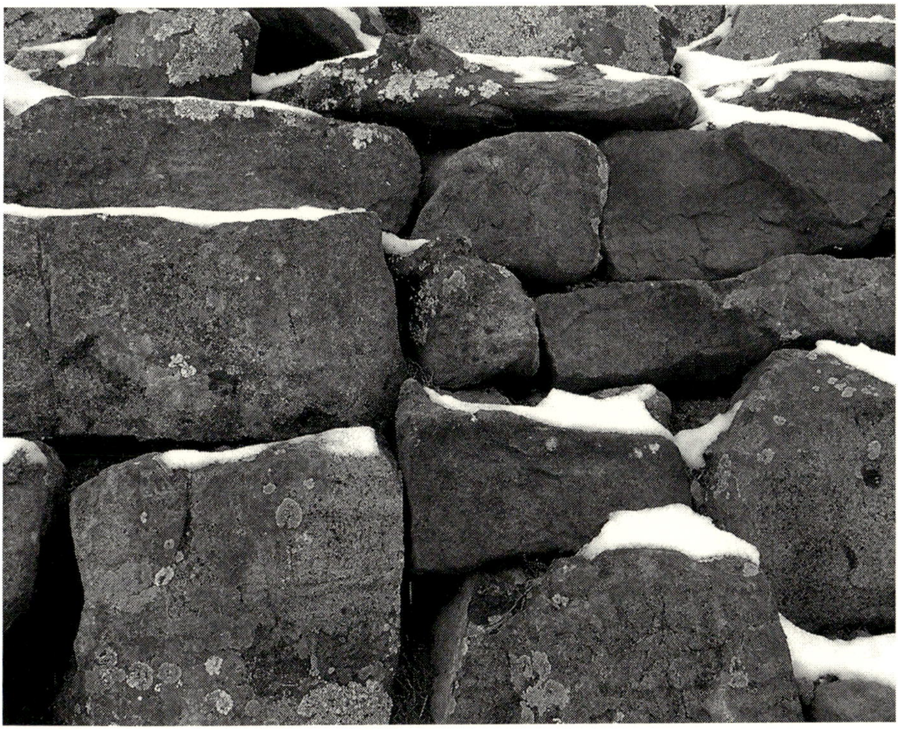

> This is perfect, gorgeous, and out of your very own sense of place and spirit. It gave me the chills!
>
> Claudia M. Reder
> author of *My Father and Miro*
> Brighthill Press

BOOKS BY NANCY KING

NOVELS

Morning Light
A Woman Walking

NONFICTION

Dancing With Wonder: Self-Discovery Through Stories
Playing Their Part: Language and Learning in the Classroom
Storymaking and Drama
Storymaking in Education and Therapy, co-written with Alida Gersie
A Movement Approach to Acting
Giving Form to Feeling
Theatre Movement

THE REVIEWERS SAY —

READING NEW MEXICO

FICTION BY AUTHOR

Morning Light by Nancy King
Tasora, ISBN 978-1-934690-17-8, $14.95

Nancy King puts this tale together like a jigsaw puzzle — flashes of memory, multiple points of view, immersing readers in the minds and hearts of people who influence the heroine Anna for good or bad. Anna's story reverses the old movie 'It's a Wonderful Life.' Instead of the main character realizing the influence she's had on others, she discovers how to thank others for their influences on her.

Nancy King strikes a balance between the darkness of abuse and major illness, and lightness of discovering life's unexpected joys. *Morning Light* is for readers who know the tough road to growth when coming of age.

Ms. King handles the craft of writing with style. Her shifts in character point of view work well . . . the blend of family stories, traditional tales, and fictional narrative make the book intriguing.

> The beauty of this book lies in its layered use of the healing power of story. Not only does Nancy King gift us with the courageous journey of Anna out of the vortex of abuse, but she nests stories within stories that lead to a victory both brave and hard won.
>   = Lisa Dale Norton, *Shimmering Images* and *Hawk Flies Above*

READING NEW MEXICO
FICTION BY AUTHOR

A Woman Walking by Nancy King
Tasora, ISBN 978-1-934690-16-1, $12.95

A *Woman Walking* is many folk tales within a folk tale. Ninan has inherited her grandfather's book of tales — and the responsibility to wander the world telling his stories. She cannot refuse this task for there is no one else in the family who has been given the gift of storytelling.

At first she rebels, questioning why she should be deprived of a normal life. She reluctantly begins her travels, but finds she cannot tell her grandfather's stories. She is compelled to tell the stories that come from within. She travels far and wide, stopping at villages and towns to tell her tales. Each time she stops, she makes friends and wonders again why she must spend her life alone. She asks herself again and again, "Is storytelling enough to fill my life? Will I never be able to put down roots and have a normal life?"

When Ninan meets a man who says he loves her and wants to spend his life traveling with her, she makes a decision that shows she accepts her own identity as a storyteller and a woman.

> We tell stories to make sense of our lives. Storytelling is not only a source of meaning but of survival. In Nancy King's mythic tale *A Woman Walking*, a young girl has to chose between staying home in an ordinary life and taking on the task of travel and storymaking. A bit of fairy tale, a bit of Ursula LeGuin, and the author's own vision bring these tales to life.
> = Miriam Sagan, *Gossip*, Tres Chicas Press,
>   and *Map of the Lost*, University of New Mexico Press

THE STONES SPEAK

Nancy King

Tasora

The Stones Speak © Nancy King 2009
1224 Vallecita Drive
Santa Fe, NM 87501
nanking1224@earthlink.net
www.nancykingstories.com

All rights reserved. No part of this book may be reproduced or transmitted in any form or by any means, electronic or mechanical, including photocopy, recording, e-publishing, print-on-demand, or any other information storage and retrieval system, except for photocopies or electronic files of no more than five pages, without prior permission in writing from the publisher.

Itasca Books
5120 Cedar Lake Road
Minneapolis, Minnesota 55416

Cover and first page photos by the author; author portrait by Kim Kurian; text photos by Douglas Bullis

ISBN 978-1-934690-18-5
LCCN 2001012345

Printed and bound in the United States.

For Andrew Adelman

and

Suzan Hall

"And the day came when the risk it took to remain tight inside the bud was more painful than the risk it took to blossom."

Anaïs Nin

1

It was 1959. Naomi had been teaching junior high school gym for a year, dreading the seemingly impossible task of trying to interest girls who despised everything about the class, from putting on their gym uniform, to learning sports they loathed, to having to take showers, dress, and put on makeup in less than five minutes. When she saw the ad in the local paper, she couldn't react quickly enough.

> *Looking for dancers who can learn folkdance patterns quickly. No salary, but travel in Europe with expenses and room and board provided.*

Naomi had been saving her money, and she could dance. Perfect—the way to see Europe, as she'd been longing to do, without having to travel alone. She immediately called the number in the paper but was so disconcerted by the sexy male voice on the other end of the line she couldn't think what to ask.

"Auditions on Saturday," he said. She said she'd come. He gave her the address.

Without thinking about possible consequences, she turned down the summer job she had worked so hard to get, and applied for a passport. Only after she mailed the letter did it occur to her that the folkdance man might not hire her. Then she'd be out of a job, luck, and money.

The place for the audition turned out to be an unimposing two-family house, which surprised her. She had imagined the audition would be held in a studio or commercial office. The furniture in the living room was moved to one side, the rug rolled up. The handsome man with the sexy voice greeted her at the door looking like an ad for Esquire. Eric's white shirtsleeves were rolled up to his elbows, and the buttons were opened far enough to reveal the blond hair on his chest. His blue eyes bored into her, checking her out as if she were a blind date rather than a prospective employee. Naomi felt overwhelmed and anxious, and excited.

"How many other people are coming to audition?" she asked.

"You're the last one," he said, his seductive voice as smooth as dark chocolate.

Naomi began to doubt the wisdom of applying for a job that meant traveling with a man she hardly knew. Never before had she acted so quickly and so rashly. Further unnerved when he asked if she had a boyfriend, she was so taken aback she lied. "Yes."

Only when he put on Israeli music did she begin to relax. He was a good dancer and it was easy to give herself up to the pleasure of moving with him. At first the dances were relatively easy. Always able to pick up steps pretty quickly, she began to enjoy herself. But then he switched to tricky Balkan music, with steps that were fast and complicated. Even though she managed to keep up, when the music ended she was sure she wasn't good enough for his troupe.

Eric told her she wasn't bad. As he talked, he kept looking her up and down. She almost told him she'd changed her mind. "How many languages do you speak?" he asked.

"I had three years of high school Spanish and two of French."

He laughed. "I can say boy, girl, forward, backward, stop, go, hello, and good-bye in all the languages we'll need. For the rest of the instruction, I just say 'people' and demonstrate what I want them to do. That works for folks in every country. I show the dancers what to do and then they follow our lead, doing the steps we do. By the way, you got a valid passport?"

"I just applied for one. So, how many of us are going?"

"Two. You and me. We're all I can afford. I'm leaving on Tuesday to teach at a conference. I'll meet you in Vienna, in the lobby of the Hotel Schott, on the twenty-fifth of June. You'll need to bring at least two circle skirts, some white blouses, and shoes to dance in that don't scuff wood floors."

Business finished, he put his arm around her, said good-bye, and ushered her out the door before she could ask any questions. As she walked to the bus stop, Naomi wondered how she was going to tell her parents she was about to spend the summer with a strange man, no matter that he was a folkdance teacher and it was a job. She could still feel the touch of his arm as it massaged her back.

Even after she finished teaching on the twenty-third of June and headed home to her parents and friends in New York City, she was still trying to figure out how to explain her sudden recklessness. Any thoughts about postponing the discussion were shattered when her mother gave her an application for a summer job at a school for delinquent children. Normally, this was the kind of job that would have interested Naomi. Not willing to lie, and not able to tell the truth, that she would be traveling with a strange man, she told her parents that she had taken a job teaching folkdance in Europe. She made it sound as if she would be part of a group. Forestalling all questions, she told them how excited she was to have the opportunity to travel in Europe, teach, and meet people rather than simply go as a tourist. She hoped her enthusiasm masked her anxiety.

The night she flew to Amsterdam there was a horrible storm that only increased her nervousness, especially when the soldier next to her kept muttering that he hoped the plane would crash. Naomi was so startled she asked why he wanted to die. "I'm from Alabama, Ma'am. Being stationed in Iceland is more cold and ice than I can bear." The conversation was so surreal she stopped worrying. After landing in Austria, she found the train to Vienna, crossed borders and time zones, and arrived at the hotel around ten in the morning, too tired to worry about how she would meet Eric, too exhausted to feel anything except the sheets of the bed.

She awoke a few hours later, still tired. Through the fog in her brain, she saw a man and a woman standing at the foot of her bed, their arms entwined. A male voice was chirping, "Wake up, Sunshine, time to rise and dance."

Naomi yelled in surprise. "What? How did you get into my room?"

Eric laughed. "Mona works here."

"What time is it?"

"Six-thirty. In exactly one hour and twenty-seven minutes we're expected to lead an evening session for Mona's folkdance group. Get up."

That was easier said than done. Her head ached and her brain kept asking, *Where am I?*

Even though she didn't speak German and didn't know the dances, a pasted-on smile, limp wrists that let the man do the leading, and feet that knew how to waltz got her through the evening without making a fool of herself. But when she looked at Eric and Mona, dancing as if they were one body, Naomi wondered why Eric had invited her to join him. She felt sure she was not a good enough dancer to be teaching anyone. Afterward, while sitting with them in a restaurant thick with smoke, flowing beer, and language she couldn't understand, the next ten weeks loomed large and difficult.

As people started to leave the restaurant, Eric gave Naomi directions to her hotel and then took off with Mona, holding her close to him. Naomi stood there, not sure if it was safe to walk the dozen blocks so late at night. She had remembered to take a card with the hotel's address and phone number in case she got lost, but who would she ask? In what language? Naomi felt abandoned. Not seeing any taxis, she began to walk, hoping she was going the right way.

Suddenly, a motorcycle roared to a stop beside her and a man she vaguely remembered from folkdancing asked in broken English, "Vant ride?" Naomi didn't like his looks but quickly decided that riding with him was the lesser of two evils. She showed him the hotel card. He nodded, helping her onto the seat. She reluctantly put her arms around his waist but all hesitation about holding on to him vanished as they zoomed off. She clutched his body as if they were lovers.

When they arrived at the hotel she held out her hand and said, "*Danke shein*," hoping it sounded like thank you in German. The man ignored her hand and hugged her. Naomi didn't respond and managed to free herself, thanking him again. When he followed her into the hotel, she felt afraid. At the elevator, when it was clear he intended to go with her to her room, she shook her head and said, "No." He ignored this and followed her into the elevator. She waited until the doors were almost closed, then rushed out and ran to the desk clerk, who was dozing in a chair. She hoped he understood English. "Excuse me, I need help."

The clerk stood up just as the motorcyclist came from behind and put his arms around Naomi. She tried to get away, but he held her too tightly. Not knowing how much English either man spoke, she said to the clerk, "I want to go to my room. I don't want this man to come with me. Help me!"

The clerk looked at the man, who was a head taller than he was, shrugged, and sat back down. Naomi wrenched herself away, ran into the elevator, and pushed the button to close the doors. They shut just as the man caught up with her. He banged on the doors, hard. Just to be safe, in case the other elevator arrived before she got to her room, Naomi pressed the button for the wrong floor and then walked down the stairs to her room. It was a long time before she felt safe enough to sleep.

The next morning she arrived at the train station early and narrowly avoided bumping into Eric, who was kissing the tears on Mona's face. When she saw Naomi, Mona pulled away from him and picked up her purse.

"Aren't you coming with us?" asked Naomi, trying to hide her embarrassment.

"No, I have to work," said Mona.

Eric looked at his watch and said to Naomi, "Let's get going; our seats aren't reserved." He reached for Mona, but she had moved away from him. Her eyes were focused on Naomi, who turned toward Eric, unable to bear the look of agony on Mona's face. Naomi picked up her suitcase, gratefied that she'd had the presence of mind to pack lightly, and walked slowly toward the ticket counter thinking that Eric would soon follow.

Instead, Eric shrugged, waved to Mona, and walked briskly to the information center, never looking to see if Naomi was following him. Naomi felt uncomfortable, beginning to sense that Eric expected her to pay attention to where he was and to act accordingly.

Shortly after the train started moving, he put his arm around her and pulled her to him. "I've been looking forward to being with you."

Naomi moved away. "What about you and Mona?"

"We're friends. Nothing special. Now how about you and me getting to know each other." When Naomi got up and sat down on the seat opposite him, he said, "You signed on to work with me, remember?" As the train lurched to a start, Eric grabbed her, holding her too tightly, forcing his tongue deep into her mouth.

Her mind said no. Her body said yes. Although Naomi responded, she felt disgusted with herself. When the conductor came in to check their tickets, she left and walked to the bathroom, promising herself she would set better boundaries. She wanted to teach folkdancing, not take the place of someone else's lover.

To save money spent on hotels, Eric convinced her to share a bedroom, telling her they would split any money left over from the courses after he had paid their expenses. All the rooms had twin beds, and she kept him away from her the first few nights by telling him she had her period, even though he was quick to say it didn't bother him. She was so busy fending him off that she didn't think to refuse when he asked for her passport so he could buy their tickets. When she asked for it back, numerous times after that, he always had a sensible-sounding reason to keep it.

Since they taught mostly at night, their days were free. Naomi had thought she'd be able to walk around the old towns, visit museums, and get a sense of each place, but Eric had other ideas. Claiming he didn't want her to get into trouble, he refused to let her out of his sight. He had no interest in museums and galleries, so every time Naomi tried to go, he found a way to stop her.

Naomi began to feel that she was Eric's prisoner. His notion of relationship, such as it was, had everything to do with her meeting his needs and nothing to do with what she wanted or needed. On their last night in Geneva he jumped into her bed and crashed on top of her. She fought him off as best she could, but he was strong and determined. Afterward, she felt like a whore who'd been paid too little to give too much. When she was sure he was asleep, she pushed him off of her, got up, and searched for her passport. Cold sweat poured down her face as she rummaged through his suitcase and camera bag and toilet kit. He had obviously taken pains to hide it. After not being able to find it she lay down in his bed, wondering how she was going to recover her passport and leave him.

During the summer before her senior year in college, Naomi had slept with her boyfriend of three years. Afterward, she wondered what all the fuss was about. They'd slept together a few more times before Naomi finally had the courage to ask him to take more time. He declared her frigid and broke off the relationship. Naomi considered herself sort of a virgin because she felt there had to be more to sex than what she'd experienced. Her encounter with Eric only deepened her worry that maybe her boyfriend had been right.

The next morning, when Eric came to the bed in which Naomi was sleeping, she leapt up, ran into the bathroom, and locked the door. In the shower she tried to figure out how to get away from him, but she didn't know their itinerary, he had her passport, and she didn't have much money. During breakfast he said, "I don't know what's bothering you, but figure it out fast. We're a team, remember?"

"What do you mean?" she asked, stunned.

"You don't think I asked you to come along for your dancing ability, do you?"

"Yes, I do" she said.

"Think again," he said with a sneer.

Naomi wondered how she could ever have found him attractive. Even worse, she couldn't imagine how she would survive being with him for two more months. From that point on, she watched and waited, letting him have what he wanted. The quicker it started, the sooner it ended. She searched the groups they taught, looking for possible allies, but his reputation preceded him. People flocked to his dance sessions—his voice as seductive with a hundred people as with one.

Her apparent surrender eased his watchfulness. One morning, at a railroad station in Italy, she noticed he was busy making last-minute arrangements, so she said in what she hoped was a casual tone of voice, "Why don't I buy the tickets to Rome? You've got enough to take care of."

Eric handed Naomi the money and their passports. She walked to the ticket counter trying to look relaxed, as if this day were no different from any other. After buying their tickets, she waited until their train was announced and then rushed back to join him. Eric was furious. "Where were you? The train's already here. We need to board right now."

"The line was really long. Let's put our stuff on and then I'll give you the tickets and passports." Naomi held her breath while he nodded, picked up his suitcase, and walked up the steps. Just as the train started to leave, Naomi threw him his passport and ticket and jumped off. Even as she watched the train disappear, she couldn't stop shaking. Though she had no idea where to go or what to do, her relief at being free of Eric was so great she couldn't worry about what to do next.

As she was trying to calm herself, an elderly nun spoke to her in Spanish, asking if Naomi could show her the platform for the train to Madrid. Naomi took this as a sign, exchanged her ticket for Rome to one to Barcelona, and helped the nun find her seat. It was only when she crossed the border into Spain that Naomi felt able to breathe. Yet before she had a chance to relax and feel free, she had her first confrontation with the Guardia Civil, Franco's personal police force.

The Guardia Civil were everywhere, rifles slung over their shoulders, checking suitcases for contraband. One man who tried to convince the soldiers that his hidden *Playboy* magazines were literature ended up being dragged away. The magazines, of course, were picked up by a grinning Guardia, who then dumped the contents of a woman's cosmetics bag on the floor. When they asked her what "this" was, she picked up her diaphragm, still in its case, and had the presence of mind to say, "It's for a skin condition." The Guardia shrugged, signaled for her to pick up her belongings, and turned their attention on Naomi.

"Do you declare anything?" She shook her head "no." Ignoring her protestations, they turned her suitcase upside down, but the blonde standing next to her distracted them so they let Naomi go. She gathered up her things and hurried out to the street.

2

As she left the train station, Naomi quickly realized that most people in Barcelona spoke Catalan, not a word of which she understood. But she was determined to find people with whom she could speak, not wanting her three years of high school Spanish to have been in vain. She managed to find her way to the housing office, where the clerk told Naomi she had to check in with the local police before she could choose a place to stay. The visit to the police station was unsettling. A stern uniformed officer warned her to be careful to avoid any contact with dangerous-looking persons, not bothering to identify who they were or what they might want. Naomi wondered why he was warning her. She was in Spain to relax and improve her Spanish.

After searching the list of available rooms, she finally chose an inexpensive *pension*. The landlady registered her, outlining the house rules and warning Naomi, in Spanish spoken slowly enough for her to understand, that if Señorita Rosen was not in the *pension* by eleven at night, she, Señora Vasquez, was required by law to notify the police, who would then find and arrest her. Even though Naomi sympathized with people who were trying to overthrow Franco, she had no intention of getting involved in Spanish politics.

While trying to escape from Eric, all Naomi could think about was regaining her freedom. Now she worried about money, having come to Europe with less than three hundred dollars, all her savings. She had thought it would be more than enough, given Eric's promise to cover living expenses. But when she left him she had eight weeks until her flight home, a long time to live on so little money. She briefly considered changing her ticket and going home earlier, but she didn't want to admit she'd made a mistake, nor did she want to give up the opportunity to see Europe, the main reason she'd signed on with Eric.

Naomi sat on the bed in her small room, the slanted ceiling making it seem even smaller, yet the coziness felt comforting. She didn't want to deal with her rising fears about traveling in high season with so little money and no reservations, knowing no one, and having no idea how to travel in a foreign country, especially if she didn't understand the language. How was she going to manage for eight weeks?

After unpacking her bags she realized she was hungry, so she put a pension card in her pocket and left to find a restaurant that fit her budget. Even though the peso had been devalued, the restaurants she passed were too expensive. About to give up and find a store to buy bread and cheese, she heard laughter and saw young people who looked like students eating on a large patio outside a restaurant. There was no menu posted, but she figured if they could afford to eat there so could she. Although the long line gave her a chance to decide what she wanted to eat, when it was her turn to order she couldn't remember the words and settled for food she could point to. She gave the cashier a bill and put the change in her purse without bothering to count it, not wanting to hold up people in the line.

Walking with her tray, she looked for an empty table but the place was crowded and there didn't seem to be any open seats. The noise and confusion was so unsettling she was about to dump her tray in the nearest garbage can when she heard a friendly male voice. A young, well-built man with dark hair, bright eyes, and a welcoming grin was standing, beckoning her to come to his table. Naomi knew enough Spanish to know he'd said something like, "Miss, come here. Sit, please." She felt comforted by his using the familiar *tú* rather than the polite *ustéd*. Naomi hesitated, not sure she wanted to sit with four strange men, but when he pulled out a chair for her and introduced himself, she couldn't resist, took a chance, and sat down. Pablo said his name slowly enough for her to understand, but she lost the names of his friends in a blur of language.

She introduced herself in Spanish, the first time she had tried to have a casual conversation, pleased that the men seemed to understand what she was saying. Suddenly, just as she had begun to relax and enjoy her food and the company of the men, there was a cacophony of shouting and screaming. Four members of the Guardia Civil were barreling toward Naomi and the men, guns aimed at them.

Pablo exchanged quick looks with his friends, then with an urgency that defied resistance, grabbed Naomi's arm and pulled her out of the restaurant, down a busy side street, into a warren of old houses, through alleys, and into a wooded area, continuing to run even after the shouts of the Guardia had died down and then faded out. Naomi was out of breath and tried to slow down, but Pablo put his arm around her waist and practically carried her. By this time it was dark and she had no idea where she was, who these men were, where they were going, or why they had forced her to come with them.

The wooded area was hilly, and even the men had to slow down to maneuver around rocks, underbrush, and tree stumps. Suddenly they stopped. Two of the men pulled branches and rocks away from what looked like the mouth of a cave. Naomi became even more terrified, refusing to enter a cave with four strange males. Ignoring her, the three men lit matches and disappeared into the blackness. Pablo stayed with Naomi until she was breathing more normally, then steered her toward light from a candle on a makeshift table surrounded by benches where the men were seated around the table, in high spirits, passing around a wineskin. The arc of red liquid defied gravity, landing neatly in their mouths. When Naomi was persuaded to copy the way they drank, all she did was stain the front of her blouse. The bright red looked like blood and she started to shiver. Terrified, she barraged them with questions in English since her Spanish had disappeared, but none of them understood a word she said.

Naomi didn't know what time it was, but she was sure it was past eleven, the time when she had repeatedly been warned to be in her lodgings or suffer the consequences. She tried to tell Pablo in baby Spanish that she needed to go, that the police would arrest her if she didn't get in by curfew, but he kept shaking his head. "*No! No es possible.*"

Too scared to remain in the cave, she ran toward its entrance. Pablo followed and grabbed her, speaking words she didn't understand in such a caring, worried voice that she gave up. The three other men looked relieved when they saw her, but asked no questions. They seemed too drunk to care about anything. At some point during the night Naomi fell asleep with her head on her hands, leaning on the hard wood of the table. When she felt herself being gently lifted up and laid down on something soft, she was too exhausted to care about anything.

She woke up disoriented, rumpled, and dirty, surprised to feel Pablo lying next to her, his arm wrapped around her body, and even more surprised to notice how protected and safe she felt. As soon as she moved he woke up, smiled, and spoke in a soft, loving voice. All Naomi understood was "Good morning, Miss." The rest was just soothing sounds. He patted her shoulder, perhaps for reassurance, but she found herself turning to him, leaning against his body, enjoying his strength. The other men were still asleep, snoring contentedly. It seemed this was not the first night they had spent here.

Pablo and Naomi lay next to each other, his hand gently stroking her back. She felt herself relax, snuggling against his body, Pablo's gentleness a sharp contrast to Eric's predatory demands. Pablo talked to her in Spanish, which sounded almost like music. Something unexpected and out of character drew her to him. Naomi felt loved and cared for. Her boyfriend had been wrong. She was not frigid. She had also been wrong. Having sex was not the same as making love.

When Pablo stood up and stretched, Naomi couldn't help admiring his body. She was so embarrassed to be caught in the act she closed her eyes for a second. When she looked again, Pablo was gone. Her terror returned.

She was no longer frightened of the men but she didn't know what to do. How would she find her way to her lodgings? What could she tell her landlady? What if the police arrested her? She was a Jew in a Catholic country, a woman in the midst of patriarchy, adamantly opposed to the Franco regime, though too scared to say or do anything against the rules. All her life Naomi had been a "good" girl, taking care not to disobey any regulations or laws. Now, with no intent on her part, she seemed to be an outlaw with no protection.

She washed her face in a bucket of water, keeping her lips tightly closed, not wanting to think about what might be in it or who had used it before her. At least the water helped clear the fog in her brain while she sat on a bench trying to think about what to do next. When the men woke up they nodded to her and then, one by one, they left. Part of her said she needed to leave, and the other part trusted that Pablo would return. After a long wait and furious arguments between her two parts, a young woman appeared, a feminine version of Pablo. Much to Naomi's relief, she spoke English.

"I am Nina. My brother asks me to say thank you." Naomi noticed her smile was exactly the same as Pablo's. "He sends his apologies to you for what happened yesterday but he did not have the words to explain. He hopes you are not angry with him for bringing you to this place. He hopes you are not upset with his taking care of you." Nina wrinkled her nose in disgust, making it clear she did not approve of the smells and the mess. "He also said to tell you that you are a brave, wonderful woman and he longs to be with you again. As soon as possible."

Naomi blushed. Nina laughed, then turned serious. "I have asked a friend to go with you to your lodgings to explain everything to your landlady. You will need to look ill. Act as if you are in pain, perhaps a terrible hurting in your head. Can you do this?"

Naomi nodded, yet she knew she wasn't ready to confront her landlady on an empty stomach. "Is there any way we could stop first for coffee and something to eat? I'm really hungry."

"Of course." Nina's dark eyes closed and she shook her head. "Allow me to express my sorrow that I did not think of this." She looked disapprovingly around the cave at the empty wine bottles. "Men!" Naomi giggled. Nina grinned.

The sunlight hurt Naomi's eyes, but it was good to breathe fresh air after the dankness of the cave. Nina took Naomi to a tiny café tucked between two large buildings, camouflaged by a false front that made it look like a store that sold women's lingerie. A group of men and a woman were talking intently, but when the two women entered they stopped abruptly. Nina nodded to them, but they continued to stare at Naomi as Nina led her to a table hidden by draped fabric. Without asking what Naomi wanted to eat, Nina ordered breakfast. The food smelled and tasted so good that Naomi gobbled it down. Only after her second cup of coffee did she feel ready to ask what had happened and why the men had dragged her with them.

Nina glanced at the group, whose conversation was now whispered. Before speaking, she drank her coffee slowly, as if thinking about what she wanted to say. With a seriousness that made Naomi shiver, Nina said, "It is not good for you to know about us, just in case . . . My brother and his friends are wanted by the Guardia. They knew the Guardia saw you sitting with them, talking. My brother was afraid that if they left you alone, the Guardia would think you were part of our movement and arrest you. Even if you protested your innocence, the Guardia would never believe you. In this country, women do not eat or talk with men they do not know."

"But I'm an American, on vacation. I don't even speak much Spanish."

"That is of no importance to them. If you are with people they consider to be subversive, you are subversive. End of story. Believe me, by the time they finish with you, you agree to say whatever they want. That is why my brother would not leave you."

To quell her rising panic, Naomi changed the subject. "How is it you speak such good English?"

"I studied medicine for two years in your country, but my visa was revoked by my government. Your government refused to grant me asylum."

Naomi sighed. "What happened to your studies?"

Nina shrugged. "I am alive. There are worse things than losing one's dream."

"Are you also wanted by the Guardia?" Naomi had been planning to spend a month in Spain, but now she was wondering if she should leave the country and go straight to Portugal.

"No questions, please, it is safer that way." Nina looked at her watch. "We must go. The woman is waiting to take you. She will do the talking. Remember, you do not understand what she says. Act as if you are still sick."

Naomi guessed it wasn't safe for Nina to take her, but the loss of a woman with whom she could talk made her feel like she was being abandoned. "At least tell me what she's going to tell the landlady, just in case."

"Manuela lives near the restaurant. She will say she is passing by and sees you crumpled on the sidewalk. She asks you what is wrong. You tell her you are sick from eating bad food in the student restaurant. When she sees you are too sick to go to your lodgings, she takes you home with her."

"But what if the landlady asks about my running away from the Guardia with Pablo and his friends?"

"I do not think she will know about this. But if she does, cry. Say you were minding your own business when a bunch of hooligans grabbed you. You felt ill and got away from them as soon as you could. The rest of the story is the same. But it is always best to say as little as possible. That way you do not have to remember details that are easy to forget. The Guardia forget nothing."

"Will I see you and Pablo again?"

Nina grinned. "If my brother has his way, the answer is most definitely yes. How long do you plan to stay in Barcelona?"

"I thought about a week, but now I'm not so sure."

"After a good night's sleep this will all seem like a bad dream. There is much to enjoy here, in spite of Franco. Practice your Spanish. My brother yearns to talk with you. He has a lot to tell you."

Naomi noticed that Nina never called her brother by name and wondered why. Too embarrassed to say how much she wanted to see Pablo again or to ask how she might meet with him, she simply said, "Thank you. I know it's dangerous to help me. I . . ."

Suddenly a tall woman with graying hair and large tortoiseshell glasses appeared. Manuela nodded to Nina, looked at Naomi, and then, before Naomi knew how or where she went, Nina disappeared. Apparently she and her brother were masters of the art of invisibility. Maybe that was why they were still alive and free.

Although her English wasn't as good as Nina's, there was no mistaking what Manuela said or the importance of following her directions. "I find you on street. You sick. No talk. I call taxi. Bring you to my house. In morning you still sick. I take you to your lodgings. You want to sleep. You hope landlady will bring you tea and toast. Understand?"

Naomi understood. She didn't have to pretend. By the time they got to her pension, her stomach hurt, her head ached, and she felt she would throw up any minute. Her landlady took one look at Naomi and murmured, "Pobrecita." Naomi could not understand any of the conversation between the landlady and Manuela. After Manuela left, the landlady helped Naomi to her room, and even before the door closed she collapsed on the bed and passed out, only to be assaulted by nightmare images of an army of furious, gun-toting males chasing her into black caves with no way out.

It was dark when Naomi felt someone nudging her. "Señorita, your friend is here." Naomi was afraid to ask if it was a man or a woman. She knew three people in Barcelona and only one, Manuela, was free to visit.

Pushing away her fears, she spoke with more bravura than she felt. "Tell my friend I need to take a bath and change my clothes. I'll be ready in about half an hour."

"But Señorita, he is waiting for you." The words filled Naomi with terror. Now she was sure it was no one she knew, yet she craved a wash so badly she decided whoever it was would have to wait. "I'm sorry, I need to bathe. Please tell him that I'll be ready in half an hour." Naomi walked to the bathroom and turned on the tap despite the landlady following, anxiously trying her best to convince Naomi that she didn't need to wash. Naomi couldn't stand feeling dirty for another moment. When she started to undress, the landlady left her to her terror.

A few minutes later the landlady was back, knocking on the door too insistently to ignore. She shouted, "Señorita, please hurry, he is waiting."

Naomi knew there was no way she could not go downstairs, so she yelled through the closed door, "Sí. Sí, I am coming."

She dressed and walked down the three flights of stairs as slowly as she could, wishing she knew who it was and what he wanted. She saw only one man in the small lobby, a tall, heavy-set man with a dark mustache, wearing a shiny navy blue suit, white shirt, and navy tie. He was pacing back and forth.

Naomi wasn't ready to hear her landlady say, "Ah, Señorita, you are here. Bueno." The landlady spoke to the man in Spanish, too rapidly for Naomi to follow, but his smile did nothing to allay her anxiety.

"Buenas tardes, Señorita," he said, extending his hand.

Naomi decided it was safer to speak English. "Good evening, Mr. . . . ?"

"Nevarez, Enrique Nevarez."

"I'm sorry to have kept you waiting, Mr. Nevarez. What do you want?"

"I am happy to meet you," he said in heavily accented English.

"Why are you here?" she asked, hoping whatever he said was true, thinking that no matter what he said it wouldn't be.

"I am a friend of Pablo."

The hair on the back of Naomi's neck stood up, but she forced herself to speak in an innocent voice. "Pablo? Who is he?"

The smile on Mr. Nevarez' face hardened. "Señorita, do not play games with me. You were seen last night holding hands with Pablo Muñoz, a wanted criminal. For your sake, I advise you to tell the truth."

Anger replaced fear. "The truth is I don't know who you're talking about. I ate at a student restaurant because it's cheap. It was crowded and there were no empty tables. A man invited me to sit in a chair next to him. All of a sudden there was a lot of yelling and one of the men grabbed my hand and pulled me as he ran. I struggled and finally got free of him. They kept running. That's all I know."

"Not quite. You did not return here until this morning. Why not?"

"I guess the food at the student restaurant was bad. After I ate I felt sick. I collapsed in the street. A woman found me and was kind enough to take me home with her because I was too ill to go anywhere. This morning I felt a bit better and was able to travel. She offered to bring me here since I still felt unwell and don't know my way around the city."

"And what is this woman's name?"

"Manuela."

"Her last name?"

"I don't know."

"Her address?"

"I don't know."

"Very convenient, your memory."

His tone of voice irritated Naomi. "It has nothing to do with memory. I didn't ask. But Manuela spoke to the landlady. Perhaps she knows her last name and address."

"This illness of yours seems to have happened rather suddenly. According to your story you were not ill when you sat down at a table with four strange men. Nor were you ill when you ran off with them."

"I began to feel ill while eating, but when the man grabbed me, I struggled to free myself. When I did, I collapsed. Who knows what would have happened if Manuela had not been so kind." The man's stare frightened her, but Naomi pretended to feel irate. "I've told you all I know. Now if you'll excuse me, I need to go upstairs and lie down. I still feel sick."

"You will please come with me. The police want to question you."

"For what? I've done nothing wrong."

"That is what you say. We decide if this is true."

He followed Naomi upstairs while she got a shawl, waited outside the bathroom door, and then gripped her arm as he led her outside to a waiting car, black with shaded windows. Naomi couldn't stop shivering. Her imagination was working overtime.

They rode in silence to a large, square building on the outskirts of the city. He helped her out of the car, gripping her arm so she couldn't run, and led her into a small, windowless room, where he left her without a word. She stood for a long time, waiting, staring at the desk and chair and telephone and overhead light bulb, afraid to sit in the chair. Her fear increased when the door opened and a tall, gaunt man dressed in an immaculate uniform entered the room and sat down. Ignoring Naomi, he opened a notebook and began reading.

"Excuse me but I need to use the toilet," she said.

The man took no notice. Naomi was so desperate that she walked to the door and tried to open it, but it was locked.

"I need to use the toilet," she repeated, unable to remember the word for toilet in Spanish, something she'd practiced enough times to have remembered it automatically.

He answered in rapid Spanish and then went back to reading. Naomi's fear spoke for her. "I don't speak Spanish. I don't know why I'm here. I don't know who you are. I need to use the toilet. I'm an American citizen and I've done nothing wrong. I have a right to contact the American Embassy." The man kept on reading. Naomi wondered how much longer she could hold in the urge to pee. At least thinking about it kept her larger fears at bay. When a woman, dressed in a similar uniform, wearing a skirt instead of pants, unlocked the door and beckoned Naomi to follow, Naomi hoped she'd come to lead her to a toilet.

After the interrogation Naomi was summarily deported, given less than an hour to pack before being taken to the airport. On the plane en route to the United States, Naomi's seatmate asked about her trip. Naomi hesitated. "Fine. Tell me about yours."

When she arrived home, Naomi felt broken, unable to call her parents or Sam. Instead, she sent them notes saying she was well and was busy getting ready for the new school year. Systematically, she broke off contact with friends and saw her family so sporadically, she would have missed her mother's funeral had she not noticed her mother's photograph in the obituary section of the newspaper. The more Naomi closed herself off from people, the less able she was to reach out and make friends.

Even fifteen years later, Naomi still refused to allow herself to think about what had happened to her in Spain after being taken to the police station. Feelings of powerlessness and helplessness continued to plague her, no matter that she eventually succeeded in getting a PhD, a university teaching position, and becoming a tenured professor. To keep her thoughts focused on the present, she gave herself to her work and was rewarded for her efforts by having books and articles published regularly, as well as being invited to conferences to present papers, some only peripherally related to her primary expertise—language acquisition and literacy.

At first, when Naomi opened the letter inviting her to be one of the main speakers at a conference on children's development in third world countries sponsored by the American Anthropological Association, she was tempted to throw it away. Though she'd worked with many groups of children in the United States whose lives resembled those in third world countries, she knew her colleagues. They were not given to considering ideas from academics whose expertise was different from theirs. Besides, she had a book contract and the deadline was fast approaching.

Naomi might have tossed the letter into the garbage without a second thought had it not been for Emily, the Director of Multidisciplinary Studies, the woman to whom Naomi reported. They were walking to a meeting when Emily stopped and asked, "By the way, did you receive an invitation to speak at the Anthropological Association annual meeting?"

Surprised, Naomi asked, "Yes, how did you know?"

"Bob Nelson, the Chair of the conference, is a friend of mine. I've been telling him about your work and we both thought you'd give an interesting and challenging presentation. He's the sort of man who likes to shake things up—give people different ways to look at issues."

"So I guess that means you'd like me to accept?" asked Naomi, hoping Emily would say, "It's up to you."

"Yes, I would. It's good advertising for us, and with funding tight and getting tighter we can use all the positive attention we can find." Naomi's sigh was more audible than she realized. Emily laughed. "You can do it. Just start talking about the children you've been working with on the literacy project and you'll have them hooked."

"They're anthropologists. What do they care about kids from inner city Boston?" protested Naomi.

"Make them care. That's your job."

3

Naomi walked into the conference ballroom, sighing as she looked at the sea of men in dark suits relieved by an occasional bright tie. When she noticed the woman, in clothing so bright, so different from the men's, she burst out laughing and threaded her way across the room, ignoring the men who made comments as she passed their tables.

"Thank goodness, another woman. I'm Naomi Rosen."

"Priscilla Jordan. Very pleased to meet you. Why don't you put your jacket on the chair next to mine and claim it. Nice not to be the only woman in the room."

"Where are you from?" asked Naomi, unable to stop looking at what Priscilla was wearing—the deep coral tiered skirt and matching blouse, the many rings, the turquoise necklace, earrings, and bracelet.

"Santa Fe. Home of women who aren't afraid to dress like women, no matter what—or where." She grinned.

Naomi couldn't help comparing Priscilla's look to her own, her long gray skirt, white blouse, and soft gray jacket. At least they were both wearing black boots. "Sounds like an interesting place."

"It is, in more ways than one."

"Tell me about it," asked Naomi, out of politeness rather than interest. She loved her job and community back east and had no intention of moving anywhere, ever. She had even taken a dislike to traveling—too much discombobulation for too little pleasure.

Just then a voice boomed, "Gentlemen . . . and ladies, please take your seats. The program is about to begin."

"No time for a long talk now. How about meeting for breakfast tomorrow?" suggested Priscilla as they sat down.

"Sounds good. The hotel coffee shop at seven?"

"That's a bit early for me. Let's make it eight-thirty. Never know what the night will bring." Priscilla winked at Naomi.

Naomi gave her a quizzical look but said nothing.

Later, over dinner, the two women laughed as they took note of their obvious differences. Naomi, short with dark hair, had just celebrated her fiftieth birthday while Priscilla, tall and blonde, was turning forty.

"You married?" asked Priscilla.

"Nope. I've sworn off marriage. Two disasters are more than enough. Besides, between teaching and writing, my life is pretty full." She wasn't about to tell Priscilla that in spite of her effort not to want a man in her life, something in her continued to yearn for one who would love her in ways that felt safe and nourishing, someone she could feel free to love in return.

"How about you?"

"I'm a widow. My husband died in an accident just before my thirtieth birthday."

"Oh. I'm so sorry."

"Well, it was a shock, but even though our marriage was happy enough, I decided that living alone was better than being half of a couple. I never forgot the time when Franz wanted to go to Italy and I wanted to go to Bolivia. We ended up in Italy. I suppose I thought I should follow my husband since he was older and more experienced, but I resented going. Soon after Franz died I was invited to participate in an international dig in Peru and discovered that making professional decisions without having to consult a husband opened up a world of possibilities." Her blue eyes sparkled mischievously. "Since then there've been more than a few men in my life, but each time I come close to making a commitment, I remember how easy it is to come and go when you don't have to justify leaving. Sooner or later the man and I decide to go our separate ways."

Even as the two women talked, Naomi noticed that the men at the table continued to eye Priscilla, who smiled in return. She was more curious than envious, wondering how Priscilla managed to exude so much sexual energy with no obvious effort. There was one awkward moment, when Priscilla said, "You seem to have such love and energy for teaching children, how many of your own do you have?"

Flustered, Naomi managed to say, "Uh . . . none."

Priscilla teased. "You don't sound very sure. Now me, I've had two abortions, so if you'd asked me I would have said, "Two, sort of."

Over the years, Naomi had learned to change the subject seamlessly when the talk grew uncomfortable. "I noticed that you're interested in the education of children and the way women transmit their history and culture to the next generation. Tell me about your current research."

At breakfast the next morning the two women exchanged home addresses and phone numbers, each wanting the friendship to continue. Priscilla's research, which in part explored the role of childhood in various cultures, was of interest to Naomi, whose work included helping at-risk children find their voices and express their feelings through the stories they told and wrote.

Back in her office, the week after the conference, Naomi got a phone call from Tamara, the secretary to the director of the Multidisciplinary Studies Program. "Emily wants to see you. Do you have a few minutes?"

No matter how successful she became, Naomi felt a flicker of fear every time someone in authority asked to see her. "Sure. You know what it's about?"

"No, she just asked me to call you."

"Okay, I'll be right there."

Naomi walked downstairs slowly, thinking back over her interactions with students and faculty since she had last talked with Emily. Her annual review was coming up in two weeks, and even though Naomi tried to stifle it, her anxiety had been growing exponentially. She stopped mid-stair, wondering. Surely her recent confrontation with the assistant director couldn't be the reason the director wanted to see her. Caitlin, young and ambitious, had taken a dislike to Naomi the moment they met, and nothing Naomi tried changed that dynamic. Their last encounter was particularly unpleasant.

When Naomi had walked into the Office of Student Affairs, Caitlin hadn't waited for Naomi to say hello, nor had she bothered to hide the hostility in her voice. "I understand you want to do a program for first year students in the honors dorm."

"Yes, the program committee invited me. I just need to check with you that the space is available. They'll take care of setup, refreshments, and publicity," said Naomi, politely. She had learned to ignore Caitlin's tone of voice.

"I'm sorry, it's booked."

"You haven't even looked at reservations," said Naomi, trying to keep her fury tamped down, her voice impassive.

"I know the students' calendar of events. It's not available."

"They were told it was available," insisted Naomi.

"I told you, it's booked."

Naomi knew she needed to confront Caitlin, yet she dreaded doing so. Already her stomach hurt. Taking a deep breath, she said, "I'm sure you know that I'm entitled to see the room reservation book." She tried to keep a pleasant expression on her face.

Caitlin gave her a murderous look, got out the book, and pretended to look. "I guess I made a mistake. Seems the room is available after all."

"Good, I'll just sign the room reservation section so the students can be sure they have the space they need."

Without a word, Caitlin turned her back and picked up the phone. Naomi signed her name and left, wondering if there would be repercussions. There usually were.

The door to Emily's office was open—a good sign. Emily was pacing the floor in front of her desk—a bad sign. Forcing herself to sound cheerful, Naomi smiled and asked, "What's up?"

"What do you want first, the good news or the . . . not so good?"

"Your choice."

"Caitlin's filed a grievance against you. Says you abused her."

"What? That's impossible. I've never been anything but cordial to her."

Emily sighed. "You know it and I know it." She pointed to two chairs and said, "We need to talk. Sit down."

"I can't," said Naomi. "My mind's racing too fast for me to catch up to it. How do I disprove something that didn't happen?"

"Apparently she's referring to an incident concerning a room reservation, but she says in her complaint that this is just one of many incidents where you abused your power over her."

"Hah! If anyone has power, it's her. She's in charge of student affairs. Professors have to go to her to make arrangements for trips, and if she says no, it's no. She's always been jealous of me because I began teaching here with an MA and she couldn't. When I got my PhD, as you remember, she refused to come to the faculty celebration . . . Oh, never mind, what's the good news?"

"Her complaint was thrown out by the Committee on Faculty Grievance. They pointed out there was no evidence, except what she said had happened, and she couldn't provide anyone who had witnessed your supposed maltreatment of her. I told the committee I thought her complaint had to do with personal feelings rather than professional interaction and that it had no basis in reality."

Naomi sat down. "Why didn't you start with the good news?"

"It's a warning. You need to be extremely careful when you deal with her. Caitlin reports to me so I can monitor her actions, but her husband has friends in the administration, who have friends in the administration . . . Fortunately, you have a splendid professional record, there's no history of difficulty with any staff or faculty, and your teaching evaluations are excellent. Still, she's the sort of person who'll try to dig up anything she can to discredit you. Is there anything in your past I should know about?"

Naomi grew noticeably pale as she shook her head. Emily decided to note Naomi's tension but not inquire. If there was something troubling, it couldn't have anything to do with her teaching or writing. Naomi's personal life was her business.

The friendship that Naomi and Priscilla had begun at that first conference continued to develop, and despite their geographic separation, they managed to stay in touch, sharing their lives as professional women. For more than fifteen years, they talked regularly on the phone, met when Priscilla was on the East Coast, or got together at conferences.

Naomi enjoyed increasing professional success. She published two books, wrote articles that were accepted by refereed journals, and received a good number of invitations to speak, not only at universities but also at social service agencies that dealt with battered women and children.

Her personal life was another matter. Despite the rigors of her career, she could never keep herself busy enough to fill the hole in her heart. Occasional encounters and brief relationships with men only made it larger.

When she opened the letter and read its contents, Naomi immediately called Priscilla. "Pris, you'll never guess what happened. I've gotten an invitation to spend my sabbatical in California. All I have to do is teach one seminar for graduate students the first semester. The second semester I'm free to do research. They're even giving me an apartment and a living allowance."

"That's great. Now you can come see me for a change. All these years, you've never been to Santa Fe."

"Too much open space. It's intimidating."

"You'll get used to it."

"What are you talking about?" Naomi poured herself a glass of wine, prepared for a long conversation.

Priscilla's voice was filled with the excitement. "I'm going on a dig for a couple of months and it would be great if you would come house-sit for me in Santa Fe, even for part of the time. I hate to leave the house empty, and besides it would give us a chance to have an uninterrupted visit."

"Sounds enticing. Let me think about it."

"Stop thinking and start acting. Just say yes."

Naomi laughed. When Priscilla wanted something, watch out.

"What's so special about this time? You've gone on digs before and—"

"I know," she interrupted. "It's just that this time you're on sabbatical. You can come without worrying about having to teach."

Priscilla didn't mention the phone call from her younger brother. She was ten when her mother died, old enough, her minister father said, to do the cooking. He'd hire a woman to do the cleaning and the shopping. They'd get along without a woman in the house. Pa set the rules. Her older brother, George, let her know he was boss. Richard, five years younger than Priscilla, let her know he was the baby and hadn't asked to be born. She'd had the wherewithal to find a university that offered her a scholarship to study anthropology, far away from the South Dakota hills. Thankful for the opportunities, she studied hard, seldom partied, and felt rewarded when she received a research fellowship to Harvard. She never went back, not even for her father's funeral. Instead, she sent flowers and a note saying she was out of the country on an anthropological dig.

Richard, now in his mid-forties, had never outgrown his need to be taken care of by his big sister. "Priscilla," he whined on the phone, "you're going away for two months. I'm out of a job. Why can't I stay at your place? I could use a little sisterly support. Besides, my asthma's getting worse and the doctor says I need to get out of LA." His tone set Priscilla's teeth on edge.

"The last time I let you stay, you forgot to take out the garbage and lock all the doors when you left. I don't—"

"I already apologized. Why do you keep bringing up the same old stuff every time? What about forgiveness? Pa always said—"

"Richard, in case you've forgotten, this is my house and my life. I pay the bills and I get to choose who stays here. Besides," she lied, "I already have someone lined up." She had hung up gritting her teeth, grateful she no longer had men in her life who felt they had the right to tell her what she had to do.

Naomi's call felt like a godsend. "C'mon, Naomi, say you'll come and stay in my house. I'd love to show you Santa Fe. It's the 'Land of Enchantment,' you know." In all the time Priscilla had known her, Naomi had never made a rash decision or taken a risk, yet Priscilla persisted. "It would be great if you could come. You'll have peace and quiet so you can finish the book you're writing. Besides, Santa Fe's a strange town, who knows what might happen?" Then, afraid she'd said the wrong thing, she added, "I'm only teasing. It's just a place. You make of it what you will."

The idea was intriguing to Naomi. It would give her a chance to catch her breath and prepare for fall classes without interruption, and it meant an inexpensive vacation in a place she had never been. The muted colors of the desert could be a welcome change after years of living amidst the lush brilliance of East Coast color in the spring and fall. But it was the thought of living close to mountains that made her decide to go, despite her worries about the immensity of space and Priscilla's remark that Santa Fe was "strange."

As the plane neared the Albuquerque airport, Naomi stared at the landscape, the mountains rising from the desert floor, the river cutting its way through the flat land—irrigating trees, the only green amidst the brown terrain. For an instant she felt her old fear of being a stranger, knowing no one except Priscilla. Still, the muted colors of the desert felt soothing and welcoming.

Naomi's rental car, though small, had four-wheel drive at Priscilla's insistence. "You never know when you'll have to navigate muddy roads. In this town, the higher priced the home, the less likely the road will be paved." Naomi wasn't used to driving seventy-five miles an hour, and she had to force herself to keep her eyes on the road. The stark, beautiful landscape and enormous brilliant blue sky demanded attention.

She arrived at Priscilla's house in Santa Fe just before dark, in time to enjoy a scrumptious dinner of green chiles rellenos on the patio. Naomi drank more than her usual one glass of wine, but she still had enough wit to deflect Priscilla's probing questions about her adventures before becoming a professor.

Noticing how often Priscilla stared at the sky during their conversation, Naomi asked her to talk about the stars shining above them. Priscilla, who had thought seriously about being a cosmologist before choosing to be an anthropologist, loved looking at the stars and eagerly shared her knowledge of the cosmos. Naomi listened to Priscilla's story of the constellation Orion with the rapt attention of a youngster hearing a bedtime story.

As a child, Priscilla had escaped her unhappy environment and her brothers' prying eyes by sneaking outdoors at night, wrapping herself in a blanket, and gazing at the stars. The small telescope she'd bought with baby-sitting money gave her a sense of possibility, of limitless space. Years later, when Franz asked her to marry him, it was his passion for astronomy that helped her overcome deep-seated fears of commitment. The hours they spent telling each other stories about the stars and planets convinced her they could live together. His Argentinean culture had different names and ways to explain constellations, which added to Priscilla's pleasure in astronomy. It also stimulated her desire to understand the differences in stories that people in various cultures told about the stars and planets and their effects on human life.

After Priscilla finished telling the story of Orion, she became thoughtful, lost in memory.

"Where are you?" asked Naomi.

"I was thinking about my marriage to Franz. Our first shared purchase was a telescope. Our first argument was who would use it first. The best gift I ever got was the powerful telescope he gave me for our fifth wedding anniversary."

"Are you still using it?" asked Naomi.

"You've been looking through it," said Priscilla.

The next morning, when Naomi offered to help her get ready for her trip, Priscilla declined. Naomi watched with a feeling close to awe as her friend packed the car as precisely as she had played Mozart minuets on her flute the night before. The way I pack my life, thought Naomi wryly. Maybe that's why we get along so well. Shaking her head to rid herself of worries about being alone in a new place without teaching to keep her busy, she made coffee, whipped up a batch of biscuits, and set the table for breakfast.

"I haven't got time to eat," protested Priscilla.

"If you don't eat something, you'll be in no shape to meet Juan. From what you've told me, he can go forever, with or without food. Who wants to make love with a growling stomach?"

"Naomi!" Priscilla's tone was a mixture of outrage and amusement.

"What?"

"Juan and I are just meeting for coffee before I leave for Peru."

"Methinks thou dost protest too much," said Naomi, leering as she put a basket of biscuits on the table.

"Methinks thou dost know me too well," grumbled Priscilla.

"Be careful, I just took them out of the oven." Naomi gave Priscilla a wicked grin. "On the other hand, eating them hot might be good practice for being with Juan."

Priscilla threw a biscuit at Naomi.

A few days after Priscilla left, Naomi answered a knock on the door. The woman who stood before her had a lacquered hairdo, expensive clothes, and a deep voice. "Oh, I'm sorry to bother you. Has Priscilla left?" Naomi nodded. "I'm Alicia, a friend and her realtor. I'm going to be looking at some houses that just came on the market and I was hoping she'd come with me." The woman laughed. "Priscilla says she's not interested, but she keeps asking if I've seen anything unusual."

"Sounds just like her, always searching for the extraordinary. I guess that's why she's so good at what she does." Naomi stood in the doorway, not knowing whether to invite Alicia in or say good-bye.

"Say, why don't you come with me? It's fun looking at houses, seeing what the owners have done. I've got five on my list for today. Who knows, you might even find a house you can't bear to leave."

"Me? I love my home and job back east. There's not a house in the world that could make me give all that up. Besides, I intend to teach until my memory goes."

"This is Santa Fe. You never know what's going to happen."

Looking at houses just for the fun of it was something Naomi had never done. When she and her first husband bought their house, they had looked at only two, so pressed for time and money they had to focus on finding one that was affordable and move in as quickly as possible. With her second husband, she'd agreed to move into his house—and regretted it the moment she unpacked her suitcases, trying to fit her clothing into the too-small chest of drawers.

But now I'm on vacation, she thought. Work can wait a little while.

As Naomi got into Alicia's huge BMW she was impressed by its elegant interior. As Alicia drove, pointing out aspects of the landscape, Naomi noticed that the bumps and ruts that felt like boulders and canyons in her rental car now seemed like nothing. The muted colors of the gold-green chamisa plants scattered everywhere, the purple and orange wildflowers that dotted the roadsides, the soft pinks, greens, and browns of the rocks, were so different from the landscape back east that Naomi could not stop staring. She was lost in thought when Alicia drove up in front of a sprawling adobe that looked uncared for, as desolate as Naomi too often felt.

"I can't believe they're asking three-quarters of a million for this," commented Alicia. "Just because it's within walking distance of the Plaza." Alicia's frown deepened as she jiggled the lock, straining to open the heavy door. A thick layer of dust covered every surface. The abundance of mouse droppings indicated that the house wasn't exactly empty.

"If this house costs three-quarters of a million, it's a good thing I'm not thinking about moving here. Not on my salary," said Naomi as they walked through the diminutive, putrid yellow rooms, made smaller by low ceilings. The house smelled moldy, exuding depression. She couldn't imagine what anyone could do to revitalize it.

"Let's get out of here," muttered Alicia. "This place is giving me the creeps."

"Me, too," said Naomi. "How do the owners expect to sell a house like this? Even if they gave it to me, I wouldn't want it. It needs a huge dose of Prozac."

As they left the house, Naomi felt herself becoming depressed. "So, where are the houses you said were so interesting?"

"Coming right up, I hope," said Alicia with a laugh. "By the way, there's a house that just came on the market two days ago and the owners have agreed to let me take a look. Do you mind? It won't take much time, and the other houses on the list are close enough so they won't take long to get to."

Naomi shrugged. "What's one more house? Besides, I'm only looking."

It seemed they had just gotten into the car when Alicia drove up a short, steep driveway and stopped. Naomi's heart began to beat so wildly when she saw the house that she wondered if she was suffering from delayed altitude sickness. Forcing herself to breathe deeply, she got out of the car and followed Alicia up a winding path to the house. The walls had no edges, only soft curves that invited the eye to follow and explore. Naomi had never seen such a house. Mesmerized, she walked up the stone path to the front door. Caressing the stucco wall warmed by the sun, she almost didn't hear the homeowner's invitation to come in.

While the well-dressed elderly couple chatted with Alicia at the door, Naomi kept staring at the house. Unable to move until Alicia gave her a friendly shove, she walked in, amazed. The light filtering through the rounded windows was extraordinary. Whatever architect designed the house must have had a great sense of possibility and imagination, she thought. Where most people saw straight lines, this architect had imagined gentle curves. The staircase rounded its way up to the second floor where the kitchen, dining room, and living room fit together like a puzzle, with no competition for space. The only jarring note was the décor. Dark, heavy upholstered chairs and couches fought for attention with ornately framed paintings covering most of the apricot walls. Naomi imagined off-white walls, sparsely furnished rooms, the large weavings she loved to make providing color and focus.

I need to live in this house, she thought.

Ridiculous, she told herself.

"What's the asking price?" she asked Alicia, trying to keep her voice neutral. Alicia gave her a sheet of specs. Naomi gulped. The asking price was more than twice what she thought she could afford, if she were looking. She tried to dismiss the idea of living in this house of light, but the worm of desire had wriggled its way into her imagination and refused to let go.

"Actually, for this area it's a fair price," Alicia said, noticing Naomi's shock. "I doubt it will last a week given the demand for houses so close to downtown, especially one that's so unusual."

Naomi ran her fingers over a curved wall in the living room, imagining large numbers of pillows snuggled against the wall. Even over decorated, the house felt so good she was not ready to leave when Alicia headed for the door.

She wanted this house.

She coveted it with an intensity that stunned her.

She couldn't bear the thought of someone else living in it.

The next three houses were a blur. One looked like a bordello, not that Naomi had ever been in one, with mirrors everywhere. What kind of person puts mirrors on the kitchen ceiling? The second had no vegetation, and the wind practically swept Naomi off her feet. The third, elegant inside and out, was located on a street with designer houses too big for their tiny lots. The last one was so filled with the stench of cigarettes that Naomi could not even go in to look at the house. As they walked to

Alicia's SUV, Naomi tuned out Alicia's explanation as to why each house was interesting. Suddenly very tired, Naomi was relieved when Alicia asked if she would mind stopping at her office before driving Naomi home. "I'll just be a minute," said Alicia. "I need to check my list for showings tomorrow. Make yourself comfortable."

Naomi walked right through the tastefully decorated waiting room, following Alicia into her office. "I want to buy the curved house," she said, feeling like someone else was speaking. Even as a familiar inner voice reminded her how much she enjoyed her job and community, another voice, one she'd never heard before, urged her to feel the warmth of the Southwest sun and the vastness of the blue sky, and to acknowledge her love of the mountains, to re-create herself and leave the misery of her distant past behind. If New Mexico really was the Land of Enchantment, maybe its magic could help her bury her past forever.

"Are you sure? Do you want to look at it again? I don't think the owners will mind. Priscilla will never forgive me if she thought I'd bewitched you into buying something you didn't really want," said Alicia, hiding her bafflement behind a well-practiced realtor's facade.

"I'm ready to buy it. What do I do?"

Naomi made an offer of slightly less than the asking price. Alicia figured out the details and Naomi signed all the papers with barely a glance. It was as if she had entered a parallel universe where a previously unknown part of her had taken over. She had never felt so calm or clear.

"I'm going to ask the owners to give us an answer before ten tomorrow morning. I just know the house isn't going to last long in this market," said Alicia as she dialed the number. Looking at the pleased expression on Naomi's face, she said, "It's not over yet. They have to agree to your offer, there has to be an inspection, the mortgage has to be approved . . ."

All Naomi could think was: I want it.

Driving back to Priscilla's house, astounded by the sudden change in her life, Naomi imagined living in the house, basking in the sun-drenched light. She was filled with a quiet joy she could not ever remember feeling.

The next morning, certain that the owners would accept her offer, Naomi called Emily, to tell her about the house and her plans to leave the university. After a shocked silence, Emily's questions came at Naomi with gale force. "You're doing what? You're leaving? I thought you loved your work? Do you know anyone in Santa Fe? What about your house here? Didn't you just remodel the kitchen and put in a new heating system? What about the literacy program, which took you how many years to get going? All the students who've signed up. Who's going to run it?"

"I've fallen in love with this house," said Naomi.

"But you're a full professor, with tenure, designing your own courses and programs. How can you just give it up? Naomi, I've known you more than twenty years. You're a sensible, practical woman. You never make rash decisions. Are you in trouble?" Emily's voice deepened, taking on a confidential tone. "Is it a legal problem? Do you want me to ask Richard to recommend a good lawyer out there? I know how expensive houses are in Santa Fe. Are you sure you want to take on such a big debt at this stage of your life?"

Naomi bristled at the thought she was too old to change her life. "I can't explain what happened. All I know is that after I saw the house I wanted to live in it. If the owners accept my offer, I'll consider it an affirmation. Out here I keep hearing people say, 'If it happens, it's meant to be.' When the owners accept my offer, I'll know I'm supposed to be buying the house."

Emily snorted. "Just because they live in *wu-wu* land doesn't mean you can. Think about what you're giving up."

"I know it sounds weird, but I've never felt more clear."

Emily's voice took on its usual, comforting tone. "Well, it's possible the owners won't accept your offer. You're sure nothing is wrong? You're not running away from something? You can tell me. I'll help if I can."

Naomi shivered, not wanting to think about how long she'd been running away. "What do you mean?"

"Call me as soon as they've rejected your offer and you've come to your senses. I need to know when you're coming back so we can implement the new literacy program. By the way, Dr. Mackintosh at the juvenile detention agency just called to ask if you had time to start a writing program for incarcerated teens. He feels your way of working with those young people could make a big difference in their rehabilitation."

Feeling slightly guilty, Naomi hung up the phone. She stared out the window at the sunset, awed by the ever-changing palate of orange, pink, yellow, gold, and purple.

When the phone rang Naomi danced to answer it, certain that it was Alicia calling to say the owners had accepted her offer. "I'm sorry," said the realtor, "they've already had two offers for more than the asking price. We'll find something else you'll like."

It's my house. They can't sell it to anyone else. "Have they accepted an offer?"

"Not that I know of. But you don't want to make a counteroffer, do you? Getting into a bidding war with people who have deep pockets could get pretty expensive. What about the house on Camino del Sol? You liked it, didn't you?"

"I want the curved house."

Alicia sounded like an adult trying to soothe an upset child. "Look, you didn't even know that house existed before I showed it to you. You'll find another house. People always do."

Naomi's anger surged. She didn't enjoy being patronized, nor could she explain why it wasn't about finding a house, it was about living in that house, with the curves and the light and the welcoming feel.

"What do you want to do, if anything?" asked Alicia.

"I'll call you back in a little while," said Naomi, her mind racing, going nowhere.

"Look, Naomi, I've been selling real estate for over twenty years. Interesting houses come on the market all the time. Your not getting this house isn't the end of the world."

Yes it is.

Suddenly the landscape that had felt so soothing seemed less friendly. Despite the warmth of the day, Naomi could not stop shivering. Priscilla's house, which only minutes before had felt spacious and welcoming, now seemed small and alien.

She grabbed the car keys and left. Driving without knowing where she was going, she found herself in front of the curved house. She sat in the car trying to marshal her thoughts, but there were too many. Taking a deep breath, she got out of the car, walked briskly up the stone path, and rang the bell, suddenly remembering she didn't know the owners' names.

The woman opened the door, looking puzzled, "Do I know you? Oh, are you the woman who came by with Alicia yesterday?"

"Yes. I was wondering if I could talk with you."

"About what?"

"Well . . . I know you have offers for your house that are more than mine, but I really want your house. I'm ready to quit my job at the university and leave the community I've been living in for years. Please, can we talk?"

"Who's at the door, dear?"

"It's the woman who came by with Alicia yesterday."

"What does she want?"

"She wants to buy our house."

The husband came to the door slowly, a tall, painfully thin, gray-haired man leaning heavily on a cane. "Didn't Alicia tell you? We've received two offers that are more than our asking price. We were just talking about which one to accept."

"Yes, that's why I'm here. I can't make a higher bid. Even the offer I made is more than I can afford, but I thought that maybe we could work out something." She looked at the husband, pleading with her eyes. "I'm expecting a large grant in a few months. When I get it I could give you some additional money."

"How do you know you'll get the grant?" he asked.

"What's the grant for?" she asked.

"Could I invite you to join me for a cup of coffee, or tea? Maybe we could make an agreement," said Naomi, so nervous her voice was barely louder than a whisper.

"Dear, that's what we have realtors for. To work out contracts, so we don't have to be involved," said the man.

"I know." Naomi took a chance. She looked directly at the woman. "Alicia told me how much you love this house. Do the people who've offered more than the asking price love the house? Do they want to live in it, like I do, or will they just use it for vacations, maybe a few weeks each year?"

The man put his arm around his wife's waist, ignoring the intensity of Naomi's plea. "I'm sure you'll find another place you love just as much, maybe more. After all, it's only a house."

Naomi thought she saw sympathy in the woman's eyes. "Ma'am, I'm a single woman, a professor. I'm not known for making quick decisions, but the minute I saw this house I felt something I can't explain. Please, couldn't we work something out? I might be able to sell my house back east for more money than I think. Please!"

The woman turned to her husband. "Harold, she sounds like me. Can't we at least talk?" Without waiting for his response, she invited Naomi in. She followed the couple as they laboriously made their way up the stairs, trying to think what she could say to persuade them to sell her the house. As they sat in the dining room, the phone rang. She prayed it was not another offer for more than the other two. It was.

"Lillian," the husband said, "we now have three offers that are higher than the one this young woman made." He stood up with difficulty and said to Naomi, "Please excuse me but I need to take a nap." His wife helped him lie down on a couch in the living room and covered him with an afghan.

When the woman returned, Naomi spoke quickly, "I know it sounds crazy, a house is just a house but . . ."

The woman seemed lost in thought, staring at a photo of a bride and groom. "When Harold and I were first married, I had a chance to participate in a pilot project helping pregnant women in a Mexican village learn about nutrition and health care. It was only for six weeks and I was really excited about the opportunity to go someplace new and help people. But when I told Harold, he said no. He didn't want his wife traipsing around, as he put it, in some godforsaken place with no running water or electricity. He said I owed it to our future children not to put myself in danger or impair my health. I was young and in love, so I didn't go."

The woman looked out at the piñon trees covering the hillside. "It's hard to want something and not have the power to make it happen."

"Your house is too expensive for me if I think about it just in terms of numbers, but it feels as if my life depends on my living here. Please, please accept my offer. I'll do whatever I can to make it up to you."

The woman looked at Naomi, intently studying her face. Naomi met her gaze, hoping the woman believed her. The woman stood up and walked across the room to check on her husband who was sleeping. Naomi anxiously waited for the woman to return. She came back with a wistful look on her face. "I find it hard to believe that Harold and I have been married fifty-two years. Most of the time we've been happy, but sometimes he loses sight of what's important, at least to me. I'm going to accept your offer. He might be upset, but he'll come round. He loves me."

Naomi tried to hug the woman but she moved away. "I don't want to move, but Harold's health is getting worse and we need to find a one-story house. He knows how much this house means to me. Your loving it feels comforting, like I'm not just abandoning it to the highest bidder."

"You're welcome to visit anytime you like," said Naomi. "I'll pick you up and drive you here whenever you want. If ever—"

"I think you better go, dear. I'm rather tired." A flash of worry crossed Naomi's face. "Don't worry. I'll call your realtor, and mine," added the woman. "It might take a few days to get everything straightened out, but I'll make sure you get to buy the house."

Word spread quickly. The barrage of questions from friends and colleagues, whose opinions and platitudes were meant to "bring you to your senses," did nothing to change Naomi's mind. Instead, each time she heard another bit of "good advice," Naomi imagined running her hand over the softly rounded walls and felt an inchoate sense of pleasure. Perhaps she was bewitched, as some people suggested, or living in a dream world, as others thought. What she knew was that after seeing the house she never had a second's doubt or hesitation. The moment she made the offer, something within her had shifted and opened. She hoped she was ready for whatever might happen.

After the phone call from Alicia, telling her in an astonished voice that the owners had changed their mind and agreed to her offer, Naomi stood in the kitchen staring into space, unable to take in how much her life had changed. An old song ran through her mind. "What a difference a day makes . . ."

Still shaky, she called Emily to say she would be leaving the university after fulfilling her sabbatical obligations. Emily's stunned silence did nothing to disturb Naomi's feeling that her life had changed according to a plan she had not conceived. She thought of Pascal: "The heart has reasons reason cannot know." She wished Priscilla were in the country so she could talk with her. They had never lived close enough to see each other regularly. Would this move affect their friendship? Naomi dismissed the worry. They'd been good friends. They would remain good friends.

She made herself a cup of tea and took it out to the patio, settling into a comfortable lounge chair to enjoy the shadows of the sun playing hide-and-seek with the mountains. She felt strangely protected and cherished, until she smelled fire and saw black smoke rising from a nearby field. She jumped up in alarm, knocking over the cup, barely registering the sound as it crashed on the flagstones. The smell of smoke took her back to another fire, long ago.

She was about five years old and had been sleeping soundly. The hands shaking her and the voice urging her to wake up were so frightening she hid under the covers, pulling them tightly around her body, wanting to be left alone. With even more urgency, the hands grabbed and the voice shouted, "There's a fire. We have to get out of here." Still half asleep, she fought to stay in bed, but she was picked up and rushed out of the apartment house wearing only her nightgown. In the darkness of night the fire lit up the sky, too bright and too hot to bear. Yet shivering with fear, all she could think of was her cold feet. She wished she were wearing her slippers. She wished someone would hold her. She wished she were still sleeping in her bed

Discomfited by the memory, Naomi ran into Priscilla's house, called the non-emergency police line, and reported the fire. Quickly closing the windows and doors, she stood transfixed, like a moth pulled to light, watching flames shoot into the air, billowing black smoke obscuring the landscape that had recently seemed so magical. She marveled at how quickly life could change.

4

Preparations for the move across the country had been long and difficult. Sorting the too-many books she had acquired after decades of living and teaching meant looking at each one before deciding whether to take it or give it away. Even though she had kept only the books she loved, donating more than sixty cartons to libraries and colleagues, boxes of books piled to the ceiling now filled her new study. Having to close down her university office and go through eight file cases of papers and projects containing the heart and soul of her life with students resulted in a sometimes uncomfortable revisiting of her past. Naomi arbitrarily decided to take just three cartons of material, yet the selection process took months. Equally difficult were the questions her colleagues asked: "Who will you be if you're no longer a professor?" "What will you do if you're not teaching?" "What's it like to be making a whole new life for yourself at your age?" "How will you meet people?" "Is a house worth all this upheaval?"

Just before moving to Santa Fe, she'd had dinner with Sam, her oldest friend, who asked his usual searching questions: "Are you sure you're moving because you want to live in that house, or is there something else going on? Are you in trouble?" When Naomi assured him that she was fine, that she'd fallen in love with the house and was looking forward to creating a new life for herself, he gave her a hug and said, "Okay, leave me a message when you've arrived and I'll call you."

Like always. "Remember when we first met?"

"Yeah, the only two Jewish kids in our first grade class. Remember how mad our teacher was when all the Irish Catholic kids went off to religious school on Wednesday afternoons and she had to stay because of us?"

"I don't know what I would have done if you hadn't made jokes about her. The way she looked at me was scary. I still remember her disapproval."

"Maybe she would have liked us better if we'd been Irish Catholic. Then she could have gone home early."

"Sam, you were always my friend—even beating up the boys who stuck my blonde braids in the inkwells. As it was, when I got home my mother would joke about my remarkable ability to grow green hair." Naomi raised her glass of wine to toast Sam. "Here's to you. When I was teased about getting the highest mark in composition, you defended me. Even more impressive, you allowed me to ride on the handrails of your bike to go to the subway and then came with me to Manhattan to go to ballet performances you didn't really like." Naomi closed her eyes, lost in memory.

"What are you thinking about, Nomi?" asked Sam.

"I remember when your family moved away after we finished sixth grade. I came home crying and I told my mother, 'I've lost my best friend.'" Sam shook his head. "Yeah, it didn't help when your mother told you, 'You shouldn't be friends with a boy. What about the girls in your class?'"

"I never could explain to my mother why the girls in my class didn't seem to like me. I just felt comfortable with you."

"Well, I felt the same way you did, only with me it was my father asking why I hung out with you instead of the boys."

"You've always known when I was in trouble. Remember when I came home after the first day of seventh grade, in a new school, and you called and asked, 'What's your new school like?'"

"Yeah, you said, 'It's okay,' and then I knew it was horrible."

"You even asked, 'What does that mean?'"

"Didn't do me much good. You said it was like being blue in a green world."

"That was the best I could do," said Naomi. "Even now it seems apt."

"So, are you ready for the movers?" asked Sam.

"I guess. They're more worried about my loom than anything else.

When the packers came, they kept looking at the loom, wondering what to do about it."

"What did they decide?"

"They're going to wrap it in some kind of clingy paper that's supposed to protect the weaving and prevent anything from coming apart."

Sam raised his glass. "Here's to you, Nomi. May the things that come apart lead to new discoveries."

"Is that a blessing or a curse?" asked Naomi.

"I guess it's whatever you make of it."

"I'll miss you, Sam."

"Same here, but that's what telephones are for."

In Santa Fe, before the movers left, they insisted that Naomi check her loom to make sure it had survived the trip without damage. She unwrapped the packing material. "It's fine," she said, and the men helped her place it against the wall.

"How do you do it?" asked one of the movers, a stocky man in his late twenties.

"I'll show you, " she said. Sitting on her stool, using her fingers and a fork, Naomi wove deep red yarn back and forth, moving in a slow, soothing rhythm that never failed to center her.

"It must take you forever to make a piece," said the second, a grizzled older man.

"I'm not in a hurry."

"Well?" asked Sam. Even on the telephone his voice felt welcoming.

"The loom and I have arrived with all our parts intact. There are boxes everywhere. Just looking at them makes me tired."

"So don't look. Take a walk. I'll call you tomorrow."

Naomi hung up, thinking about how she and Sam were as close as if they were brother and sister. Although they continued to see each other frequently as they grew older, their early relationship seemed to set the

59

tone, and neither of them sought to change it into something romantic.

Naomi didn't want to think about the four years when she had disappeared from his life, returning only when she saw his father's obituary in the paper. Acting on impulse, she'd gone to the funeral, staying in the back. When the service was over, he confronted her. "Where the hell have you been?"

"In hell, but I'm back," she'd quipped. "Can I help with the reception?"

Later, when he tried to get her to talk about what had happened, she finally told him, "Sam, it's something I can't talk about, at least not yet."

"When you're ready, will you tell me?"

Naomi had nodded, but the time never came.

Ignoring piles of boxes and furniture still not in their right places, Naomi walked up the road in front of her house, marveling at the brilliance of the blue sky, admiring the variety of adobe houses, each managing to look unique in spite of the commonality of their design. She came home feeling energized.

When the phone rang, she knew it was Sam.

"Did you take a walk?" he asked.

"Yes. You were right. It cleared my head."

"How's it going?" he asked.

"I'm inundated by boxes, and most of the furniture is in the wrong place, but other than that, everything's fine."

"How does it feel to be there?"

"I can't quite believe the house is mine."

"Any second thoughts?"

"None, but I'm wondering what kind of person I am to just up and leave where I've lived and worked for so many years without the slightest regret or worry about what's going to happen. Weird, eh?"

"Maybe not. Moving to Santa Fe gives you a chance to be known as you are, not as you were. I'm kind of envious."

"So come. Bring Rebecca. I have a guest room."

"Yeah, well, I'll talk with her about it."

"Something wrong, Sam?"

"I think so, but I don't know what. Anyway, I have to go. Call me anytime."

"Same here."

Days later, even after Naomi had unpacked most of the boxes, placed her furniture where she wanted it, and hung her weavings, she walked around the house reminding herself that it was hers, that no husband or lover would walk in and, horrified at the way she had taken over, ask her to leave. She needed to do something to make it her own, but what that was, she didn't know. She wished she could call Priscilla and ask her for ideas—an anthropologist ought to know something about house ownership rituals—but she wasn't due back for another four days.

Naomi sat on the rug in her study, drinking a cup of black tea, thinking about the difficulties of having packed up her house and office. She arranged the move so that she could meet the movers when they arrived and spend the first night in her house. Priscilla had offered to let Naomi stay in her house while she was off on the dig, but Naomi didn't want to impose, not that Priscilla had even hinted that this would be an imposition. Naomi needed to manage on her own. She'd been relieved that the university hadn't insisted she fulfill her sabbatical obligation by making her stay another year. Emily had tried her best to persuade her to do this, but Naomi had finally convinced her there was no point in her starting a new program when there was currently no person to take it over when she left.

Tired of dealing with boxes and mess, Naomi walked down to the Plaza, the heart of downtown Santa Fe, only a mile and a half from her house. The walk in the sun felt good after being inside. Naomi had been told that all she had to do was follow Washington Avenue and she'd arrive at the Plaza, so she walked with confidence, excited about being part of Santa Fe. A large tree-lined square with a bandstand and areas of grass filled with mostly young people milling around, talking, smoking, and playing badly tuned guitars, the Plaza seemed like a scene from the sixties. In the center of the Plaza was a monument, a memorial to soldiers killed in battles against Indians. Naomi read the inscription and was shocked. She knew that Santa Fe was a city of three cultures—Native American, Spanish, and Anglo, and she wasn't naïve enough to think that the city was a cultural paradise where everyone got along, but a monument in the middle of the town square to commemorate soldiers who had killed Native Americans in their quest to colonize Santa Fe seemed in bad taste, as well as historically suspicious. Naomi thought about an African novel she'd read where the mother says to her daughter, "Until the lion learns to speak, the tale is told by the hunter." She couldn't help thinking there should be a memorial honoring the Native Americans who suffered all manner of atrocities by U.S. soldiers and settlers who expropriated land and resources that didn't belong to them.

Had she moved to the wrong place? Maybe falling in love with a house wasn't reason enough to change her life. Surprised by her anger, she walked toward the Palace of the Governors, unable to stop thinking about the unfairness of history always being told and commemorated by winners and conquerors. Despite the number of people meandering around, Naomi suddenly felt lonely, keenly aware that she knew no one in Santa Fe except Priscilla, who spent as much time away on digs as she did at home. If she were with me now, thought Naomi, in less time than it takes to blink, Priscilla would find ten interesting people to talk to. Naomi wondered how she was going to make friends in Santa Fe given her shyness and discomfort meeting new people, especially in groups.

Naomi stopped when she came to the Palace of the Governors. This historic building with a block-long portal sheltered Native American craftspeople who sat on blankets, their jewelry, pottery, figurines, and sculpture arrayed on the pavement on colorful cloths. Tourists sauntered by looking at the offerings, asking prices, trying on rings, matching earrings with necklaces, while the artists sat watching.

Naomi was walking slowly, taking in the scene, when she spotted a silver ring with a long pink stone, a rarity midst all the turquoise. The boy's eyes met hers. "Try it," he urged. "It will look good on your hand. Your fingers are nice and long."

She smiled, thinking what a good salesperson he was. "Thanks, but I don't need another ring."

"It's not about need," he said. "It's about beauty. You deserve to wear something beautiful. My mother says the world needs more people who appreciate beauty."

"Did your mother make this ring?"

"No," he said, not bothering to hide his outrage. "I did." He paused. "But she helped."

"What did she do?"

He picked up the ring and put it on the tip of his finger. "She has a good eye, my mother. I'm just learning. She looks at a whole mess of stones and shells and goes right to the good one. I . . . well, I miss a lot." He looked embarrassed, as if he'd said too much. "This is the best ring I ever made," he said, holding out the ring. "Try it, please."

Naomi shrugged and put it on. It was too small for her middle finger. Feeling unaccountably disappointed, she said, "Well, even if I wanted to buy it, it's too small."

He grinned. "No problem." He took it back and worked on it, stretching the band slowly and carefully. "Here, I bet it fits perfectly now."

She tried it on, not sure if she was hoping it would fit or was now too big. He watched intently. The ring fit perfectly. His eyes lit up, his pride apparent. Naomi looked at it for a long time, then shook her head. "It's a lovely ring but . . ." She gave it back to him, avoiding his eyes.

She walked away, hoping someone else would recognize the fine workmanship. At the same time she asked herself why, if she liked it so much, she hadn't bought it. She had the money. Didn't she deserve to wear something beautiful and lovingly made? By the time she got home and began unpacking boxes in her study, her mood had plummeted. Her thoughts split into two warring camps: one wanting her to go back down and buy the ring, the other—unbearably prissy—congratulating her for not wasting money on something she obviously didn't need.

After unpacking too many boxes, she felt dizzy and decided to take a rest. Out of habit she looked at her watch. Five minutes to five. Without thinking she jumped into her car and rushed down to the Plaza, found a parking spot, which in itself seemed like a miracle, and hurried to the portal. Most of the Native Americans were leaving, but the boy was still there, talking to an older woman whose hand rested lightly on his shoulder.

When he saw her he looked away. Who wants to be disappointed twice in one day, she thought. He had begun packing up his jewelry, and she wondered if the ring had been sold. She felt stupid and embarrassed. What was so special about a ring, even if it was beautiful? It wasn't as if there were an important occasion, or a partner with whom she could share it. Still, she walked up to him and said, "You're right, it is beautiful. I'd like to buy it, if you still have it, that is."

The woman smiled and moved away. With ritual solemnity the boy put the ring on Naomi's finger. Shyly, he told her how he and his mother had found the stone, actually a shell that was quite rare, and he'd had to convince his mother he was ready to make it into a ring. "Thank you," he said.

"I think I'm the one who needs to thank you."

Walking to her car, gazing at the ring, she tripped on uneven pavement and fell, putting her hands out to catch herself. She worried that she'd damaged the ring. Only after she got home did she notice her bleeding knee and elbow.

Within weeks of her move to New Mexico, friends began posing variations on the question, "Have you met anyone yet?" Since her track record for finding caring, healthy, interesting men was abysmally poor, Naomi did not relish the thought of more misery. She had no confidence that she'd learned whatever she needed to know to avoid repeating history. Nor did she want to think about certain past relationships that definitely constituted unfinished business. The loneliest she had ever been was lying next to her first husband. Even when their bodies were inches from each other, it had felt like miles. She had no desire to revisit the need to please a man at the expense of losing herself. Since she had no confidence she could be in a relationship and stay centered, she focused on house improvements, overseeing repairs to outdoor wires chewed by squirrels, replacement of the wooden deck floor that was deteriorating, and changing the chandelier in the dining room to a series of track lights that lit the table, a weaving, and a group of small African statues she'd inherited from her parents. She hired a man to design a garden that used native plants and required little maintenance. Best of all, she started working again on a long-deferred book about the power and place of stories.

Friends, a cousin, even a neighbor in her seventies who knew someone who knew someone who met someone online began pushing Naomi to try Internet dating. She learned to grit her teeth and say "Thanks but no thanks" with some degree of equanimity. Priscilla, for whom having a man in her life meant fun and no angst, was undeterred by Naomi's insistence that she wasn't interested in meeting men, especially via the Internet. Within hours of arriving home from her latest dig, she was on the phone. "Nomi, it's fun, try it. I'm still writing to one of the guys I met."

"Pris, if I'm going to meet a man, it's going to have to be in a normal situation, whatever that is, with mutual desire. The whole idea of Internet dating raises hopes that can't be satisfied. Besides, who knows who you're really contacting."

"Your problem is you look at every guy as a potential life partner. Who wants to have a partner for life? Too much work and too little fun. Take my advice; stop trying to meet the perfect man. He doesn't exist. What's the problem? You think you're too old to meet a man?"

"Pris, stop pushing. I'm not interested."

Naomi seldom looked at herself in the mirror. Years ago, after a difficult time, she hadn't been able to face herself, and replaced the bathroom mirror with a painting. Even now, with a large mirror above the bathroom sink, she generally managed to avoid looking. But sometimes, when she brushed her hair, her eyes wandered to her face and she wondered if she looked her age, knowing even the thought was stupid. Every woman she had ever known worried about growing old, even women in their twenties with flawless skin and no wrinkles. Naomi took some comfort from knowing she did her best to stay in shape, eating healthy foods and taking good care of herself. At least for the moment, the number sixty-seven didn't interfere with what she wanted to do or how she chose to live.

She called Sam, knowing she'd feel better about herself after talking with him. She had helped him through many relationships with women before he met and married Rebecca.

He immediately sensed her sadness. "What's the matter?"

"Everyone keeps asking me if I've met someone, and if not, they've got a suggestion as to how I should go about doing it. Priscilla's the worst. She's absolutely relentless. She says I'm too serious, that I need to have more fun. Of course, her idea of fun is having a man in her life. I know she means well, but it makes me feel bad."

"Well, knowing you, if you want to meet someone, you will. But if you want my advice, if you do meet a guy, stop asking questions."

"Why not tell me to stop breathing? Asking questions is a big part of who I am. When I'm teaching, if I didn't ask questions, we might sit in silence for the whole session, or I'd have to lecture—two fates I prefer to leave to those with no choice or imagination."

"Going on a date is not the same as teaching."

"I know. I try to switch gears, but it's not so easy. Settling for superficial chat makes my jaw muscles ache and my stomach hurt. It's worse than having an elephant in the living room. It's like having a whole herd that grows exponentially."

"Have you ever thought you might not be as interested in finding a man as you think?" he asked.

"Yeah, I've thought about it, and I sure as hell would rather have no man than the kind I've had in the past."

"You think that's your only choice?"

"Sam, can we talk about something else?"

"Sure. I just want you to be happy."

A few days later, Naomi got a call from her cousin Daniel, almost six years younger than she. They had spent a lot of time together when they were children but had become close only as adults. She had helped him through the rocky period after his wife died, especially when his young daughter needed a woman to help her deal with the loss of her mother. Now Naomi couldn't help smiling. He sounded so happy as he told her about a woman he had met online a few months before. "Elizabeth and I are having a great time. We share lots of interests, she knows how to deal with her stuff, and we really get along."

"That's wonderful. I'm happy for you."

"You sound a little down. What's happening? How's the house? What's it like to be living in Santa Fe? Do you miss teaching? Have you made any friends?"

His barrage of questions made Naomi laugh. "Hey, Daniel, you may be a lawyer, but I'm not on the witness stand."

"Sorry. It's just that I haven't heard from you in a while and I've been worried. How are you?"

"I'm okay."

"That's what you always say. So, how are you really?"

"I don't exactly know. My house is beginning to feel like mine . . ."

"But . . ."

"I just feel down, for no reason that I can figure out."

"Any way I can help?"

"You help just by being in my life."

After Naomi hung up the phone, she went to her study to read and edit what she had written the day before. An idea that had been amorphous yesterday suddenly seemed promising. She began to write, feeling a sense of satisfaction as ideas flowed easily, one thought leading to the next. Writing seemed to lift her spirits. It was something she had always turned to when she didn't want to think about her life.

The phone rang again. Sighing, she reluctantly picked up the receiver just before the answering machine kicked in. A male voice she didn't recognize said, "I'd like to speak to Naomi Rosen."

5

She didn't know the voice and had a bad feeing when the man didn't identify himself. Suddenly afraid, she said in her most anonymously professional voice, "Dr. Rosen is not available at the moment. Who may I say is calling?"

The man hesitated. "I prefer not to leave a message; it's a private matter. Can you tell me when Ms. Rosen will be in?"

"Dr. Rosen does not return phone calls unless she knows the name of the caller and the purpose of the call."

Click.

She was angry she had acknowledged that the man had the right number. Why hadn't she just said, "You have the wrong number"?

Who was the man? What did he want? As if rummaging through file drawers, she kept pulling out memories, trying to connect the voice with a person. Some drawers had been locked so long, she'd lost their keys.

Naomi couldn't explain the feeling she had that the man was making the call for someone else, but it was too strong to ignore. Yet what could she do about it other than ask him what he wanted, and she was unwilling to do that. How had he gotten her number? The conversation, such as it was, kept replaying in her mind. Did this mean she would have to monitor all her phone calls to make sure she didn't have another encounter? She realized she couldn't stop shaking.

The next time the phone rang she tried to let it ring, but habit and curiosity made this almost impossible. The warmth of the voice and the request came as a surprise. "Hello, Dr. Rosen, my name is Phillip Bockman and I'm calling from Cimarron University. I'm pleased to tell you that you've been chosen by the events committee to be the keynote speaker for our conference in August. We hope your schedule will permit you to accept." Flattered, Naomi felt herself relax. She knew only too well that once you stop university teaching full time, it's not likely that colleagues will remember your professional existence.

After she accepted, trying to hide the excitement she felt, he said, "We'd like you to send us your bio and a casual four-by-six color photo within the month so we can mail it to the printer with the rest of the program material."

Naomi had no recent photographs. Not wanting to bother the few people she might ask to take a snapshot or end up with photos she couldn't use, she decided to hire a professional. Opening the telephone book and seeing so many listings made her head spin. After calling four studios that sounded less than promising, she tried the Pomegranate Studio. Getting a recorded message in a pleasant female voice that assured she would call back within the hour felt encouraging.

In fact, barely ten minutes later the phone rang and a woman with a vibrant way of speaking asked to talk to Naomi Rosen. After introductions, Jessie asked, "What made you decide to hire a photographer?" Naomi told her about being the keynote speaker. "Congratulations!" Jessie sounded genuinely pleased. "You say the pose needs to be casual. What kind of setting did you have in mind? Is there one that interests you?"

"I like to climb on rocks."

"Huh?"

Naomi grinned at the photographer's bafflement. "Would a high rock wall be a good setting?"

"I guess . . . ," she said, "if you like rocks."

"Do you retouch your photos?"

"No. If you want me to do that, I have to send the film off, but it's usually not necessary. What matters is a person's energy, and you sound like you have lots."

Naomi liked her immediately.

"I'm free this afternoon," Jessie continued. "Why don't I pick you up and we can check out the setting and light."

Jessie drove up in a purple jeep, sporting a cowboy hat and a smile that melted half of Naomi's fears. She looked to be in her mid-thirties, a tall, rangy woman with long blonde hair and jeans that fit perfectly. As they drove, Naomi instructed her how to get to the place she'd found by accident walking off a hiking trail.

"This is a great spot for photos," commented Jessie as she pulled up to the site. "Show me the rocks." The photographer's enthusiasm felt genuine, yet it wasn't enough to allay Naomi's concerns. "You look worried," said Jessie.

"I am," Naomi admitted.

"About what?"

"Well, I can kid myself all I want about not caring how old I look, but when it comes to having my photo taken, there's no hiding place. Still, I don't want to be one of those people who sends in an old photograph and then has to deal with people's shock when they see the real you."

Jessie laughed, waving her hand as if to shoo all Naomi's fears into a nearby mound of leaves. "You look great, nothing to worry about."

Naomi rolled her eyes as she led Jessie to the clearing where she'd seen the wall, relieved she was able to find it. Touching the wall of rocks, warmed by the sun, feeling their strength, she wondered what stories the stones would tell if they could speak.

"How on earth did you find this place?" asked Jessie. "It looks like somebody built this wall, but why would they do it here, in the middle of nowhere?"

"Back east there are lots of stone walls built by farmers in the 1700s to demarcate their farms. Now the land is mostly forest, and the stone walls seem to have no use, so maybe the same thing happened here."

Jessie looked at the wall. "It's got to be at least ten feet high. Why would a farmer build such a high wall just to mark the boundary of a farm?"

"I don't know, but I'm sure glad someone built it. What do you think? Will it make a good background for the photographs?"

"Well, it will be unusual, that's for sure." After checking her light meters and camera angles, Jessie said, "I think I have what I need. Ready to go?"

Naomi nodded, reluctant to leave the silent grandeur. Driving back, they set a date and time for the photo shoot. Watching Jessie drive off, her cowboy hat at a rakish angle, Naomi's anxiety lessened.

Trying to decide what to wear for the photo shoot, Naomi emptied the better part of her closet and two drawers. Nothing felt or looked right. She contemplated buying something new but couldn't even make up her mind whether to wear pants or a dress. Two days before the shoot, Naomi worked herself into such a tizzy she felt disgusted. Where were all her high-minded principles? Her concern for the world and the mess the government was making of international relations, the economy, health care, the environment . . . ?

Wear the black pants, black is slimming.

I'm not fat.

So wear the purple skirt.

It might balloon out.

By the time Naomi heard Jessie's jeep roaring up the driveway the day of the shoot, her closet was empty except for hangers. Clothing lay in heaps on the floor. Fearing Jessie would see her foolishness, Naomi grabbed a pair of sage cotton pants and a matching tee shirt. "I'll be right out," she yelled, quickly brushing her hair and daubing makeup on her face.

When Naomi opened the door, she was so nervous she spoke through the screen door, uttering banalities she normally wouldn't admit knowing.

"Am I going in or are you coming out?" teased Jessie.

"Sorry. Guess I'm a little nervous," apologized Naomi, opening the screen door.

"About what?"

"Posing for a stranger."

"After two minutes I'll be like an old friend." On the way to her jeep, Jessie stopped. "You look great," she said. "Trust me. This will be fun."

I'd rather go to the dentist.

"C'mon, the light's perfect. Take me to your rocks."

Everything changed the minute Naomi began climbing up the large stones that formed the base of the wall. Worries, anxiety, doubts about the way she looked, all disappeared. Naomi even forgot about Jessie as she clambered up the rocks, enjoying the warmth of the stones and the feel of her body snuggling into curved spaces.

"Hey!" Jessie said with a laugh, "what about me?" Naomi turned around and Jessie began snapping. "How do you feel about being the keynote speaker?" Throwing her arms up into the air, butt resting lightly on a large stone, her face turned toward the waning rays of the sun, Naomi felt as if she were flying.

For the next hour, while the light was still good, Naomi responded to Jessie's questions and suggestions, joyfully moving about on the rocks, ignoring the click of the shutter. After a while, the pleasure of being on the rocks made Naomi forget about the reason for the session, aging, even how she looked. It was almost as if she were a child again, free of any thoughts except the pleasure of clambering up warm stones. As they drove back to her house, Naomi remembered the day the rocks had brought her home.

Her family had moved just after her eighth birthday. Too shy to introduce herself to the kids on the block, Naomi practiced invisibility despite her mother's dire threats about what she would do to her if she didn't go out and meet the other children. But all the punishments in her mother's large repertoire and all the threats in her vocabulary weren't enough to make Naomi play with kids she didn't know. She stared longingly out her bedroom window toward the woods, where she'd been forbidden to go by herself. When her mother left for a meeting, sternly reminding her to stay close to the house, Naomi took off with an apple in her hand and raisins in her pocket.

The forest felt safe, like an old friend waiting for her to visit. She paid no attention to where she walked and stopped only when she heard water splashing. At first, despite looking everywhere, she couldn't find the water. It was only when she looked at her shoes and noticed they were muddy that she began to step gently on the increasingly soggy earth. The sound grew louder and she bent down to dig. After she cleared away some earth, water splashed up, washing her face and lifting her sagging spirits. She drank, gulping down the cold, refreshing spring water without worrying about its purity. Gazing at the underground spring pushing its way to the surface, she delighted in having helped in its liberation. She sat down on the nearest patch of dry earth and watched the spring bubble, imagining how pleased it was to be released from its earthy prison. When she noticed that the sun was going down, she realized she needed to hurry home if she wanted to be there when her mother returned. Then it occurred to her—she was lost.

Before she began to panic, she noticed a stone wall off to her right and climbed onto it. She had heard that all roads led somewhere and hoped it was also true of stone walls. Someone must have built them for a reason, and this one looked to be in good condition. As she made her way, enjoying the feel of the various rock shapes under her feet, she noticed a fallen tree that looked familiar and then a rock formation she remembered. The stone wall was like a guide, taking her where she wanted to go. And it did, ending in a clearing not far from her house.

Naomi shook her head, not wanting to remember another time, much later in her life, when rocks had led to misery.

She'd been rock climbing with a man, much taller and heavier than she, partnered by the leader despite her protests about the disparity in their sizes. The man had laughed at her. "Hey, Babe, I climb every weekend. If anyone's going to fall it'll be you, so stop complaining and let's get going." Naomi hadn't thought she was complaining, only pointing out the obvious, especially since she wasn't as experienced as he was. The group began roping up and Naomi followed along. Carefully, she made her way up the rock wall, trying to ignore the increasing distance from the ground. She made it to the top, joyful, inordinately proud of herself, having once again triumphed over her incipient fear of edges.

After sharing fruit and cookies, the group members began their descent. Her partner suggested he start down first so she could belay him using a strong foothold available only at the top of the rocks. His cockiness irritated Naomi, and perhaps that was why she wasn't paying close enough attention. When the rope lurched from the weight of his fall, she almost fell off the top. The rope burned through her jacket, turtleneck, tee shirt, and bra before she managed to stop the slippage. She kept him from bashing into the rocks at the bottom of a ledge, but not by much.

Shaken, they made their way down the rest of the climb without incident, but when they unroped he let loose a torrent of anger. His fury at her "incompetence" seared. "If you can't belay, you shouldn't be climbing. You almost killed me." As the group walked to the van, Naomi's shame and embarrassment made it impossible for her to talk. She vowed she'd never climb again. But her love of rocks, of climbing, of feeling powerful and strong eventually outweighed all other feelings, and she found another climbing group.

Jessie's comment, "See you next week when I have the photos," interrupted Naomi's thoughts. She nodded, pleased to be back in the present. "You looked so happy scuttling about on the rocks, I'm sure the photos will show it."

Five days after the photo shoot, the purple jeep was once again thundering up Naomi's driveway. Jessie hopped out, waving two brown envelopes. "Wait till you see your gorgeous mug," she crowed. "Let's look at the black and white shots first. I know you need yours to be in color, but I really like shooting in black and white and you might have a use for them later on." Sitting at the kitchen table, Jessie spread out all but one.

"What's the one in your hand?" asked Naomi. "Is it too bad to show me?"

Shaking her head, Jessie waved it in front of Naomi, who burst out laughing, remembering her response to Jessie asking how it felt to be the keynote speaker. She had raised her arms and legs, barely balancing on her butt, feeling as if her joy would lift her into the air. In the photo, Naomi looked like she was flying. Something in her relaxed. Whatever her age, she radiated vitality. That was more than good enough.

As they looked at the color photos, Naomi admitted that the pleasure she had felt being on the rocks showed. Even the ones where Jessie asked her to look serious or thoughtful had a quality that suggested Naomi was about to break into laughter. Picking out the photo for the conference publicity was easy—they both chose the same one. "If you like, I can scan two black and white and two color photos for you. Then if you want to send them to anyone, you'll have them."

"Sure," nodded Naomi, thinking she now had one less excuse for not writing a profile and trying Internet dating.

"So, have you gotten online yet?" asked her cousin Daniel.
"What's the problem?" asked Sam.
"Let me know how it goes," said Rebecca.
"What's stopping you? They're only men," reminded Priscilla.
Why does it feel like such a big deal? Naomi wondered.

The photos arrived online, and she sent them to various friends. All their responses were similar: "Great photos." "Neat shots." "You look terrific."

Daniel e-mailed suggestions about how to use his favorite dating service.

Naomi went online, starting with the questionnaire required by the service that Daniel favored. But she gave up halfway through, feeling equal parts frustration and irritation. If she was going to meet a man, why couldn't it be casual, without all this nonsense? She tried another service but wasn't willing to pay twenty-five dollars a month. The third service offered free usage for a week but asked for her credit card number before she could begin. Clicking on the red X, closing down all the sites, she felt a measure of satisfaction as she watched them disappear.

The process depressed her, reminding her how seldom boys, and then men, had chosen her to be their partners at dances or on dates. She knew she wasn't unattractive and had a reasonably good figure, so she never understood how less attractive girls attracted streams of males. Maybe it had to do with confidence, which she had never had, or being serious, which she was. Naomi knew these thoughts were a one-way descent into a black hole, so she focused on preparing for the workshop she was to give in a week. She had been told by several colleagues that when she stopped working, requests for workshops would stop, but so far this hadn't happened. She was still being invited to return to places where she had previously given workshops, and new requests were coming from referrals. Figuring out eight hours of activity for twenty-five teachers she had never met was absorbing and a welcome challenge. Planning helped to restore her sense of self.

At this moment her life was better than it had ever been. Yet she couldn't stop yearning for a relationship with a man, even though she had enough sense to know that it wouldn't fill the void inside her. She wondered why she continued to want something that had, for the most part, caused unhappiness rather than connection. Maybe she wasn't capable of a healthy relationship with a man, which was why she didn't attract healthy men. Maybe she had just been fooling herself, thinking that if she had a good man in her life she would know joy. Even as she thought it, a voice inside her screeched, "Hah!"

The phone rang. Was it that man? She turned off the answering machine, went to her loom, and unwove the weaving she had done two days before. The colors clashed and the pattern was too regular. Then she noticed an earlier section where the bold burgundy gave way to a quiet moss pink. It looked soothing and comforting yet it was not satisfying. She ripped out that section as well. "I will find a way to make this work if it takes me all day," she said out loud. For the next two hours, Naomi wove and unwove, struggling to find colors and patterns that pleased her. If asked, she could not have explained why, but when she stopped she felt satisfied.

6

Returning from a three-day conference some weeks later, Naomi felt energized. It had been her first time as a keynote speaker, and her speech was well received. She had dispelled her initial nervousness by admitting to the audience that she was a virgin when it came to being a featured speaker. The audience had laughed encouragingly, one person yelling out, "You can do it." After her first seminar, more people wanted to take the second seminar than the room could hold. A few of the participants in her final session invited her to dinner. They spent the evening talking about teaching literature and sharing ideas about their favorite books.

Doug, a professor in his late fifties who taught comparative literature at a small eastern liberal arts college, sat next to Naomi and ordered a bottle of champagne in her honor. So much attention felt simultaneously uncomfortable and good. Full of questions, Doug listened intently to her answers despite frequent interruptions from colleagues. After dinner, he asked if she wanted to take a ride to the beach. Everything in her yearned to hold his hand as they walked along the shoreline and talked, but she had grown up at a time when a woman let the man lead. He didn't and she couldn't. They exchanged business cards, and later Naomi sent him an e-mail thanking him for the champagne and the walk. No response. She wondered what she'd done wrong.

At home, the conference euphoria faded quickly. When the phone rang, Naomi answered tonelessly. Priscilla knew this meant Naomi was having a difficult time. The first time it had happened, and Priscilla had asked what was wrong, Naomi had changed the subject. This time was no different.

"You sound as if the world's fallen in on you."

"Do I? I'm sorry. Don't know why I sound that way, nothing's wrong."

"Nomi, how long have we known each other?"

"I don't know—fifteen years? Why?"

"And how many times have I told you what was going on in my life?"

"Pris, I know where this is going. I told you, nothing's wrong."

"You don't sound as if nothing's wrong." She heard Naomi sigh.

"Well, maybe it's this Internet dating business. Everyone I know is pushing me to do it, as if having a man in my life will solve all my problems."

"Like what?" asked Priscilla, wishing for once Naomi would talk about what was bothering her.

Naomi automatically changed the subject. "I'll meet you for supper at Mucho Gusto. Six-thirty. Okay?"

At dinner, Priscilla could see that Naomi was making an effort to be cheerful. Naomi never complained about her life, but even after all their years of friendship, Priscilla sometimes felt she had no idea who Naomi was. There were unaccounted gaps in Naomi's history that she refused to talk about no matter how Priscilla couched her questions or showed her caring.

"Maybe you'd feel better if you had a man in your life," suggested Priscilla, wishing Naomi wouldn't be so uptight about men.

"Maybe I'd feel better if I slit my throat."

Priscilla's horrified look shocked Naomi. "I'm only kidding. I think the constant noise of the workers putting a new roof on the house is getting to me. I'm okay, really," she said, drifting away from the conversation, privately wondering how one went about finding a kind, caring, healthy, fit, politically liberal man who didn't obsess about age. She had fantasies of a mail-order catalog where one could choose a model with a money-back guarantee.

Priscilla interrupted her reverie. "Naomi, you need to make a plan. What's yours?"

"I don't have one. Do I even want one?"

Naomi disliked making long-term plans, especially after the one time she did make one she'd experienced the worst sense of loss and pain of her life. She'd learned the hard way: making plans too far ahead leads to heartache. She wasn't willing to ask for more.

"Nomi, are you listening?"

"Sorry. What were you saying?"

"If you want a man in your life, you have to work to make it happen. And if the first plan doesn't work, you need a backup. Lots of backups."

"Sounds like a campaign."

"Well, in some ways it is."

"Going through all that rigmarole isn't worth it. I quit."

"Give it a try. I'll pay for the on-line fees."

"It's not the money."

"So what is it then?"

"Having a man in my life isn't worth the trouble."

Driving home from the restaurant, Naomi felt both restless and exhausted. She sat down to write but couldn't concentrate. She kept thinking about how most men she'd met had never been attracted to her. The few who had been were outsiders, like her, though not necessarily in the same way. It probably was no help that she didn't know how to stop being an observer. And then there was the issue of needing to be good.

Even as a young child, she couldn't break rules. It wasn't about being good, it was about trying to be safe. If she obeyed the rules, she might not get into trouble, and if she stayed out of trouble, there would be less chance of experiencing misery at home. Growing up, to protect herself, she had practiced the art of being invisible to avoid being noticed. If you were in the habit of being invisible, it was hard to flirt or act as if you felt desirable, or available, or interested.

Except with Adam—attractive, sexy, and the ultimate outsider—who had watched and waited and then walked right through her defenses, into her heart, breaking every rule that stood in his way, leaving without saying good-bye. Even now, years later, she had put her feelings about him into the unresolved emotions box, turned the lock, and thrown away the key.

They had met in a rock climbing group, four men and one other woman, part of a larger group of people who hiked and skied together. Adam was the leader, the expert. Naomi was the least experienced, somewhat intimidated by the sheer rock face and the long climb ahead of them. She told him she'd never done such a difficult climb before. He told her that it didn't matter—he'd teach her what she needed to know and by the end of the day, she'd be looking forward to the next climb.

Her first experience was so exhilarating she'd signed up for the rest of the season. He gave her a hug, unashamed to show his pleasure at how quickly she learned and how courageously she moved up and down the steep rock walls. That was the first of many trips. She got to be so good that she belayed him, even stopping his fall when he slipped on an unexpected patch of ice. But then she noticed, the better she got, the less interested in her he seemed. She wondered if she was imagining things and chided herself for making problems where there were none.

The day of the last trip of the season was cold. It had rained the night before and the rocks were slippery. "I don't think it's safe to go," said Naomi.

The look Adam gave her was chilling. He turned to the group and asked, "Anyone here want to change their mind?" No one spoke. "Don't come if you think it's not safe," he said to her, busily checking gear.

Embarrassed, she shrugged and helped organize the group to prepare for the descent. All went well until Beth, a woman with little experience, slipped on a patch of ice and brought two others down with her. Naomi, who was roped in behind her, hit her head on a rock and lost consciousness. When she came to, lodged against the rock outcropping that had broken her fall, blood was pouring from cuts on her face and head. The rocks were cold and wet. She felt betrayed.

Later, she could not remember how she had gotten down the rest of the rock wall, and had no memory of the trip to the hospital. She could not forget Adam's arms around Beth, tenderly caring for her. He never returned Naomi's calls or responded to her letter. Does a man always have to be better than the woman he's with in order to feel good about himself, she wondered?

Annoyed at how much and how often she thought about men, a topic that seemed pointless, for the next couple of days after her dinner with Priscilla, Naomi forced herself to work on the chapter of her book she'd promised her editor. After tossing away too many false starts, she decided to begin with a story about a student who had complained in class, "Why do we have to choose topics that are personally meaningful? Why can't you just assign one and let us write up our research?" Before Naomi could answer, the student added, "No other professor asks us to choose topics that are meaningful." The student hadn't said, "What's wrong with you? Why can't you be like everyone else?" yet she definitely implied it.

Suddenly Naomi's fingers stopped typing. The question loomed large, even though the incident had happened years ago. She knew she wasn't the only professor to demand that students make a connection between themselves and what they were learning. Yet she felt an urge to defend herself, all the while knowing how foolish this was. Even the other members of the class had laughed at the ridiculousness of the student's complaint.

As she sat at her desk, this memory triggered another, of a time when she was only nine but, for some unknown reason, the teacher had put her in a ballet class with eleven year olds. Naomi was determined to keep up with them. At the end of the term her class began preparing for their first performance. Each student was asked to choreograph a short piece to dance after the class exercises. All the mothers were carefully instructed about how to make or purchase the required pink tutus and ballet slippers.

At home, Naomi had always found it comforting to look at a set of three framed watercolor paintings on a wall in her parents' bedroom. They were scenes of Mexico: two men working in a field with scythes, three women around a well, and two women washing clothes. Naomi decided to base her dance on these images.

During each of the last few classes before the dance performance, two or three students showed their work for the teacher to criticize. When her turn came, Naomi danced her dance, proud and happy to have accomplished something she thought was important. Afterward, instead of the usual suggestions, there was silence. The teacher glared, and then yelled at her. "What is wrong with you?" Shocked, Naomi stood, paralyzed, waiting for the yelling to stop.

When she got home and told her mother, the first thing she heard was, "What's wrong with you? Why can't you be like everyone else? You're in a ballet class. Your teacher told you to make something beautiful."

"She said to choreograph a dance. That's what I did."

"Well, she just phoned to say that if you don't make a new dance, one that's beautiful, like the other girls, you can't be in the recital."

"I guess I won't be in the recital, then."

"And what about the costume I made for you? All that work? For nothing? What's wrong with you?"

Naomi stood up and paced, trying to send the memory back to wherever it came from. When it refused to cooperate, she closed the computer file and went into the living room where she put on a CD of Nigerian drumming, and turned up the volume. She danced as long as her body was willing. But the question continued to reverberate: "What's wrong with you?" Then a second question came barreling in after the first: "Why can't you just forget the past?" Good question, thought Naomi. I would if I could—if I knew how.

Unable to concentrate on her writing, she called Sam. "How do you forgive and forget? I'm up for a permanent case of amnesia for everything that's happened in the first thirty years of my life."

"What triggered this?"

"Memories that refuse to stay where they belong. Feelings that continue to hurt long past the time they should have drifted off into the emotional graveyard."

"I don't think I'm the right person to ask. Rebecca left this morning."

"Oh, Sam, I'm sorry. Why?"

"You described it pretty well. I can't forget about the affair she had last year. She can't live with constant reminders of what she calls my lack of trust. If you figure out how to stop remembering, I'll hire you."

"Can I help?"

"What do you know about living with bad choices?"

Too much. "What are you going to do?"

"What I feel like doing is getting drunk. What I will do is leave tomorrow for Toronto, where I have a big consulting job. But if she should call, pretend you don't know anything, okay? She hates that you and I talk about our personal lives. The fact that we've known each other all these years and have never been sexually interested in each other is inconceivable to her."

"Seems to me she's the one with the trust issues."

"Not to hear her talk."

"Sam, you're a great guy. Stop beating up on yourself"

"I hope, dear Nomi, you take your own advice."

Naomi went to her loom and looked at the yarns hanging on the wall. Without hesitating, she selected colors she'd been avoiding. The dull browns and off-whites felt comforting. She worked slowly, the pace calming her racing thoughts, the feel of her fingers moving under and over the warp centering her. Slowly, the rhythm of interlacing yarns and creating pleasing patterns eased her tension. After weaving for a few hours she walked back to her desk. The chapter wrote itself.

7

The first minutes of a conference always overwhelmed Naomi. Excess air-conditioning. Too many people. Too much hustle and bustle. As she was standing in line to register, she heard a voice she had hoped never to hear again.

"Hello, Sweetie."

Being reminded of a one-night stand that should never have happened was not her idea of a good way to begin meeting people at a professional meeting. He caressed the back of her neck, his fingers lingering on a spot just below her ear. "You've come up in the world. Keynote speaker. Well done. How about us doing a little speaking of our own? I've got a king-sized bed that's much too big for one person."

"Hello, Stan." Naomi moved away from him, pretending she hadn't heard his invitation and busied herself with registration materials.

He grabbed her wrist. "What's the matter? Too high up in the world to remember the old friend whose pants you couldn't wait to get into?"

"Friends don't hurt friends." She pulled away from him, afraid of the look on his face, grateful that they were surrounded by people lining up to register. It was only when she reached the safety of her room that she discovered she'd left her conference materials on the table. Unwilling to chance another encounter with Stan, she hailed a porter who was just leaving an adjacent room. "There's five dollars waiting for you if you rescue my registration packet from a table in the Eldorado Room."

She woke up with every speaker's worst nightmare—a throat so sore she couldn't speak. Her neck was so tight, she felt she was being choked. In three hours she was supposed to address a roomful of colleagues.

Naomi told herself that not speaking was not the end of the world, but the platitude did not comfort her. She called to see if there was a hotel doctor on duty.

"No, Dr. Marsh comes in at noon. Is it an emergency?" asked the desk clerk, concern in her voice.

Despite the pain, Naomi forced herself to say, "I'm the keynote speaker."

"Oh dear, you sound terrible. If you come down to the desk, I'll find out if there's a doctor on call who can see you now."

The best the clerk could do was to find a GP, an elderly, white-haired man with bright blue eyes and a caring manner whose office was around the corner from the hotel. After looking at her throat, Dr. Rivers paused, and then choose his words carefully. "I don't see any redness or swelling, but when I palpate your neck, it's very tense. I think this could account for most of the pain. If I were a psychologist, I'd be asking, 'What are you afraid to say?'"

"Can't you give me something? I'm supposed to give the convention's keynote address in a few hours."

"I can prescribe a tranquilizer to ease the pain, but if you try to talk with your throat as tight as it is, you could damage your vocal cords. Absolutely not worth it, in my opinion."

"Isn't there anything else?"

"The old remedies work pretty well, with no side effects. Hot tea with lemon and honey. A warm towel around your neck. Time. Figuring out what's bothering you. Do you want a prescription for a tranquilizer?"

"No. They make me feel like I'm living in a fog."

Dr. Rivers shrugged.

She paid him and left, asking herself, "What don't I want to say?"

As she walked out of his office, Naomi remembered her second-grade teacher. Miss Brown obviously didn't like her, and told her she was too smart for her own good. When she taught arithmetic, she made Naomi sit outside the door so she would "know what it was like to be stupid."

The day of the first arithmetic test, Naomi woke up with a throat so sore she couldn't talk. Her father took her to a throat doctor. Although Naomi was in the room, the doctor talked to her father as if she weren't there. "No pathology, but the throat's very tight. Give her these pills, three times a day with meals." The pills made her woozy, and she hated the feeling, so she made believe that she took them. Naomi's mother told her she could tell she was just pretending to be sick. When Naomi asked her how she knew, her mother turned her back, ignoring the question.

Naomi failed that first arithmetic test. But the boy who sat in front of her was smart in math, and she figured out how to cheat. When Naomi got a good grade on the next test, Miss Brown said that she was just pretending to be stupid in arithmetic.

This was only the first of many times when her throat was so sore she could not eat and could barely talk. Yet each time, the doctor's report was the same—no sign of pathology.

As Naomi walked back to her hotel from Dr. Rivers' office, she stopped at a drugstore. "What am I just pretending?" she asked herself as she gazed at the shelves of cold remedies. Twenty minutes later she had stocked up on lozenges, cough syrups, aspirin, ibuprofen, and creams to relax muscles in spasm.

"Do you know where I can buy herbal teas?" she asked the checkout clerk.

"There's a convenience store about five or six blocks farther down the street."

Walking there required more energy than she had, so Naomi headed back to the hotel, talking herself into feeling better.

The message light was flashing when she entered her room. Trying to ignore it, she closed the drapes. The red light flickered everywhere. She shrugged and pushed the play button. It was Marian, the conference coordinator, who wanted Naomi to call her back as soon as possible.

Naomi brewed a cup of black tea supplied by the hotel, hoping the hot liquid would ease her throat. After drinking it, she rubbed cream on her neck, and sucked on a lozenge. When she felt able to return the call, Marian didn't recognize her voice—what there was of it. Nothing Naomi said reassured the woman that she'd be able to give her speech.

"It's short notice, I know, but Professor Harvey's just back from working with Aboriginal educators in Australia. I'll ask him to fill in for you."

"I'm drinking tea. I've got more than an hour. I'll manage."

"And if you don't?" Marian's tone of voice was not pleasant.

Naomi wanted to give the talk. She needed to stand up in front of the audience and tell them what the children had accomplished despite the dire educational diagnosis each of them had received. If she didn't give the talk, she knew she would feel she had let the children down.

"I will manage, so no more talk about Professor Harvey. I'll meet you at two-thirty in the Gold Ballroom." But she knew Marian—she was probably on her way to Harvey's room right now.

Naomi massaged her neck using all the cream in the container. Then she wrapped her neck in hot towels, sucked on more lozenges, drank more tea, and paced the room. The vulture of despair loomed large, but Naomi refused to give in, unwilling to admit that, after all this time, something inside her was still capable of choking her words.

As she paced back and forth, she noticed bath salts in the basket on the bathroom counter. She emptied the package into the tub and filled it with the hottest water she could stand. She sank into the lavender foam and pleaded with her body and brain to relax her neck muscles so her vocal cords could do their work.

An image of Annie came to mind from Naomi's graduate school days, when she was doing a two-week tutoring stint at an elementary school in a poor neighborhood. Naomi was in the principal's office when Annie's fourth-grade teacher dragged her in.

"I'm sorry, Mr. Barnes, but this is the last straw. Annie simply won't learn. All she does is distract the other children. I want her out of my room." After thrusting the skinny girl into the office, she stormed out.

The ten year old who stood in front of the principal met his gaze with a poise that belied her years.

"What do you have to say for yourself, Annie?"

"Nothing."

"Mrs. Baxter will tell me what happened, but I want to hear it from you."

"Won't do any good."

"Why not?"

"She doesn't like me."

"What am I going to do with you?"

"Find a teacher who likes me."

"And where, pray tell, will I find such a person?"

Annie looked at Naomi. "That lady there? She looks nice."

"She's a tutor, not a teacher."

Something about Annie touched Naomi. She volunteered to work with her each morning for the two weeks she had off from graduate school. After that, she offered to come for an hour twice a week.

The fifth-grade teacher, Ms. Gonzales, a graduate student like Naomi, agreed to let Annie stay in her classroom during the afternoon if Annie promised not to cause any disruptions. Naomi's curiosity was aroused when Annie asked her, "Can I ask questions when I'm in that lady's class?"

When Naomi arrived at the principal's office to pick up Annie and take her to Ms. Gonzalez' room, Annie was reading a *National Geographic* magazine. As they walked down the hall, Naomi asked Annie to tell her about the story she'd been reading.

Annie asked, "You really want to know, or is that a teacher question?"

More than a little taken aback, Naomi answered, "I'd like to hear about what you find interesting." Annie nodded and recapped the theme and essence of the story. She was obviously intelligent and articulate. Naomi saw no signs of defiance or intransigence. Curiosity got the better of her. "Why did your teacher throw you out of class?"

"She thinks she knows everything and she doesn't."

"There must be something more."

She shrugged. "Ask her."

"Is there something I can do to help you?"

"You're only here for a few more days. If you want to help, ask Ms. Gonzales to let me stay in her classroom. She's really nice."

Naomi never found out what made the fourth-grade teacher act as she did, but Annie was allowed to stay in the fifth-grade classroom, with a teacher who encouraged her to go beyond workbooks and worksheets.

The image of Annie was so strong that Naomi had to remind herself where she was—in the hotel bathtub—and what she needed to do to reclaim her voice to give the keynote address. As she stepped out of the steaming bath, Naomi looked at herself in the mirror and said to her image, "Annie, if you can figure it out, so can I."

Armed with lozenges, a bottle of hot water with lemon and honey, and more chutzpah than confidence, Naomi met Marian. "I think my voice will be good enough."

"And I think you sound like a duck with a sore throat. Professor Harvey agreed to take your place. He'll be here in a few minutes."

Instead of arguing, Naomi smiled, walked past her onto the stage, and took her seat, massaging her neck until the room quieted and introductions began. Before Marian could introduce Professor Harvey, Naomi walked to the dais, took the mike off the stand and leaned into the audience as if speaking to each person individually.

"I'm told I sound like a duck with a sore throat." People laughed. "Professor Harvey has graciously agreed to take my place, but I think that how I sound is less important than the material I've brought with me to share. I hope you agree." The applause had a releasing effect on the pain and tightness in her throat.

"The children whose work I will discuss were relegated to low achieving or special education classes, for the most part without formal testing. As a result of this process, these students learned that they had no value and no intelligence and, like most of their education, what they learned was wrong. The study, done by five researchers, sponsored by the Council on Learning, followed one hundred boys and girls between the ages of eight and twelve over a period of two years. The complete account of the methodology and results will be printed in the November issue of *Learning* magazine."

Naomi was grateful she had put their work in a computer presentation. Making time for the audience to read meant less strain on her voice and a chance to sip honey-lemon water and suck on lozenges. The children's writing moved the audience as much as it had Naomi. And even with extra time for questions and reflection, there were still arms raised and issues to be addressed when the session was almost over. By then Naomi was hardly noticing the throat pain.

"If you don't mind," she told the audience, "I'd like to end the session with a poem I wrote for a girl named Annie. I call it *The Cant of Can't*."

> You there, the one who's just been told you
> can't spell,
> can't write,
> can't think,
> can't talk,
> can't draw,
> can't do.
>
> You there, the one who says, 'I can't.'
> You come to us.
> We'll show you that you can.
> Always."

Naomi whispered, "Thank you, Annie."

At the reception that evening, her voice once again disappeared, but she was too happy to care. Colleagues bombarded her with questions.

Whispered answers popped out with unexpected ease and depth. Her absence at professional meetings the past two years was noted, giving everyone a chance to catch up on what had been happening. The story of how Naomi quit teaching at the university to move two thousand miles west because she fell in love with a house evoked a lot of talk about being open to possibility. Even though she didn't feel as brave as her colleagues gave her credit for, Naomi was happy to be looked at with awe and amazement. No one quite believed it happened as it did—so many "ifs," all having to fall into place for the house to be hers.

Mike, who taught at a university in Montana, sat on her left at dinner. Years ago they had worked on a complicated and ultimately successful theatre project. At the time, they had both been unhappily married and had had a brief affair. It didn't quite work, so after a short time they mutually agreed to return to their previous status as friends and colleagues. Naomi enjoyed his hug.

The seat on her right remained empty until the salad was served. Stan sat down with a jovial, "Is this seat taken?"

"No," answered the woman on his right with a welcoming smile.

Naomi's appetite disappeared. When Stan put his arm around her shoulder and looked as if he was about to kiss her on the lips, she moved her head and he kissed her cheek. Not wanting to make a scene, she gave him a weak smile and hoped the woman next to him was as interested in him as she appeared. When his arm remained on Naomi's body, she stood up.

"Be right back," she said to Mike.

Stan followed her. "Your talk was wonderful."

"Leave me alone."

"Give me another chance. I know last time wasn't that great but—"

"I said, leave me alone." Pushing past him, she walked into the ladies room and tried to figure out what to do if he was waiting for her when she walked out. He was.

He blocked her path, grabbing her arm. His tone was menacing. "Last year you couldn't wait to unzip my pants."

"If you don't leave me alone, I'll call security."

"Go ahead. Who'd believe a teacher like me would hassle an 'important person' like you?"

For a moment, Naomi felt paralyzed. So many times in the past, even when she found the courage to speak up, no one had paid attention. But now she hoped her determination not to be a victim would give her the courage to defend herself.

"You just played your last card."

She yanked her arm from Stan's hand as she pushed past him. Without looking back to see if he was following her, she walked to the concierge, who was sitting at his desk. "I'm being threatened by a man and I need help. I'm afraid of what he might do."

The concierge made a call. Within minutes Mr. Margolies of the hotel's security force, a solid-looking man in a dark blue business suit, introduced himself and began to ask her detailed and relevant questions. She described Stan and gave a brief account of what had happened. Mr. Margolies' responses were polite and reassuring.

"He says you won't believe me," said Naomi, silently cursing her trembling lip.

"He's wrong."

Mr. Margolies followed her back to the table, where Stan was laughing, his eyes fixed on the woman next to him. When he saw Naomi, his smiled wavered momentarily.

"Hi, Sweetie, where've you been? Your meal's getting cold."

"That's him," whispered Naomi, sweat running down her body.

Mr. Margolies walked over to Stan, discreetly showed him a badge, and asked him to come with him. At first Stan refused.

"I haven't had dinner, but I'll be happy to talk with you afterward." The security guard said something to him in a voice too quiet for her to hear. Stan reluctantly stood up. "I'll be right back, don't go away," he said to the other woman before leaving with Mr. Margolies at his side.

People at the table gave Naomi questioning looks, but she smiled and pretended to eat her salad. Mike asked in a low voice, "Are you okay?"

"No, but if you order me a scotch, and he doesn't come back, I'll be fine."

Mike's grin was just what she needed. Naomi wondered if it was a coincidence, but after Stan left, her throat muscles soon relaxed, the pain went away, and her voice returned to normal.

On the flight home, as she nervously breathed through the plane's bumps and jolts, feelings of a job well done overwhelmed her flying fears. Two publishers had showed interest in her book about stories and language acquisition, and a colleague from a graduate school of education had invited her to do a weeklong seminar. To celebrate her newfound bravery, she splurged, ordered a cognac, and vowed she would no longer be a pretzel, twisting herself into a shape that wasn't hers just to assuage her fear or someone else's need or want or wish. Just to make sure, she wrote in her diary: <u>NO MORE PRETZELS!</u>

8

Priscilla had trouble understanding Naomi's reluctance to use Internet matchmaking sites. At dinner one night, she told Naomi, "In my opinion, if you want a man in your life it's no big deal. Privately, Priscilla wasn't even sure Naomi wanted a man. Maybe she just wanted the wanting. Still, knowing Naomi might become angry, she talked quickly. "I wrote you a profile. I'll read it to you. You can make whatever changes you like."

"Priscilla, I told you, I'm not interested."

"C'mon, just listen. It won't kill you."

"How's your grant coming along?"

"Nomi, don't be mad, but I signed you up with an Internet dating service, Meetings.com and submitted your profile and photo. You should be hearing from men soon."

"How could you do that without asking me? I told you I'm not interested.

Priscilla laughed. "So shoot me. But before you do, let's go to my place and open up your e-mail. We can see what you got and what you think."

Sitting in front of Priscilla's computer, Naomi grumbled as she looked at the profiles of two men. Neither interested her. She closed out the site and said, "Okay, Pris, that's it. I'm tired of hitting delete."

"Well, at least now you know what to do, that's something. Keep me posted if anyone interesting shows up."

Three more profiles soon appeared. Naomi decided that only one seemed even remotely appealing, a lawyer who worked for legal aid. At least his heart was in the right place, and she figured they would probably agree politically. His photo showed a shock of white hair, gorgeous green eyes, and a friendly smile. He wrote:

> *Hi!*
> *You sound like an interesting woman. I love your smile. Your profile's fascinating. Tell me more about you. I look forward to hearing from you. Can't believe you live in Santa Fe.*
>
> *Larry*

They corresponded for about a week, moving from service-protected e-mails to giving each other their personal e-mail addresses, to exchanging phone numbers.

Larry called when she was out and left a message, his voice deep and friendly. Despite knowing that the odds of meeting someone with whom she connected on the first try were abysmally low, Naomi felt a quiet excitement. When she learned that they had been to see the same movie, an obscure foreign film, at the same time, she sensed they might be compatible on many levels. With Priscilla's encouragement, she continued to exchange e-mails and talk with him on the phone. It was only a matter of time before they decided to meet. Larry invited her to a Mexican restaurant not far from her house, with good food, a casual atmosphere, and a low level of intimacy

She didn't think she was nervous, but while getting ready she dropped a glass and cut her toe. Then she took out half the clothes in her closet before deciding what to wear. To make matters worse, an accident closed down her side of the road towards the restaurant and the detour had made her unfashionably and uncharacteristically late.

He was waiting in front of the restaurant, an amused smile on his face, as Naomi hurried to cross the street. He looked like his photo, a definite plus. As soon as he opened his mouth, she knew he was from New York. When she learned that they had gone to the same high school, although he had graduated a year ahead of her, something in her relaxed.

The more they talked, the more she felt she knew him. She had to keep reminding herself that affinity and common experience were not the same as knowing.

When the waiter came to take their order, Larry smiled and ordered for both of them. Naomi was about to protest, but she liked his selection and decided not to make a fuss. He was a raconteur with wonderful stories to tell about helping clients fight for their rights, and his passion for defending undocumented workers was so moving that she couldn't help admiring his enthusiasm and concern. But after a while she realized that he had not asked about her life. His conversation was a monologue, albeit fascinating, from appetizer to dessert.

A waiter interrupted him to ask if they would like to try, on the house, a new wine they'd just imported from Spain. Tasting it, Naomi was transported back to a time when she had shared a similar wine with a man who had exuded warmth and safety. She remembered his gentle caresses, feeling his loss with an intensity that took her by surprise. When Larry pounded the table for emphasis, she jumped, catapulted back to the present. Larry hadn't even noticed that she'd been gone during much of his story.

After a meal that lasted more than two hours, Larry walked Naomi to her car. Without thinking, she gave him a hug. His body was unresponsive, and from the look on his face when she got into her car, he seemed taken by surprise. He waved good-bye, saying nothing about future meetings. She wondered if he would call. She wondered if she wanted him to. She wondered where the hug came from.

When he invited her to go hiking a few days later, she said yes. Walking in the mountains, especially in spring when the wildflowers were a banquet of color and smell, was part of what made living in Santa Fe so appealing.

When they first started walking, Naomi tried to begin a conversation with Larry, but his terse replies exhausted her interest. She gave up and walked at her own rate, not caring that, in spite of frequent stops to wait for him to catch up, the distance between them quickly increased. Larry didn't hide his surprise at Naomi's pace, even though she was not trying to impress him. When she walked in the woods, she had an unfortunate tendency to get lost in thought. Her feet usually found their way with little direction from her brain. Sometimes, though, she lost the trail because her feet had found another path, in the wrong direction. She had been known to bushwhack down steep mountain inclines after missing turns on well-marked trails.

As she reached a level place after a significant climb, Naomi turned around to look for Larry. He was walking some distance behind. Waiting gave her a chance to drink water and catch her breath. The smile he forced when he reached her did not include his eyes or his tone of voice.

"Trying to set a speed record?"

"Nope," she said, waiting for him to take a drink before she asked if he was ready to move on. Without responding, he took out a handkerchief, wiped his face, and opened a roll of candy, popping several into his mouth without offering her any. She started walking up the next incline.

They were about three-quarters of the way to the top when he called out, "Hold up, this is as far as I like to go."

"How come?"

"Too many people at the top. Too much yammering."

Naomi decided not to point out that they hadn't passed anyone nor had anyone passed them. "That's interesting. In all the times I've climbed up Atalaya, I've met people only once—a couple who were so quiet I almost bumped into them."

"Well, go to the top if you want to. I'll wait for you down by my car."

You don't want to go to the top because you're already out of breath and we haven't even come to the steepest part. "That's okay. I'll do it another time," she said, trying to keep the irritation out of her voice.

They walked back down in silence. Naomi had stepped aside to let him go first, but he waved her on, and she wasn't about to make an issue of who led.

When they got to his car, he opened the door, put his backpack and poles in the trunk and then sat in the front seat without a word to Naomi.

She put her gear in the back seat and sat down in the passenger seat. "Is something wrong?" she asked.

"No. Why? Do you think something's wrong?"

"I don't know; that's why I asked."

Shaking his head as if to dismiss her question, he turned on the radio, twisting the dial until he found a country music station where an off-key singer was wailing about the fickleness of women.

So much for Internet dating, thought Naomi.

When they got to her house, he said, "Thanks for the hike. I'm sorry but I need to run. I've got a client waiting."

"No problem." She waved good-bye, feeling she had narrowly avoided stepping on a land mine.

She was reminded of what her father said when she kept beating the neighborhood boys at Ping-Pong when she was a teenager. "If you want them to ask you out, you have to let them win." She had been stunned and irate. Even then she thought the price was too high.

She called Priscilla after her hike with Larry. "I tried. I learned. It's enough."

"Why quit after one not so great experience?" asked Priscilla.

"Why not?" countered Naomi.

In little more than a week Naomi received two more phone calls asking for "Dr. Rosen." When the man called a third time, Naomi confronted him. "What do you want? Why do you keep calling? Who are you?"

"I'm not at liberty to tell you. All I can say is that it has to do with your past."

"The past is the past. I'm not interested." She slammed down the receiver, got into her car, and drove to a trailhead on one of the mountains just north of Santa Fe. She walked up the trail, her pace fueled by anger and fear. At the top of a long climb, she sat, watching the clouds move, wishing she could sit there forever. But when she saw how low the sun was in the sky, she started down the trail, moving quickly to avoid having to walk back to her car in the dark.

The man must have been waiting, keeping himself hidden until she put her key in the lock. She didn't hear his footsteps, but when he said, "Good evening, Dr. Rosen," Naomi fell against the door, too startled and terrified to look around.

"I am sorry to frighten you, but I'm a lawyer and my mission is important. Since you wouldn't talk to me on the phone, I had to resort to other tactics. Now that I am positive you are the Naomi Rosen I've been searching for, I want to arrange a meeting between you and my client. The issue needs to be resolved. It's gone on for much too long. Nothing is gained by denial. You can't keep ignoring reality."

"I don't care who you are or who you're representing. I want you to leave immediately."

"Please, be reasonable. One visit is all he asks for."

"That's one visit too many. Good night." Naomi opened the front door and slammed it closed without looking to see where he was. She turned off the answering machine and lights, hoping the darkness would discourage further interaction.

A week later, Naomi was at the Albuquerque airport waiting for a plane to Philadelphia, where she was scheduled to give a talk to a group of educators examining the place and power of stories in literacy programs. She looked forward to sharing her ideas and experience, and hoped she had the wherewithal to do justice to the students and tutors whose work she was going to present. Remembering her last speaking experience, she'd come prepared with chamomile tea, honey, lemon, lozenges, and analgesic cream.

The plane, scheduled to depart at 11 a.m., was delayed due to bad weather in Chicago. No new departure time was listed. She watched people read the information on the illuminated board. Some grumped, others got mad, a few sat resigned. She had given herself an extra two days, so for the moment she had plenty of time and told herself to relax. She bought a large cup of coffee and sat in the least crowded area she could find.

As she was opening a baggie of homemade muffins she had packed to eat en route, she heard a voice that made her want to run and hide.

"Well, well, well, look who's here."

There, standing in front of her, was her former husband, Gabe. His hair, which had been grayish-white, was now dark brown. He'd gained weight and now looked like a prosperous accountant. The sexual energy that initially attracted Naomi had disappeared. Beside him was a much younger, pudgy woman with a baby face, holding the hand of a small child—a dark-eyed, dark-haired boy who stared at Naomi.

"Long time no see," said Gabe, with no irony in his voice, no sign that once upon a time he hated clichés.

Naomi hoped he couldn't see her trembling hands as she tried not to spill the hot coffee. "Hello, Gabe."

The woman looked questioningly at Gabe. "Naomi, this is my wife, Bonnie, and our son, Peter."

Bonnie nodded, obviously knowing who she was.

Peter took this as his cue to leave his mother and move toward Naomi. "I'm three. I had a birthday party at Gramma's. When we go home I'm having a birthday party in my house. Jimmy and Billy and Ethan are coming. I'm gonna get lots of presents."

Naomi forced herself to smile. "That's nice."

"Peter, that's enough," said his mother, taking her son's hand, moving him closer to her. "Nice to meet you, Naomi."

Naomi nodded, unable to utter the conventional, "Nice to meet you too." She hoped they would turn and leave, but Gabe seemed to be enjoying himself.

"Our plane is delayed. Mind if we sit here? Give us time to catch up. How many years has it been?"

Naomi shrugged, making no move to remove her computer and coat from the seat next to her. "I don't remember. Do you?"

He looked uncomfortable for a moment, then recovered. "Bonnie and I've been married five years. I was transferred from Boston and we live in Chicago now. Life is good. We're expecting our second child, so Bonnie quit her job to take care of the kids."

Naomi was sure that the next questions would be about whether she'd remarried and had children, neither of which she wanted to talk about with Gabe. She looked at her watch, gathered up her things, and said, "Time for me to go. My plane's due in a few minutes, and I need to use the ladies room before I board. Glad you're doing so well. Have a good flight."

She hurried toward the rest room, hoping Bonnie didn't plan to use it anytime soon. When she emerged, she saw the three of them still sitting there. Gabe was working on his computer. Bonnie was reading to Peter. Making sure they didn't see her, Naomi checked her flight departure. Noting that it was still listed as delayed, she headed toward the bar farthest from her gate. She ordered a shot of brandy and took it to the most secluded table she could find.

Unbidden memories flooded through her carefully constructed mental barriers. She remembered the day she had gone to her university mailbox and found two letters. The first explained that her sabbatical was dependent on her being promoted in May. The second informed her she'd been denied a prestigious grant that would have given her a year free from teaching to do research on stories and literacy development. Then, just minutes after she got to her office, the doctor's secretary called to say her mammogram was suspicious and she needed to come in for further tests. Reeling from the relentlessness of the bad news, she decided she would visit a friend who was worried about her marriage. At least, she thought, we can console each other.

She had called Gabe. "I'm going to visit Mira after work. We'll probably have dinner together, so go ahead and eat without me. I should be home around ten."

Mira was weeping when Naomi arrived. Her husband had asked for a divorce. Instead of their usual tea, they drank wine and cooked and talked until they had nothing more to say. They put the food they'd made on the table, but neither of them was hungry. Naomi laughed mirthlessly. "It can only get better, right?"

Mira decided to take a bath.

Naomi decided to go home.

When she got there the house was dark, but the full moon lit her way as she walked to the bedroom.

She saw her husband in bed. He was not alone.

"You're home early," he said, his voice devoid of emotion." I thought you said you'd be back after ten."

Naomi couldn't speak. She walked into the kitchen and poured herself a tumbler of scotch, downed it, and poured another.

"How about pouring one for me?" said her husband, now fully clothed, smelling of soap and aftershave lotion.

Naomi looked away.

He put his hand on her shoulder.

"Don't touch me."

"I love you."

Naomi left the room.

He followed her. "Did you have dinner? If not, I'll heat up some stew for you."

"I'm not hungry."

She sat in the living room. He came in and turned on the light.

"Turn off the light."

They sat in the dark silence while she waited for him to say something, to acknowledge what had happened, to tell her how he felt about her, how he felt about being in their bed with another woman.

The next thing she knew it was morning. A blanket covered her. Her shoes were next to her purse on the floor beside the sofa. Her husband was gone.

In the kitchen she found a note.

> Sweetheart, I'm picking up lobsters for dinner. Let's eat at six.
> -Love, Gabe.

Naomi finished her brandy, remembering how crazy she had felt finding him in bed with another woman, wondering how she could have continued to live with Gabe for so long without confronting him, and how she began to move through her life with him on automatic pilot.

She stood up and stretched, then ordered another brandy. Nothing stopped the flow of memories. She cringed when she thought about how she had been unable to ask Gabe about his infidelity. Who would believe she'd never brought up the subject, that he'd never offered an explanation. Who could imagine they had lived together for two more years increasingly avoiding all intimacy until all that was left of their marriage was polite proximity.

To get away from Gabe, Naomi had applied for a year's position teaching at a university in London, leaving a few months after finding her husband in bed with the other woman. Her husband's letters were frequent and loving. Hers focused on what she was doing. Not so frequent. Not so loving. When he wrote asking her to join him in Switzerland to ski, she accepted, thinking that perhaps living apart for a few months had eased the tension between them enough to finally talk about what had happened.

They met in London, spending a week together before flying to Geneva. She had introduced him to her friends and couldn't help observing how overbearing he was, particularly when the conversation turned to politics, how embarrassingly quick he was to make fun of anyone who talked about their feelings. Naomi took refuge in silence, hoping no one noticed. He didn't. Her friends did. She refused to acknowledge their unspoken questions and displeasure, but she couldn't ignore their reactions.

She also couldn't ignore that she no longer found Gabe sexually attractive and wondered why she even pretended to respond. But after their arrival in Geneva, skiing all day provided an excuse for her lack of desire.

Their first night, at dinner, they agreed to share their table with Hans, a young German man.

"How did you and your wife meet?" asked Hans after he had made a toast to continued good skiing.

"In bed," her husband had answered.

The two men laughed, ignoring Naomi's obvious embarrassment.

She picked up her steak knife, imagining herself thrusting it into her husband's chest.

Sipping her brandy, Naomi thought about her two divorces She divorced her first husband because living with him was like living with a stone. She'd felt emotionally starved. Gabe had asked for a divorce, ending her second marriage, because, according to him, she demanded too much from him emotionally. Naomi knew there was a lesson in all of this, but she chose to focus on her work and stop thinking about men. Most of the time she'd kept herself busy enough, yet there were times, like now, when her memories refused to stay in their boxes.

The loudspeaker announcing her flight interrupted her thoughts. Feeling uncomfortably woozy, Naomi kept her head down as she walked to the gate, hoping to avoid any further encounter with Gabe. Seeing him had brought back too many uncomfortable memories.

All through the flight to Philadelphia, and even while registering for the conference, Naomi kept thinking about her encounter with Gabe, wishing she'd been able to say something wittily devastating, to put him on the defensive, to emerge victorious, whatever that meant. When the conference coordinator invited her to dinner with the other presenters, she was inordinately grateful. Finally, surrounded by colleagues, the stimulating conversation banished thoughts of her disastrous marriage.

The next day she delivered her address to a group of interested educators, who continued to ask questions until the moderator reluctantly told them they had to stop, that their time was up. Four members of the audience invited Naomi to join them for a drink and further conversation. By the time she returned to her room, her thoughts were focused on a journal that the four were starting and the essay they had requested she write.

9

The hardest part about being away from home was coming back to hundreds of e-mails, piles of letters, and too many phone messages. The e-mails were a collage of her life: a few from colleagues responding to discussions at the conference; two from meetingplace.com, which she deleted without reading; many from friends; and a host of requests for money and action from political and conservation organizations.

Tired of responding to e-mails, paying bills, and answering the most urgent phone calls, she put on her hiking boots, jumped into the car, and headed for the mountains. One of the pleasures of living in Santa Fe was the plenitude of hiking trails within easy reach. In twenty minutes she was at the Atalaya trailhead. As soon as she started walking she felt lighter, as if each step outpaced the cloud that had been hanging over her head. The trail was narrow and well worn, so she didn't worry about drifting off of it. That was fortunate—she was in no mood to deal with the consequences of bushwhacking down the steep mountain, thick with the slippery needles of evergreens that soared toward the sky.

As the incline became steeper, she began to gasp for breath. Determined to keep going, she put one foot in front of the other, the joyful effort pushing out the last of her unexplainable depression. At the top of a rise, she headed for a favorite vista with a perfectly shaped rock where she could sit for a while and contemplate the universe. It was so secluded she imagined it to be her private hiding place. Sometimes when Naomi was alone, she felt lonely, but never when walking in the mountains. The feeling of being hidden and nestled lifted her spirits and, for the moment, decreased the size of the emotional hole in her heart.

When she heard the whistling, her body stiffened. The sound grew louder. Someone else knew about this place. The world suddenly felt dangerous. There was no place to hide. When she heard the dry branches crackle behind her, her breath disappeared.

A male voice said, "I see you found my favorite rock."

Naomi leapt to her feet and whirled around, catching her foot on a root and falling to the ground. Lying on the earth with a foot wedged at an uncomfortable angle was not exactly the best way to meet a strange man. From her prone position he loomed large, but the twinkle in his eye was reassuring.

"I'm sorry, I didn't mean to scare you. Let me help you." She allowed him to disengage her foot, then she took the proffered hands that helped her up. After checking to make sure nothing was injured or broken, he offered her a chocolate bar.

"Thanks," said Naomi. "For your help and the chocolate." She broke off a piece and gave it back to him.

"Keep it," he said. "I've got lots. I'm a chocoholic. It's the only thing I feel like eating when I'm hiking or skiing."

She sat back down on the rock. After taking a mammoth bar of dark chocolate from his pack, he found a comfortable spot next to her and sat cross-legged. She couldn't help looking. There was no ring on his finger.

Naomi stifled a giggle. He reminded her of a big bear—tall, dark, and shaggy. His slight accent indicated he wasn't born in the United States, but she couldn't tell where he was from or how old he was. His reddish beard was flecked with gray but his hair was almost white.

"Since we're sharing chocolate and the view, we ought to at least know each other's names. I'm Amos."

"Naomi, but my friends call me Nomi."

They sat in companionable silence munching chocolate until Naomi's right leg began to cramp. She stood up trying to work it out.

"I think I've been sitting too long. I better get going." She put her backpack on her shoulders.

He asked, "Do you mind if I walk with you?"

For a split second she felt trapped, then she thought better of the offer and said, "No. That would be fine. If I walk too slowly for you, feel free to move on."

"I suspect your pace will be just right."

"How can you tell?" she asked.

He grinned. "Intuition."

She nodded, thinking to herself that a man who admits to having—as well as using—intuition can't be all bad.

One of the reasons Naomi loved hiking up Atalaya mountain was the variety of views. She generally chose to go up the steep trail, taking pleasure in the knowledge that there was a less steep, more winding option for part of the way up. She hadn't hiked for a while and wasn't sure what shape she was in, but she liked testing her endurance, pleased by the feeling that just when she thought she couldn't take another step, she did.

They headed toward the top with Naomi in the lead. Although she felt his presence, she set her own comfortable pace. There was no pressure to go faster. Their ease with each other made her feel the lack of a partner keenly.

She had walked up Atalaya mountain many times and knew where the pitch got steep and her breath turned into gasps, but this time it was as if she had wings. Her steps were light, and she felt as if she could burst into song. She couldn't help laughing.

"What's so funny?" he asked.

"I feel like I've sprouted wings."

"God, I hope that doesn't mean you've turned into an angel."

"There's about as much chance of that as this mountain turning into meatballs."

"I am reassured, although the idea of a mountain of meatballs makes me hungry. Want some chocolate?"

"Any more sugar and I'll turn into a screaming meemie. I better wait for lunch. I usually have it at the top. Want to join me?"

Amos nodded, taking a chomp out of another huge chocolate bar. "That sounds absolutely perfect."

Usually Naomi found herself alone when she reached the summit and looked forward to the quiet and grandeur that always moved her. This time, as they arrived, he said, "Looks like we're not the only ones up here today."

"Maybe they'll leave soon."

He shrugged. "It's a public place. They have as much right to be here as we do."

His patronizing tone of voice annoyed Naomi. Ignoring the group, she looked for a place that felt private, assuming Amos was still behind her. When she asked, "What do you think?" there was no answer.

Looking around, she saw him across the grassy space chatting with two men and a woman. Sitting close by, clumped together, were a couple with two boys, a girl, a puppy, and an older dog. He was offering them all chocolate bars, which they took, laughing. She wondered if he was a salesman for a chocolate company. Torn between wanting to join him and feeling jilted, she ate her lunch alone, needing to be wanted more than she wanted company.

She'd experienced many moments like this—watching people enjoying themselves yet unable to join them even when she had the opportunity. Lost in thought, Naomi jumped when her hiking companion sat down next to her.

"Nice people. They're here to buy Native American pots for their gallery in Copenhagen. Said they've been wanting to come to Santa Fe for fifteen years."

"I used to teach in Denmark."

"Why didn't you join us?"

Naomi refused to tell the truth—that she felt like a fifth wheel. "I don't know." She could feel herself sliding down into the all too familiar black hole.

"So what did you teach?" he asked.

"Literacy and language acquisition."

"How many languages do you speak?"

"English, some Spanish and French. What about you?"

"Hebrew, Arabic, English, and French mostly. I can get around in a few others."

"Were you born in Israel?"

"No, in Czechoslovakia, but my parents managed to survive the war. Afterwards they made their way to Israel despite the blockade. I was too young to remember much of the language or our life there."

"What made you come to the United States?"

"I got a scholarship to study at MIT."

"How come you didn't go back?"

He shrugged. "Too long a story," he said, lying down. She stretched out a few feet from him. Convenient lumps of grass under her back and knees and the warmth of the sun encouraged her to close her eyes.

A rough tongue licking her face awakened Naomi, as did a loud voice shouting, "Beadle, come here!" Either Beadle was deaf or he didn't care. The large black dog didn't move. He kept nuzzling Naomi as if she were a long lost friend. Caught between annoyance and pleasure, she stroked the dog's face. He took immediate advantage by licking all of her exposed skin.

Beadle's owner, a tall, lanky man with a gray ponytail, rushed over to her and tried to pull the dog away. Beadle did his best to ignore him.

"I'm sorry. I never saw him act like this before," said the man.

"Maybe we were lovers in past lives," said Naomi, sitting up.

"Yeah, right," he sneered, struggling to get his dog away from her.

"I don't mind. A little loving—what could be bad?"

Naomi didn't much like dogs, especially those that approached and licked without an invitation, but Beadle's attention was making the black hole smaller. She surprised herself again by hugging the dog.

Beadle's owner shifted from being concerned about Naomi's welfare to establishing who was boss. At least for the moment, Beadle, with Naomi's support, was winning.

Amos came up from behind, grabbed the dog, and held him as if he were saving Naomi from a poisonous snake.

"You better keep your dog on his leash. He might not always be so friendly."

"If your girlfriend would mind her own business, Beadle would come when I call like he always does."

"She's not my girlfriend."

"Whoever she is needs to butt out where she doesn't belong."

The two men glared at each other. More sensibly, Beadle wagged his tail, straining toward Naomi.

The tension between the men grew perceptibly. Naomi stepped between them, trying to ease the situation

"Look, I'm sorry if I caused a problem. I was feeling down, and your dog's affections felt really good. C'mon, Amos, let's get our stuff. I need to be down by three." Without waiting for Amos to agree, she took his arm and acted as if she were his girlfriend, muttering under her breath, "Please. Let's go. No trouble, okay?"

He shook off her arm and turned toward Beadle's owner. "You have a problem keeping your dog on the leash? I believe it's the law, even here on the mountain."

"I have a problem with you," said Beadle's owner, moving toward Amos.

The situation was so overwrought and the cause so stupid that Naomi picked up her backpack and ran between the two men.

"Stop it, both of you." She bent down and buried her face in Beadle's fur, hoping the men would come to their senses. When she couldn't get them to back off, she started down the trail, hoping Amos would follow, hoping he cared more about being with her than "testosteroning" with a stranger.

Then she heard a frustrated voice yell, "Beadle, come back here!"

Turning around, she saw Beadle loping happily toward her. "Go back,

Beadle," she called but he trotted on, leash slithering after him, matching her stride, seemingly delighted. After having to unsnag his leash one too many times, Naomi wrapped it loosely around his neck, freeing him to run and leap. At first she walked slower than usual, hoping Beadle's owner was more concerned about his dog than in confronting Amos, but when she saw no sign of him she resumed her normal pace. It wasn't until they were a third of the way down the mountain that she began to wonder what would happen if Beadle's owner accused her of dognapping. And what about Amos? Why wasn't he more interested in her than some stupid power struggle more suitable to eight year olds than grown men?

Beadle tripped Naomi. Deliberately. Running in front of her, he stopped short and looked up as she fell. Although she was in no mood to be licked, he gave her no choice. His joy was contagious. She wrapped her arms around him and he snuggled close, seemingly as hug deprived as she felt. She refused to think how silly they must look—a big black dog and a small white woman blissfully entwined in the middle of a narrow mountain trail.

"Beadle!"

Naomi jumped up, and Beadle ran off before she could grab his leash.

"Beadle!" The angry voice grew louder and more insistent.

She contemplated hiding, but no tree looked large enough. Frightened, Naomi decided to run.

10

Naomi was in pretty good shape, but the dog's owner was obviously a runner. Grabbing her arm, he pulled her down.

"Where's my dog?"

"I don't know," she gasped, struggling to get away. "Let me go!"

"He followed you. Where is he?" His menacing tone made Naomi shiver. She was about to kick him when he released his hold.

"He ran off when he heard you yell."

"Why didn't you hold his leash?"

His anger frightened her. "You couldn't hold him and you're his owner. How do you expect me to? Besides, he's your problem, not mine. Where's Amos?"

"He's your problem, not mine," sneered Beadle's owner.

He was standing between her and the trail down the mountain. Naomi glared at him, hoping he would move aside or someone would come. Through the trees she saw Beadle, watching.

"Look, I'm sorry about your dog, but I have to go. People are waiting for me at the parking lot, and if I'm late they'll start searching for me."

It was a lie, but she hadn't taught acting for nothing. Taking advantage of his hesitation, Naomi pushed past him and started walking as fast as she could, forcing herself not to look back.

By the time she got to the parking lot at the end of the trail, she was drenched with sweat. There were no people, but plenty of cars. She could only hope someone would appear if she needed help. As she opened the rear car door and put in her backpack, walking poles, and hat, Beadle jumped into the back of the car, sprang forward, and settled himself in the passenger seat.

"Oh no, dog. You can't do this!"

Naomi got into her car and sat in the driver's seat, trying to figure out what to do. The dog was too big to push out easily, and she was afraid to make him angry. Beadle had no such qualms, his head nuzzling against her.

When she stroked his face, she noticed the name on his tag, but no owner's name or address.

"Beadle, what am I going to do with you?" He snuggled closer.

She drank some water, and Beadle immediately nosed the bottle. "Does that mean you're thirsty?" She put water into her palm, and he slurped it so fast that it was more tongue lick than drink. Sighing, she repeated the process until the bottle was empty. With his head resting on her legs, oblivious to the fact that her lap was soaked, Beadle closed his eyes and slept.

Naomi knew nothing about dogs. She had no idea what to feed him or how she would know when he had to go out. Had there been an address on his tag, she might have taken him to his owner's house, yet Beadle's reaction to his owner haunted her.

"Why me, Beadle?" she said. "Aren't animals supposed to sense people who like cats rather than dogs?" Beadle snored.

Stopping at a market to get dog food, Naomi found the variety of cans and dry food bewildering. She picked up one can after another, looking at the ingredients, wondering which was the healthiest. They all seemed unappetizing.

"What are you looking for?" asked a man with a shock of gray hair, leaning on a cane, who was putting cans into his shopping cart.

"Dog food."

"I sort of guessed that. What's the problem?"

"I don't know what kind to get."

He picked a can off the shelf and said, "My dog likes this. Maybe yours will too."

"He's not my dog."

"So why are you feeding him?"

"Good question." She was tempted to tell him what had happened and to ask where she could take Beadle, but the dog had wormed its way into her heart and she wasn't sure what was best for either of them.

As Naomi walked away, he said, "You better get some dry food as well. They need a mix." He handed her a fifteen-pound bag.

"Doesn't this come in smaller amounts?"

"Yeah, but it costs more."

"Right now that's not an issue." She ignored his quizzical look.

At home, when Naomi opened the car door to let Beadle out, he stood up on the seat but refused to move any further.

"Come on, Beadle, we're home. At least I am."

When no amount of persuasion worked, she left the car door open and the front door ajar and went into the house. A few minutes later Beadle appeared, stopping a few feet inside.

"Well, well, look who's decided to be brave."

Naomi wasn't used to being followed. When she closed the bathroom door, Beadle wailed so piteously that she opened it, not expecting him to snuggle against her legs. Nor did she expect him to hop into the bathtub as she took a shower. Her bed was no exception. The minute she lay down, he was right beside her. This was a bit more togetherness than she could easily manage. The dog probably weighed close to fifty pounds

"Beadle, don't you want to sleep on the rug? I'll give you a great pillow."

He watched as Naomi put a pillow on the floor, but he made no move to leave the comfort of her bed. She lay down on the pillow, hoping he would follow. No luck. Sighing, she got back into bed and found herself snuggling against his warm body. She slept surprisingly well.

Where she went, he went. Up the stairs and down the stairs. Into the bedroom and out of the bedroom. When Naomi sat, he put his head in her lap. His need for closeness moved her. Whenever they got out of the shower, leaving a trail of water, he lapped up the puddles. When she took a bath, he jumped in. Shocked, she yelled, "Beadle!" He jumped out but shook his body so ferociously she was treated to a mini shower. She got out of the tub, grabbed two towels, and wrapped one around herself and used the other to dry him off as best she could, no mean feat given his propensity to lick any part of her that wasn't clothed.

Writing with a dog too big to sit in her lap but continually trying to do so was not conducive to concentration. Naomi found herself talking to him as if he were a person even though she had to push him down and say, "Sit!" a half dozen times before he agreed to stay out of her lap while she was writing at her desk. Just when she hoped they were settled, he started nudging her thigh insistently—a new tactic. As the pushing increased in intensity, it dawned on Naomi that he was trying to tell her he had to go out. She opened the front door before putting on his leash. The sound of furious barking and human yells unnerved her as she rushed outside.

Beadle was fighting with a tan and black dog, smaller and fatter than he was. Its owner was yelling, "Lukie, Lukie, darling," while trying to separate the two.

When Naomi saw blood dripping from Beadle's mouth, she ran toward him. "Beadle, come here. Now!"

He growled. She couldn't tell if it was at her, the other dog, or the other woman, whose yells for her dog changed into screams at Naomi.

"Get your dog away from mine before he kills Lukie!"

Without thinking Naomi ran to the fighting dogs and tried to separate them. The woman's dog bit her on the arm, a deep gash that bled profusely, but the momentary distraction enabled Beadle to run away.

The woman grabbed her dog and hugged him, yelling hysterically. "Your dog attacked my Lukie!"

"Your dog bit me. Has he had his rabies shot?" Naomi showed the woman her arm.

"This wouldn't have happened if your dog was on a leash."

"Where's your dog's leash?"

"My dog wasn't bothering anyone."

"Are his shots up to date?" The woman ignored Naomi's question, put the leash on her dog, and hurried off.

Naomi knew she should have asked the woman her name and address, but all she could think about was blood. And rabies.

She rushed into the bathroom, with Beadle close behind. The gash on her arm was deep, and she had difficulty stopping the bleeding. Beadle's injuries, although numerous, didn't seem serious enough to warrant a visit to the vet, where she would undoubtedly be asked questions she couldn't answer. Naomi wondered what the symptoms of rabies were and if it was too late to get shots once the symptoms appeared. She decided she couldn't deal with the stress of having the series of painful shots. All she could do was hope the dog had been inoculated and that all the flowing blood had washed the wound of infection. She cleaned and bandaged it as best she could.

She lay down on the bed. Beadle jumped up and plopped down next to her.

"Beadle, get down." No response. "Beadle, please?" Each time she spoke, the dog interpreted it as an invitation to move closer. Too tired to push him off, Naomi gave up. He snored. She slept. It was dark when she woke up, startled to feel a warm body pressing against her. Her arm throbbed.

"What am I going to do with you?" Beadle licked her arm. "I am not a dog person." He licked it again. She wondered if she was imagining that the pain had lessened. Maybe there was something to the idea of kiss and make it better. When the phone rang, visions of his angry owner filled her with dread.

"Hey, Nomi, I'm back."

"Want a dog?" Naomi told Priscilla the whole story.

"Better get your arm looked at. Rabies is no picnic."

"What am I going to do with Beadle?" Just the mention of his name started his tongue licking, this time on her bare feet.

"Maybe his owner put an ad in the paper. What about the registration number on his tag?"

She looked at his collar. "There is no tag. It must have come off in the dogfight."

"You could take him to a shelter." Beadle's head on her lap made this a more than dubious proposition.

"Come over, would you? I need a level-headed opinion."

"Oops, that leaves me out. You know how I found Benny."

Priscilla had told Naomi the story in great detail, how she was hiking and heard crying. When she followed the sound, she found a young puppy, apparently abandoned by its owner, stuck in a hole.

"But you like dogs. I don't."

"Tell that to Beadle," said Priscilla.

"Thanks a bunch. So, are you coming over? Beadle wants to meet you."

"Check the lost and found. I'll call you tomorrow."

No matter how often Naomi pushed Beadle off the bed, when she woke up, he was snuggled against her. What was happening felt unreal. She wanted love in her life—but a man, not a dog. She asked Beadle, "How come I ended up with you instead of Amos?"

There was no mention of a missing black dog that fit Beadle's description in the paper the next morning. Naomi had a tennis game and was grateful she could still hold the tennis racquet with her right hand. She didn't want to leave Beadle in the car for two hours, yet she worried about leaving him home alone. Before changing into her tennis clothes, she took him for a long walk, feeling relieved that they met no dogs.

When it was time to leave for tennis, Naomi put fresh water in a dish and dry food in a bowl. "Okay, Beadle. I'll be back in about three hours. Please, be a good dog." As she closed the door, she heard him whine, then a loud thump, which sounded like he was throwing himself against the door. Gritting her teeth, she got in the car and drove off.

Naomi found it difficult to concentrate and missed balls she usually hit with ease. All she could think about was Beadle—how he was, what he might be doing. Part of her was tired of worrying about the dog. She hadn't invited him to be in her life. And yet, when he came romping in, his affection eased a hurting place inside her.

While driving home, her sense of dread increased. She had visions of yarn scattered everywhere with who knows what on the rugs. A vase broken, water spilled on the wood floors. Bracing herself for the worst, she opened the door and called his name. Nothing. "Beadle, I'm home!" Silence. Envisioning him dead or bleeding, she raced around the house yelling his name. She couldn't imagine where he was or what had happened until she went into the utility room and noticed the torn screen. How he managed to get through the tiny window boggled her mind. One thing was clear. When that dog wanted something, he did his best to get it. Was that his legacy?

Naomi looked around outside, called his name, and asked neighbors if they had seen him, but no one had. Her pillow was dented from his lying on it. Just as she put her head down, smelling his smell, missing his loving presence, the phone rang. Something told her to let it ring, a feat she found impossible.

"Where's Beadle?"

"How did you find me?"

"I'm coming to pick up my dog."

"He's not here."

"Oh yes he is. A friend of mine saw him jump into your car and took down your license plate number."

"Too bad your friend didn't see him jump out," lied Naomi.

"I called the police. They're going to charge you."

"Let them. I don't have your dog."

"You can't bluff me. I'm coming to get my dog."

"I told you, your dog isn't here. And if you try anything funny, I'll push the panic button on my alarm system. It rings at the police station. The cops will be here before you can drive away."

"Look, lady, all I want is my dog."

"So put an ad in the paper. Put signs up. Maybe someone's seen him and is waiting to find out how to contact you. By the way, if you love your dog so much, why didn't you put your phone number and address on his dog tag? That would certainly let people know how to contact you."

"My friend saw Beadle in your car."

"Your friend should have told you he jumped out. Or didn't your friend tell you the whole story?"

"I just want my dog."

"I don't have him."

"I know where you live. I'll find Beadle."

Naomi slammed down the phone and called Priscilla. "I need to get out of the house for a while. Want to meet me for dinner?"

"No, I've got work to do. Come here, there's enough food for both of us."

Naomi gathered up the food she'd bought for the dog. Just in case the police did come, she wanted no evidence of Beadle's presence. The torn screen would have to wait until the morning.

Suddenly, in the distance, she thought she heard a truck. Worried that it might be Beadle's owner, she grabbed the bag of dog food and bumped into the pantry door, reopening the gash on her left arm. She awkwardly bandaged it then hurried out to her car. When she saw Beadle's owner through the windshield of his truck she gunned the engine and drove off, only slightly relieved that, while she had driven through a red light, he had stopped for it.

Naomi carefully carried the bag of dog food with her right arm. When Priscilla saw the bloody bandage on Naomi's left arm, she immediately took her into the bathroom to doctor it. She'd learned to deal with cuts and bruises as part of her field training. "I guess with a dog named Lukie, especially if his owner lives in your neighborhood, you don't need to worry about rabies, but it sure is a nasty mess."

"Can you keep the dog food here for me?"

"I guess, but why not throw it out? You planning to get a dog?"

"Yeah, right. As if I didn't have enough worries in my life."

"Like what?" Priscilla's response was automatic.

Naomi's avoidance of the question was also automatic.

"Can you keep the food for a few days?" Naomi asked. "If it gets to be a problem, just dump it."

"I'll make you a cup of tea from stuff I got in Peru," said Priscilla as she finished bandaging Naomi's left arm. "The Indians there use it to heal wounds and some kinds of sickness. Doesn't taste very good, but I think it works."

They took their tea and sat underneath the portal, looking at the setting sun. "No matter how many sunsets I see here, I never get used to them," said Naomi, making a face as she drank the bitter brew. "The colors and patterns are astonishing."

Priscilla nodded, then decided she'd try once again. "You seem upset. It can't just be about the dog."

"If I believed in *wu-wu*, I'd say my spirit is being weighed down by forces beyond my control. Any ideas? I feel so stuck. It's as if my head and my heart are at war."

"Tell your heart to start talking to your head."

"Are you kidding? They refuse to acknowledge each other's existence."

"Maybe you have to do what I did when I decided to quit smoking. Just do it."

"By the way, how many times did you say you quit before you quit?"

"Point taken."

11

While still a professor, teaching full time at a research university, with all the perks and privileges of rank, Naomi often worried about who she would be when she stopped teaching. Her identity depended more on her profession than she wanted to admit. Yet after moving to Santa Fe and being repeatedly asked for a business card she didn't have, she made a new one with surprising ease, choosing to be a storyteller—even leaving off the PhD. She discovered she liked having time to write and weave, and to create her own schedule according to her needs, not those of others. When people wanted to know how she liked retirement, she shot back with too much edge. "I didn't retire. I fell in love with a house and quit my job."

She was at her desk, writing, when the phone rang. "May I speak to Dr. Rosen?" asked an unfamiliar female voice.

"Who's calling please?"

"My name is Beatrice Romero. I'm the director of Juvenile Services in Santa Fe. We've started a new program, a course in creative writing as part of a court-mandated program for delinquent teenage girls, and we're looking for a teacher. You were highly recommended by Priscilla Jordan, who's done consulting work for us."

Naomi felt a surge of joy. Someone still wanted her professional expertise.

"Would it be possible for you to come to my office to discuss salary and schedule tomorrow afternoon? I realize this is short notice, but our previous teacher . . . How about two o'clock?"

"Three would work better for me." Naomi didn't want to seem too available, especially if salary was negotiable.

As she drove to Beatrice Romero's office she wondered what kind of crimes the girls had committed and how they felt about being ordered to write. Didn't seem like the right way to go about encouraging new behaviors, but maybe whoever mandated the program knew something about motivation that Naomi didn't know, especially when it came to dealing with girls in trouble with the law.

Mrs. Romero was a stern-looking, tall, full-bodied woman with piercing black eyes. She wore a gray tailored suit, had tiny diamond studs in her ears, a wide silver and turquoise wedding band on her left ring finger, and spoke in a no-nonsense way that initially intimidated Naomi. But after they finished negotiating salary and arranging a schedule, Mrs. Romero's tone of voice changed, becoming softer, almost pleading. "I think you should know, you might be these girls' last, best, and only chance to make better lives for themselves. It won't be easy."

"The program sounds wonderful. Any judge who thinks creative writing is a better alternative than punishment must be an unusual person."

"The point is, the program has to achieve results if we want the funding to continue. As you know, budgets are tight and getting tighter."

"How are results going to be measured?" asked Naomi, wary of tests that measure what can be measured rather than changes for which no measurements exist.

Mrs. Romero hesitated. "Less belligerence, perhaps. Maybe a change in attitude. Certainly different social choices—no more shoplifting or prostitution or aggressive behaviors."

"Isn't that a lot to ask from a creative writing program?" asked Naomi.

"These girls are in crisis, but they're young enough to make new, healthier choices. Learning to express themselves in appropriate ways could be a first step. Which reminds me, I will need to see what the girls write so I have some idea of what they're feeling and thinking and how these change as the program develops."

"What about privacy and confidentiality?" asked Naomi. "How are the girls going to learn to trust me if they have to show you everything they write? Shouldn't they have the right to decide whether to show you their work? Especially at the beginning?"

"Dr. Rosen, this is a court-mandated program. The judge sets the rules. I merely carry them out. If you think you can't abide by the rules, I need to know this now."

Naomi hid her anger as best she could. "Mrs. Romero, I'm not saying you shouldn't see what the girls write, I'm simply suggesting that it be by their own volition. If these girls are in trouble with the law, it's at least in part because they don't know how to control their impulses. By allowing the girls to freely express themselves with no comment or judgment, we'll be helping them to trust that what they say won't be held against them. This will give them time to develop access to deeper, perhaps hidden, more vulnerable aspects of themselves."

"You have two choices, Dr. Rosen. Either you agree to let me see what the girls write and you teach the program, or you don't. In which case, I cannot hire you."

Faced with the either-or situation, Naomi reluctantly agreed. After hearing thumbnail descriptions of each girl and why she'd been arrested, Naomi was hired to teach an initial series of six two-hour sessions with five girls, ages fourteen to seventeen. The beginning of each session was designed to give them an opportunity to talk, and, in time, to explore their feelings. Although Naomi knew it would take a lot of work on her part for them to trust her, and some of them might never do so, she hoped the traditional stories she told would open the way for her and the girls to create a caring community.

First sessions seldom go according to plan.

Naomi arrived a few minutes early to give herself time to organize her thoughts, but two of the girls were already there, looking out the window. The taller of the two wore skintight jeans, a form-fitting long-sleeved, high-necked shirt, and high-heeled sandals. Her long dark hair gleamed in the sun. The girl next to her was almost as tall, her dark hair plaited in a single waist length braid. She wore a loose top over her ample torso. Naomi wondered if she was pregnant.

"Hi, are you here for the writing workshop?"

After looking her up and down, checking her out, the taller girl said, "Yeah." Her challenging tone disconcerted Naomi who tried to control her shock when she noticed the bruises on the girl's face that her makeup did little to conceal.

She walked toward them. They remained where they were. "I'm Naomi Rosen. I'm happy to meet you. And you are . . . ?"

"Martina. And she's Juanita."

"I can talk for myself," snapped Juanita.

"Well, how about that," mocked Martina.

Before Juanita could respond, Naomi intervened. "I'm glad you're here early. Would you mind helping me rearrange the chairs?"

"There's only gonna be five of us," snickered Martina looking at the straight rows of chairs. "We can sit in the front row, unless Juanita here does her usual and sits in the back row."

"Shut up, bitch," muttered Juanita.

Martina laughed. "Girl, you are so easy to poke, it's pathetic."

Naomi took a deep breath. No one ever said there'd be no bumps in the road, especially after hearing Mrs. Romero describe the girls, ending with the warning that Martina, seventeen, and Juanita, sixteen, were cousins, that they were always together, always fighting, and unwilling to be separated. Martina had been arrested for prostitution, Juanita for assault and battery.

While Martina and Juanita watched Naomi move chairs, a skinny, short, nervous-looking girl with black braids entered the room. Nilda, fourteen, the youngest of the group, had been arrested for shoplifting and ordered to attend the writing workshop as part of her probation.

"Would you like help?" she asked in a voice so soft that Naomi wasn't sure she had heard correctly.

"That would be great. I want to push the chairs back far enough so we can have a circle of six chairs."

The last two girls straggled in. Fifteen-year-old Lupe had bleached blond hair, blue eyes, and earrings that dangled to her shoulders. She wore jeans that barely hung on her hips and a tee shirt that ended just below her bra. She'd been declared a ward of the court after running away from home one time too many. Carolina, sixteen, was arrested for DWI and driving without a license. Her father died when she was a baby and she'd been living with an aunt since her mother's disappearance when she was about five. After Carolina's arrest, the aunt threw her out. She'd been living on the streets when the police picked her up. She was dressed in Capri pants and a tee shirt that read, "If you don't like it, go f . . . yourself

"There's only five of us," protested Nilda.

"Right! Five of you and one of me make six."

"You gonna sit in the circle?"

Naomi nodded.

The girls sat and looked everywhere but at Naomi, who ignored their stony faces. "Welcome. I'm pleased that we'll be working together. As you know, I'm here to help you with your writing, so let's begin by each of you telling a little about yourself." Naomi nodded to Martina, sitting to her left. "Martina?"

Martina sighed, looked at the ceiling, leaned back, and fell to the floor. When Naomi asked, "Are you okay?" she nodded, picking herself up, ignoring Naomi's offer of help, glaring at her as if forbidding her to ask about the bruises on her face

"Oh, man . . ." complained Juanita, staring at her cousin. Martina's ferocious look silenced further comments.

Naomi decided to ignore the incident and continue the session. "Everything we say and do here is private. Nothing will be shared with anyone without your permission." *If Mrs. Romero wants to fire me for not forcing the girls to show her their writing, so be it.* The girls nodded. Silence. "I'm here to help, not to judge." Silence.

As a young teacher, Naomi had learned to be comfortable with silence in her classroom. She sometimes found it a good way to convince a group that they had a responsibility to participate, that she was not going to be the only one to talk. Still, Mrs. Romero's last words echoed. "Dr. Rosen, these girls are tough. I just hope you're tougher. The previous instructor never finished the first session."

The tension between Martina and Juanita was palpable. Nilda appeared ready to cry. Lupe stared at a crack in the ceiling as if it were a Van Gogh painting. Carolina looked at Naomi with an amused expression.

The silence dragged on and felt so unproductive that Naomi decided it was time to change tactics. "Is it all right if I tell you a story from Brazil?"

"What's it about?" asked Carolina.

"Hummingbird and Panther."

There was another long silence that Naomi chose to respect, not wanting to impose an agenda or create a false sense of connection. After about ten minutes of increasingly unbearable silence, Martina, said, "Go ahead. Tell the stupid story if you need to," her voice thick with sarcasm.

"This is your time. What you decide matters to me."

"Is it a story with a moral?" asked Carolina. "I hate stories with morals."

"Me too," said Naomi.

"You do? How come you don't like them?"

"Because ending a story with a moral is like telling what the story means. In a way, it kills the story." The girls seemed less guarded, so Naomi continued. "The meaning we derive from a story usually depends on what we're going through or how we're feeling."

"That's dumb," said Martina. "A story's a story. How's it supposed to change?"

"So what's the story you want to tell us mean to you?" asked Juanita.

Naomi laughed. "Neat trick, but it won't work."

Juanita giggled.

"If you know so many stories, why you want to tell us this one?" asked Martina, the guarded look firmly in place.

"I like the story."

"That's it?"

"That's it."

"The lady who brought us here said we had to do stuff with paint and clay," said Lupe. "What if we don't want to?"

"Yeah, what if we don't draw good?" asked Nilda.

"Tell you what," said Naomi, "let's play with the paint and clay after you hear the story and see what happens. Then we can talk about whether you think it's a good thing for us to do. It's hard to make a decision without experience."

"You can say that again." Carolina rolled her eyes.

So, Naomi told them the story:

> Hummingbird felt terrible because she was so drab and colorless, unlike the beautiful red and yellow flowers, the brilliant blue sky, and the glorious green grasses and leaves. Nothing she tried changed the color of her feathers.
>
> One morning, while feeling particularly miserable, she heard a loud groaning, a hideous noise. Much to her horror, it was Panther, an animal who terrified her. His sharp teeth were almost as big as she was. As he moved closer, his moans grew so unbearable Hummingbird blurted out, "Why are you making such a terrible noise?"
>
> Panther told her, "Last night, I accidentally stepped on Mouse Mother's children as I was running through the forest. To punish me, when I was asleep, she put mud on my closed eyes. Now the mud is so hard I can't open my eyes. I can't see. I'm blind. How will I ever find food to eat?" He began to wail louder than ever.

Naomi looked at the girls, pleased to see they were listening.

> "You're not the only one with a problem," snapped Hummingbird. "I'm so dowdy and colorless, no one even notices me."
>
> "That's not a problem. I can fix that."

"You can?" asked Hummingbird, not at all sure she believed him.

Panther said, "I'll make a bargain with you. If you peck the mud from my eyes so I can see, I'll help you become as colorful as you like."

Although Hummingbird wanted this more than anything in the world, getting so close to Panther was almost too frightening to think about.

Yet her yearning to be colorful was more powerful than her fear of Panther's sharp teeth. She gathered her courage and flew to Panther, making him promise to keep his mouth closed. She pecked out the mud from his eyes as carefully as possible, hoping he wouldn't eat her when she was finished. When Panther could open his eyes, he leapt into the air. "I can see. I can see!"

Hummingbird grumbled, "What about your promise? What about our bargain? What about me?"

Panther took a long look at Hummingbird. "You really are ugly. No wonder you're unhappy." Hummingbird was about to tell him that he didn't have to try to make her feel bad, that she already felt awful, when he said, "Follow me."

He led her to a clearing in the forest near a bubbling stream and told her to gather as many different colored flowers and grasses as she could find. He made a roaring fire and put a pot of water over it.

Hummingbird followed his instructions. She filled the pot with flowers and grasses and stirred and stirred and stirred until Panther decided it was time to take the pot off the fire. When the water was cool he told Hummingbird to jump in and wet herself all over.

When she flew out and shook herself off Panther looked at Hummingbird and said, "Better do it once more."

After the third time of jumping into the pot and shaking off the colorful water, Panther said, "That's better. Now fly to the river and take a good look at yourself."

Filled with dread that Panther's plan had not worked, she slowly flew to the water, afraid of what she would see.

"Open your eyes and look!" commanded Panther.

Hummingbird took a deep breath and did as she was told.

"Oh," she whispered, hardly believing her eyes, amazed to see such a marvelously colored bird reflected in the water. "I'm beautiful."

"Yes, you are," said Panther. "And I'm hungry," he said as he loped into the forest to find something to eat.

The girls were silent after the story ended, but their faces looked more relaxed. Nilda was smiling. The atmosphere in the room had lightened considerably until Martina challenged, "We got to paint now?"

"I'd like you to try doing it, yes."

"What's it got to do with writing? This is supposed to be about writing."

"It is, but painting is a way of connecting thoughts with feelings. Look, this is your time. You get to say how you spend it. All I ask is that you try before you decide you don't want to do something. Can we agree on this?" The girls looked at each other.

Carolina said, "You said we have to paint with our fingers, right?" Naomi nodded. "Well, I got polish on my nails. I don't want no stuff ruining them."

"Me neither," agreed Juanita.

"I have gloves you can use if you don't want to get your hands dirty."

Their expressions clearly showed that fingerpainting was the last thing they wanted to do, but Naomi kept going. "I'm asking you to do something you've never done, and you're saying no on the basis of imagined problems. Why not try it and see what happens? In a way, isn't that why you're here? To look at the choices you've made and explore new ways and ideas?" Nilda seemed eager, but Naomi sensed that if the youngest were the first to say yes, the older girls would say it was only for children.

"Martina, you told the social worker you wanted to be an artist, didn't you?" Martina nodded. "This might help you find a medium that interests you."

"Yeah, but fingerpainting's for kids. I want to make real art."

"All this talk is givin' me a headache," complained Juanita. "Let's just do it and get it over with." The girls argued with a growing intensity.

Martina stood up, her arms tightly crossed against her chest, glaring at Naomi. "Fingerpainting has nothing to do with writing and that's what we're supposed to be doing. I'm leaving. I got better things to do."

Juanita stood up, hissing at Martina, "Oh yeah, if you're so smart, how come you keep lettin' José hit you?"

A free-for-all ensued, with Juanita and Martina yelling at each other in Spanish, Carolina and Lupe trying to separate them, and Nilda hiding under the desk. Naomi was shocked, horrified by the mess of red fingerpaint in front of her. For a moment she thought it was blood on the floor. Then Martina and Juanita began punching and pulling hair and hurling curses, knowing where each was vulnerable, knowing too much about the other's life. Carolina got pummeled and Naomi was hit on the face as they attempted to separate the two girls. Nilda's sobs grew louder and more terrified as she cowered in a fetal position, unwilling to let Lupe comfort her.

It was not the best moment for Mrs. Romero to come into the room.

"What's going on?" she asked in a tone of voice that demanded an immediate explanation.

The girls froze. Juanita wiped blood off her face. Martina straightened her clothing.

"We were practicing stage combat and it got a bit out of hand," said Naomi, avoiding the girls' incredulous looks, dabbing the blood on her face with a tissue.

"Dr. Rosen, you are paid to teach creative writing. There's enough violence in these girls' lives. Come to my office as soon as the session is over. And I want to see their writing." Seeing the shocked looks on the girls' faces, she added, "With their permission, of course."

Naomi was relieved Mrs. Romero could not read her thoughts. *Damn supervisors, always thinking they know what's best, even for people they never taught.* "When you came in," said Naomi, "we had just finished staging a fight and were going to use it as the basis for writing. I slipped and accidentally scratched Juanita. You're welcome to stay and see how we use the material we've just developed." She gave the girls a pleading look, "Right?" They remained impassive. "In fact, if you'd like to participate, we'd love to have you join us."

"Dr. Rosen, I will see you in my office." She strode out.

The silence was palpable. Naomi handed out materials.

"You lied," said Lupe.

"Yes, I did. I thought what I said was preferable to explaining what really happened. What would you have done?"

Lupe stared at Naomi. The others looked away.

Sometimes clichés are true, thought Naomi. She felt as if there was not one elephant in the room, but a whole herd. She wanted to ignore the emotional chaos she felt in the girls, but with Nilda still huddled under the table and Martina and Juanita glaring at each other, ready to finish their business, this was not possible. Naomi bent down to help Nilda stand up, but she refused to move.

The silence continued. Naomi decided to press ahead. "Okay, here we go. On the left side of the paper, write the word *fear*. Now, stick your fingers in the paint and make an image of fear. You only have a minute so there's no time to think about right or wrong or good or bad. Whatever you paint is fine."

Nilda remained under the table. No one moved to participate. All Naomi could think about was the teacher who'd walked out without finishing the first session. She refused to give Mrs. Romero, or anyone else, the opportunity to say, "I told you so."

She took a deep breath. "We have half an hour left in the session. You heard Mrs. Romero. She wants to see your writing. In my opinion, helping me helps you, but it's your choice." Silence. Silence. More silence.

For the first time in years, the quiet got to her. She stuck her fingers in the pot of black and fingerpainted, oblivious to the stares of the girls. Nilda came out from under the table and stood next to her, watching. Without a word, Nilda took a piece of paper and dipped her fingers into two pots of paint, taking obvious pleasure in smearing red and yellow over the paper.

Naomi's black swirls and jags reflected her frustration. Although she told herself to use color, her fingers refused to move from the black. As she wiped her hands, the urge to write became irresistible.

"What are you writing?" asked Carolina.

"How I feel," Naomi answered.

"How do you feel?" she asked.

"Frustrated."

"You think she's gonna fire you?" asked Lupe.

"She might."

"The other teacher we had didn't like us. Do you?" asked Carolina.

"Yes, I do," she said.

"Well, you're the only person who does," sneered Lupe.

Naomi felt Martina's eyes boring into her, daring her to do something. Taking the girls' measure, carefully choosing her words, she told them, "I know we haven't worked together long enough for you to trust me. But if you want me to come back, I need your help. You heard what Mrs. Romero said."

"I ain't giving her nuthin' I write," said Juanita. "She's always stickin' her ass in other people's business."

"That may be, but if I don't show her some of your writing, I'm out of here." Naomi found herself smiling.

"What's so funny?" asked Martina.

"I just remembered something that happened to me when I was in college doing my practice teaching."

"What?" asked Lupe.

"According to my teachers, I was obstinate, stubborn, difficult, and asked too many questions. I thought our classes were boring." The girls looked interested so she continued. "One day, I heard that my supervisor was coming to watch me teach. The students were fooling around, refusing to practice the basketball skills I was supposed to be teaching. So, feeling I had nothing to lose, I asked them to tell me what would make things better for them in class. When no one spoke, I told them my supervisor was coming soon and that I'd probably fail the course because I wasn't doing a very good job."

"Why not?" asked Carolina.

"I could tell the girls hated gym."

"Everyone hates gym," said Lupe. "It's gross."

"What happened then?" asked Nilda.

"It was sort of strange. The girls asked what they could do to help me pass. I told them that I knew they hated basketball and I understood why. There were over seventy girls in the class and only twelve could play. That meant most of the class had to watch a boring game played badly."

"What did you do?" asked Juanita.

"They agreed to help, and we created a game with players, a score, and an action. Then we practiced it, just like it was a play. In the meantime, we did gymnastics, which most of the girls liked. As soon as I got word that my supervisor was on her way to the gym, we put our plan into practice. When she came into the gym, she saw twelve girls playing and the rest of the class watching intently. As soon as she left, we went back to gymnastics."

"Sort of like you telling Mrs. Romero we was doing stage fights?" asked Lupe.

"Sort of."

"What happened after that?" asked Carolina.

"We figured out how to make gym better for the class."

Nilda started writing.

"What are you doing?" Martina asked her in a threatening voice.

Nilda kept writing.

The session was almost over. The remaining fifteen minutes loomed large.

"I asked you a question, girl!" said Martina, moving toward Nilda.

Nilda wrote a bit more, then stopped. "I was thinking about the story."

"Aren't you the good girl," jeered Martina.

Nilda edged closer to Naomi before she spoke. "I was thinking about what would happen if Hummingbird's color didn't last. If it faded after a few days."

"Interesting," said Naomi. "That never occurred to me."

"Nothing lasts. Especially when it's good," said Nilda.

"You can say that again," agreed Martina.

"I have an idea," said Naomi. "If you're willing, each of us could write one or two sentences, and we could put them into a poem in whatever order we decide is right. I'll show our group poem to Mrs. Romero. That way she'll see your writing but she won't know who wrote what line."

Nilda spoke first. " 'Nothing lasts' is my line."

"Let's write them down on these cards—one sentence per card."

The girls wrote, erased, wrote, erased . . . Naomi looked at her watch and decided her supervisor could wait. Or not.

Not, as it turned out. While they were still writing, Mrs. Romero came in. She hesitated, nodded, and left. Naomi collected the cards and gave them to Martina to read. The girls discussed each sentence until they were satisfied with their group poem.

Nothing lasts.
Not color or joy or happiness.
I'm afraid.
I want to be beautiful.
It will never happen.
Never?

"Is it all right with you if I give a copy to Mrs. Romero?"

Martina protested. "She'll probably think we're all depressed and put us on meds."

"That's why we put a question mark after the 'Never.' Remember?" said Carolina.

"I gotta go," said Martina. "We're late." She grabbed Juanita's arm and started toward the door, the others following.

Naomi hesitated, then called out. "Wait a second. Before you leave, I need to know if you want to continue."

"Why? You don't want to come back?" snickered Martina.

"I want to, do you?" They nodded. "Okay, see you next week."

Naomi watched them leave, then collapsed in exhaustion. She had expected it would be difficult to gain the girls' trust, but she wasn't prepared for the complexity of their interaction. Still, she'd gotten through the first session, which was more than the previous instructor had been able to do. She forced herself to walk to Mrs. Romero's office.

"Have you something to show me?" she asked.

"It's not much, but all the girls wrote. It's a beginning."

Mrs. Romero read the poem without commenting on it. "I'll see you next week. And, Dr. Rosen, no more stage combat."

Naomi nodded and left, wishing the supervisor had at least acknowledged her small success.

12

Despite having gotten the girls to write, Naomi felt depressed. The enormity of their problems made her wonder if she'd ever break through their defenses. She was aware that her own defenses were so firmly in place she couldn't imagine what it would take to liberate her vulnerability. How could she hope to help the girls? Driving home through the desert landscape she thought about the secrets of ancient civilizations being dug out of the earth by intrusive anthropologists like Priscilla. Why couldn't secrets stay buried? Lose their potency.

When Naomi got home, she saw the blinking light on her answering machine. Ignoring it, she put on her hiking boots and drove to the Winsor Trail near the Santa Fe ski area, her favorite hike when she needed to rid herself of demons or depression or both. The trail was steep, but when she stopped to catch her breath, unwelcome thoughts surfaced. She forced herself to keep walking, until she noticed the light was fading. It felt good to be anxious about being alone on the mountain. That, at least, was a fear she could manage.

Once she was home, her demons returned, nourished by the still-flashing light on the answering machine. She asked herself why she didn't consider that it might be Priscilla, or some college asking her to teach. Why did she assume anything about who had called? Reason didn't trump fear. Although she almost never drank alone, she poured herself a tumbler of brandy and swallowed half of it before she pushed the play button. "Nomi, come for dinner. I want you to meet a friend of mine." Priscilla's chuckle reverberated. Naomi swallowed the other half of the brandy, hoping it would calm her, and then wondered if she was fit to drive.

Despite not wanting to be late for dinner, she stopped the car and got out to watch the spectacular sunset. Purple, pink, orange, and gold light shimmered and danced, changing configurations and colors as though an artist was painting a magical universe.

Priscilla was gracious about Naomi's late arrival. "I was about to give up on you. Come meet Pablo." She laughed. "My newest love."

"*Buenas noches*, Naomi," he said, his voice warm and seductive, sounding like her Pablo from another time and place. Memories of lively brown eyes and strong welcoming arms assaulted her. She felt too dizzy to stand.

Priscilla helped her to the couch. "Lie down. Dinner can wait."

"Is your friend all right?" asked Pablo, the sound of his voice eerily familiar.

"I don't know," answered Priscilla.

Naomi tried to say, "I'm fine," but the floodgates had opened and there was no way to talk. She plunged into the waters of her past, of her time in Spain.

"Are you going to tell me what's going on, or do I have to stand here feeling anxious for the rest of the evening?" asked Priscilla.

With effort, Naomi pulled herself into the present. "I'm okay. Just felt a little faint. Probably need to eat. You know me, when my blood sugar drops, watch out." The look on Priscilla's face told Naomi that she believed her as much as if she'd said pumpkins were purple and pink.

Naomi sat up and took the proffered glass of water from Pablo. She couldn't help noticing the scar that zigzagged from his chin to just below his left eye, spoiling what was otherwise a handsome face. Hearing him talk with Priscilla in Spanish made Naomi shiver. "I think I better take a rain check for dinner and go home."

"I think you better stay and eat. I don't want to hear you lost consciousness and hit a tree or, worse, another car," countered Priscilla.

"I'm fine," lied Naomi.

"Sure you are," mocked Priscilla. "Fine as a dead noodle."

Pablo brought Naomi a plate of hors d'oeuvres, barbecued shrimp, rice balls, and steamed broccoli. The sight and smell of food she normally loved left her feeling nauseated. There was no way she could force herself to eat. "I need to wash my face."

Naomi felt Priscilla's eyes on her as she wobbled to the bathroom. The cold water helped a little, but all she wanted to do was leave. When she walked to the front door, Priscilla was leaning against it.

"Nomi, you can't fool me, something's wrong."

"I don't want to talk about it now, especially not with Pablo waiting for dinner."

"Screw dinner, I'll fix him a plate. He's a good guy. He'll understand."

"Maybe, but I want to go home."

Priscilla's gaze was steady and not unkind. "Talk to me. I'll listen. What's friendship without trust?"

"It's too long a story."

"I'm in no hurry."

"What about Pablo?"

"He's got a paper to edit. I'll tell him we need to talk. He knows not to interrupt when my door is closed."

She led Naomi into the study and poured them each a glass of wine. "I'm here. For as long as it takes. What year are we talking about?" Naomi wished she were anywhere but sitting across from Priscilla. She couldn't make herself speak. Priscilla sighed, showing her impatience. "Nomi, talk!"

Naomi was too tired to fight any longer. She began to tell her about trying out for Eric's folk dance group, and what it had been like to travel with him, when they were interrupted by an insistent knock on the door. "Prissy, could you come out for a moment?" asked Pablo.

"I'm busy. Can't it wait?"

"No. Please, I need your help."

Priscilla sighed and opened the study door. Then she heard the problem. Someone, or something, was scratching relentlessly at the front door.

Pablo said, "What do you think it is?"

Priscilla listened intently and then took out her walking staff, which had a pointed end. "Open the door, Pablo. I'm ready." He hesitated, not caring that his fear showed, but Priscilla's tone of voice was a command. "Go ahead!"

In rushed Beadle, mangled, skinny, and dirty. He ran to Naomi and when she bent down, he licked her face like a long lost lover. Pablo and Priscilla stared. Naomi was incredulous.

"Beadle! What are you doing here? Where have you been?" His bones pressed into her as he put his paws on her shoulders, snuggling close.

Priscilla brought dishes of water and food, but Beadle refused to eat until Naomi held the dish and allowed him to put a paw on her hand.

"If he's as starved as he looks, don't give him too much right now," suggested Pablo. "He'll just throw it up."

"How do you know so much about dogs?" Priscilla asked Pablo.

"Personal experience, and not with dogs," he answered, ignoring Priscilla's questioning looks.

Priscilla moved away from Beadle, shuddering. "He needs a bath." She looked at Naomi. "Maybe if we hadn't saved the bag of dog food he wouldn't have come."

"I knew there was a reason I preferred cats," laughed Naomi, unable to stop Beadle from licking her.

"I'll help if you want to bathe him," said Pablo. "He reminds me of the dog we had when I was a boy."

Priscilla wanted no part of the bathing, but she offered the use of her lavender soap. "Maybe this will improve the way he smells."

Naomi coaxed Beadle into Priscilla's bathtub, Pablo holding him while Naomi lathered him with Priscilla's soap. By the time Beadle was clean, Naomi and Pablo were soaking wet.

"If you don't want him, maybe I could take him home with me," said Pablo, as he toweled Beadle dry with one of Priscilla's fluffy mauve bath towels.

"What if Beadle's owner is still looking for him?" asked Naomi, allowing Beadle to lick her cheek. "He has no tag. Does that mean anything?"

"Not really, if his owner is still looking for him," said Priscilla, mopping up some of the water. "After this, you can never question my friendship, Nomi. There aren't many people whose mess I'd mop up."

"But how's the owner going to prove that Beadle is his dog?" asked Naomi.

"You can call the police in the morning and ask them," said Priscilla as she squeezed the last bit of water out of the mop. "It's late. Stay here tonight. Besides, I want to hear the rest of your story."

Naomi was too tired to argue. "I'll stay, but the story will have to wait."

After his bath Beadle looked even skinnier, but at least he smelled good as he hopped into bed with her, snuggling as close as he could.

When Naomi called the Humane Society the next morning, she learned that Beadle's owner was still looking for him. Now she had no excuse to keep the dog. She had the owner's name, address, and phone numbers—everything she needed to return Beadle. Yet she kept thinking something really must be wrong if Beadle preferred her to his owner.

"Eat. You'll feel better," said Priscilla.

Naomi tried. Priscilla's blueberry pancakes were famous, but just looking at Beadle's nose in her lap was enough to set her stomach roiling.

Pablo finished eating, stood up, and announced, "I will go and talk to this person. I will convince him to allow you to keep Beadle."

"I don't think so," said Naomi. "He's angry. He threatened to sue me for stealing his dog."

"I will explain that the dog found you."

"He won't believe you."

"I will make him." Pablo's tone of voice made Naomi shiver. "*Hasta la vista*," he yelled as he closed the front door.

Naomi's worried look prompted Priscilla to explain. "Pablo's mother and older brothers were killed by fascists during the Spanish Civil War, and he was tortured by Franco's goons. Just mention bullying and Pablo's ready to do whatever he decides has to be done."

"I don't need him to rescue me," protested Naomi, pushing away memories of her time in Spain. "I don't even know if I want a dog, much less one that isn't mine."

"Pablo's not necessarily doing it for you." Priscilla sighed. "He comes from a culture where almost everything is a matter of honor. But enough about him. What happened when you left Eric and took a train to Barcelona?"

"I don't really want to talk about it." Naomi avoided Priscilla's questioning eyes.

"Maybe if you talk about it, you'll feel better."

After seeing the hurt expression on Priscilla's face, Naomi had a momentary urge to tell Priscilla what happened, but her sense of shame was too strong. "Pris, just thinking about it makes me feel bad."

"Why? I can't believe you did anything wrong."

"I didn't. But in a fascist country, it doesn't matter what you did. It's what the police say you did that matters. I'll tell you this much. I went to Spain to recuperate from being with Eric and accidentally got involved with students who were wanted by the Civil Guardia. The students escaped, thank goodness, but the police found me. I was taken to prison, questioned, and finally deported." Naomi buried her face in Beadle's fur.

"You? I can't believe you'd be involved in revolutionary activities."

"I wasn't. My big crime was eating in a student restaurant and sharing a table with four guys. The Guardia came after them, saw me with them, and assumed I was part of the group. If it hadn't been for Pablo grabbing me and taking me with them, I'd have been in bigger trouble than I was."

"Pablo?"

"Pablo."

"Oh, Nomi."

"It's okay. I survived."

"At what cost?" asked Priscilla.

"Hey, I think I hear a car. Must be your Pablo. Wonder what he found out."

While the two women were talking, Pablo made a visit to the Humane Society and learned that Beadle's owner worked for the Department of Labor. Pablo considered making an appointment with the man, but then decided if he took him by surprise, maybe he would respond more civilly.

Their interview was brief. "Are you Mr. Ryerson?"

"Yes. Do you have an appointment?"

For a moment Pablo was taken aback. The man in front of him looked reasonable, not at all like a man who would threaten a woman. Perhaps Naomi had exaggerated the man's response to the dog following her.

"No. I've come to talk with you about Beadle. Have you got a minute?"

Mr. Ryerson's calm tone changed the minute he heard his dog's name. His face flushed, his fingers clenched the pencil he was holding so hard he snapped it in two. "Where's Beadle? I'm ready to sue her for stealing my dog."

"Watch it, you're talking about my fiancée."

"Tell her to give him back and there'll be no trouble."

"Your dog keeps running away from you."

"I have friends——"

"You try anything and you'll be one sorry mess."

"Big talk. No action. I know your kind."

"No," said Pablo, too quietly, "you don't."

"I'm warning you. Tell her to give me back my dog."

"And I'm warning you. Leave her alone. Your dog is where he wants to be and that's that."

"That is not 'that.' Tell her I'm not giving up until I get my dog back."

When Pablo returned to Priscilla's house, looking grim and sounding grimmer, Naomi began to worry. Would there ever be an end to this mess?

"Did you talk to him?"

"The guy is a maniac. There is no talking to him."

"What happened?" Priscilla asked as she poured him a cup of coffee.

"I spoke to Beadle's used-to-be owner."

"You didn't——" asked Naomi, worried that Pablo made things worse.

"No, but I wanted to," said Pablo.

Priscilla sighed. "Well, if there's going to be trouble, I guess it's better we know sooner than later."

"That guy is so angry at you, he could be dangerous. He threatened to take the dog back by force if necessary." Pablo's intensity frightened Naomi.

"Isn't there something like a statue of limitations?" asked Naomi.

"You said 'used-to-be owner,' " Priscilla reminded him.

Pablo hesitated, keeping himself busy by washing the coffeepot. He turned to look at Naomi. "Well, I told him you were my fiancée, and that if the dog wanted to live with you, that was the dog's choice, and if he tried any funny stuff, I'd make sure he never walked again."

"Fiancée?" exclaimed Naomi.

Priscilla frowned at Pablo. "What are you talking about? You're due to leave for California in two days."

"Maybe not. I don't trust the man."

"Wait a minute," protested Naomi. "You're both missing something. No one's asked me if I want Beadle. Everyone seems to assume that just because this stupid dog doesn't understand ownership, I have to accept what he wants. I say give the damn dog back to whatshisname if he wants him so much. Who needs all this *tzuris*?"

"*Suras?*" asked Pablo.

"It's Yiddish. It means trouble," answered Naomi.

"You don't mean that," protested Pablo. "Look how the dog adores you."

"Are you telling me that just because Beadle decided he likes to lick me, I have to take care of him, as well as deal with a maniac who says he's willing to do whatever it takes to get him back?"

"I will stay. I think you need a man to help you with this."

Naomi glared at him.

"What about your research? Aren't you giving a paper at the anthropology conference in Mexico next week?" asked Priscilla.

"I'll let Montevecito give it for me. Be good practice for him."

"Hold it, you two," Naomi interrupted. "I appreciate the offer, Pablo, but having a man protect me from a guy who only wants his dog back is not the way I want to live my life."

Pablo's jaw tightened.

"What are you going to do?" asked Priscilla.

Naomi looked at Beadle snoring peacefully on her lap, his legs dangling. "Good question." She stroked Beadle's cheek. "I think what I'm going to do is take Beadle to Mr. Ryerson and suggest we let the dog choose between us."

"What makes you think he'll agree? I told you he's dangerous," said Pablo.

"I don't care about him. I'm tired of being afraid."

"Suppose Beadle chooses you but Ryerson won't accept it? Be just like him, it seems," said Priscilla.

"Suppose Beadle chooses you, and Ryerson hires goons to get his dog back?" challenged Pablo. "Then what?"

"I'll figure out something—after I decide whether I want a dog in my life." She stood up quickly, dumping Beadle, who let out a groan of protest. "Dog, there is more to me than a lap for you to sleep on." Naomi poured her coffee into the sink, watching the brown liquid swirl down the drain, wishing she were as easily rid of the problem of Beadle and his owner.

Pablo walked over to her and put his arm around her shoulder. "Why won't you let me help? That man is a monster."

She shook off his arm. "I know you mean well, but the last thing I need is another Pablo trying to rescue me."

"Another Pablo?"

"Slip of the tongue. It happened years ago." Naomi turned and tripped over Beadle. "Shit!" She saw Pablo's and Priscilla's disapproving looks. "Look, I don't mean to be ungrateful. You've both been wonderful. But I feel like I'm sliding back into a place I've spent years trying to get out of. I need to leave before I say something I'll be sorry for later on."

"Where are you going?" asked Pablo.

"To speak with Mr. Ryerson. I will tell him that if his dog wants to live with him, it's perfectly fine with me."

"Let me go with you," said Pablo.

"I appreciate the offer, but this is something I have to do by myself. I've been running from that man for no reason. It's time to stop."

Priscilla objected. "You have very good reasons to run from that man."

Naomi took her dishes to the sink. "Thanks for breakfast. I'll let you know what happens." She started to leave, but then, remembering Beadle's inclination to go only where and when he chose, she asked Priscilla, "You didn't happen to keep your dog's old collar and leash, did you?"

"I don't know. I'll have to look."

After Priscilla left the room, Pablo said to Naomi, "I'm sorry the other Pablo let you down. Please give me the chance to make up for his stupidity in letting you go."

"He wasn't stupid, and he didn't let me go." She went into the hall and yelled, "Pris, do you need help?"

"I'm not sure this will do, but it's all I could find." She handed Naomi a fraying collar and leash.

"It's better than nothing." While Priscilla held Beadle's squirming body, Naomi put on the collar and attached the leash, cursing at the difficulty. "C'mon, dog, we're going home, one place or another."

In the car, with trembling fingers, she dialed the number that Pablo had given her.

"Mr. Ryerson, I have your dog. I'd like to meet you in the parking lot outside your office as soon as possible. If Beadle's willing to go with you, he's yours."

"Your fiancé was ready to beat me into oblivion just a little while ago. Is this some kind of trick?"

"No, it's not a trick, and in spite of what he may have told you, he's not my fiancé. Will you meet me?"

"I'm in conferences until four. Would it be all right if we wait until then?"

"Sure." She hesitated, trying to find the right words. "Mr. Ryerson, we may not be friends, but we don't have to be enemies."

There was a long silence. Naomi could hear him breathe.

"Okay. I'll do whatever it takes to work this out."

"Gotcha. See you later."

"Right. At four, in the parking lot."

Naomi hung up and leaned her head against the car headrest, relieved to have made contact. "Well, Beadle, at least for the moment the pressure's off. Now, what do I want?"

As if to answer her, Beadle snuggled against her thigh, his head in her lap.

Naomi stroked his thin body. "It seems, whether or not I want to want you, giving you up is not going to be easy."

13

Naomi avoided looking at the answering machine for as long as she could. Then, after a deep breath, she pushed the play button. "Hi! It's Karen. We need volunteers to contact Democratic voters and we're having a meeting Sunday morning at ten to discuss strategies and talking points. Let me know if you can come." Relieved, she returned Karen's call, leaving the message that she would volunteer and to please let her know where to meet.

When the phone rang, Naomi picked it up, thinking it was either Priscilla or Karen. The male voice wasted no time on pleasantries. "Dr. Rosen, we need to talk. My client will be arriving in a week."

Naomi slammed down the receiver and turned off the answering machine just in case he called back.

Beadle's whining reminded her that she needed to walk and feed him. She never realized how much work dogs could be, and found herself half hoping Beadle would go to Ryerson. And yet, outdoors with Beadle trotting happily by her side, she couldn't deny the affection she felt for him. Why had Beadle run away from his owner? Had the man hurt him? Ryerson's anger had certainly frightened Naomi. What effect might it have had on a dog?

Walking Beadle always began as a chore and ended as a pleasure. It seemed he wanted to please her. When she said, "Sit!" he sat. When she let him off the leash and said, "Come!" he came. Someone had trained him well. So why hadn't he come when Ryerson called him? By the time they returned home, Naomi felt a lot better. She was ready to think about her upcoming class with the girls.

Planning for the third session with the five girls helped to refocus her thoughts. The second class had been almost as tense as the first, beginning with a fight between Martina and Juanita that Naomi had stopped only by luck, screaming, "*Basta!*" Seconds later, when Carolina made a disparaging remark about Juanita, Martina had come to her rescue with threats of renewed violence. Go figure. Each girl had written a bit, yet none had been willing to share their writing with Mrs. Romero. During a post-session "chat," Mrs. Romero had warned Naomi that unless she gave her more of the girls' writing, her contract would be "renegotiated." Naomi's questions about the girls' privacy had apparently touched a nerve, because Mrs. Romero felt it necessary to explain that the psychologist working for the court was under pressure to show results. It seemed to Naomi that her supervisor had been unconvincingly apologetic when defending her demand to see what the girls were writing.

So, in the third session she planned to stress the importance of each girl writing something, perhaps a short poem, that would satisfy Mrs. Romero's need to see their writing without revealing whatever it was they didn't want her to know. Perhaps this would be a good time to talk about allegory and fable—even the use of legend and myth as a way to both reveal and hide their thoughts.

The ring of the alarm clock abruptly interrupted Naomi's thoughts. She had set it, knowing that when she worked she sometimes lost all sense of time.

"C'mon, Beadle, we need to go and you need to choose." With the fraying leash held firmly in her hand, Naomi got the dog into the car. As soon as she closed the door and left the driveway, Beadle began whining.

"Cool it, dog. You got us into this mess in the first place." He was not comforted. "Well, one way or another, it'll be over soon."

Naomi didn't see the man in the parking lot, so she got out of the car, wondering where he was. She was about to call when she saw him walking briskly toward her.

"Where's Beadle?" he asked.

Shocked at his abruptness, Naomi stopped and stared. He didn't look like the maniac she remembered. This time he was dressed neatly, blue shirt and dark, carefully pressed jeans. Knowing they were in a public parking lot gave her confidence.

"I'm not sure this is the best way to begin negotiating," said Naomi.

He looked taken aback. Changing his tone of voice, he apologized. "Excuse my bad manners. Sometimes I forget what I'm trying to learn.

"I don't understand."

"No reason you should. I'm Paul Ryerson."

"Naomi Rosen. Beadle's in my car."

"So, how are we going to do this?"

"I suppose we open the door and see who he goes to."

"Knowing Beadle, he could just as well run off and have an adventure."

He looked so downcast that Naomi felt sorry for him. "Mr. Ryerson, you love him, don't you?"

"Yes, I do, but I don't think he loves me as much."

"I know what that's like."

"You do?"

"Why are you surprised?"

Paul shrugged. "Guess I thought an attractive woman like you, whom my dog seems to love more than me, would have people loving her all over the place."

"Maybe in another dimension."

Paul laughed. His face relaxed a little.

"Is that Beadle barking?" asked Naomi.

"Sounds like it. I guess he's tired of waiting. Why did the guy who came to see me say he was your fiancé?"

"I don't know. He made it up without my permission."

"Knight in shining armor?"

"Something like that. He thought you were dangerous—a monster, in fact."

"And what do you think?"

"I guess I thought so too."

"And now?"

"I . . . I think we can figure this out."

Paul nodded. "I think so too.

Naomi felt herself relax. "I suppose there's no time like the present. Shall we?"

They walked to her car, each wondering what would happen when they opened the door.

"How about this?" said Naomi. "After I open the door, we move in opposite directions to give him room to decide who he wants to be with."

"Wait," said Paul. "I'd like to make a deal."

Naomi's body stiffened. "Mr. Ryerson, I thought we agreed . . ."

He interrupted "We did. And please, call me Paul. What I was thinking is that maybe Beadle wants to belong to both of us. Maybe that's what he's been trying to tell us. And we, I mean I, have been too stupid and bullheaded to listen."

"We aren't divorced parents, and he's not our child," Naomi countered.

Paul reeled backward, as if she'd hit him.

Watching him recoil, she changed her tone. "Forget what I said. Let's just see what he does."

Paul looked up and saw his colleagues watching from their second-story windows. "Would you mind if we go someplace else?"

Naomi saw the faces in the windows and thought fast. The Chamisa Trail off Zia Road was a popular place in case they wanted to take a walk, and there were lots of houses around if she needed help. She made the suggestion, adding, "That would give us a chance to walk if we want and Beadle time to decide. Besides, who wants one's colleagues watching, right?"

"I hate people knowing my business," said Paul, bitterly.

"Well, we agree on that," said Naomi. "I'll meet you at the trailhead parking lot."

Paul nodded, got into his truck, and drove off as Naomi watched the faces in the windows disappear.

Paul was standing beside his truck when she arrived. She opened her car door. "Okay, Beadle, out you go." Beadle bounded toward Paul, who knelt down, happy to receive Beadle's tongue licking his face. Naomi smiled, feeling a sense of relief.

Then Beadle ran back to her and burrowed his body into hers. Paul stood up, turned, and walked toward his truck. Beadle rushed to him, practically knocking him over.

Naomi and Paul stared at each other, wondering what to do.

"We've got a bit of daylight left. Let's walk. Maybe he'll figure out what he wants," suggested Paul.

"I think I know what he wants," said Naomi.

"Well, he can't have us both. I'm not in a dog sharing mood," Paul replied.

"Do we have a choice? Look at him. He's acting like a kid who's trying to bring his parents back together again."

"You made that analogy before. I don't find it amusing."

"Want to talk?" asked Naomi.

"Want to listen?" retorted Paul.

"Buy me a glass of wine and I'm yours."

Paul grinned. "All mine?"

"Well, for as long as you'd like to talk, but I warn you, if it's more than two hours you'll have to buy me dinner. You don't want to be around me when I need to eat."

"You might be surprised."

Naomi blushed.

Beadle sat contentedly between the two of them.

"What about Beadle?" asked Naomi.

Paul opened his truck door and called, "Beadle, come!" Beadle sat.

Naomi walked to Paul's truck as Beadle watched. The moment she got into the front seat, the dog jumped into the backseat.

"Paul, can I ask you a question?"

"Depends on the question."

"Did you ever hurt Beadle?"

He hesitated. "I don't know you well enough to answer."

Beadle's whine grew stronger as they walked away from the truck toward the restaurant. Naomi tried to ignore it, but his sounds grew more pitiful.

"Paul, what about Beadle? I wonder if he thinks we're abandoning him."

"He's a dog. He'll stop in a while."

"How do you know?"

"Okay, what do you want to do?"

"Can we drive somewhere and talk?"

"Maybe you should just take him and be done with it."

"Is that what you want?" asked Naomi.

"What I want doesn't seem to be the issue."

Naomi recognized the feeling, akin to self-pity, mixed with frustration and yearning, wanting to be understood without explanation.

"C'mon, let's go buy a bottle of wine and then you can take me to a place where we can see the sunset."

"I know just the place."

Beadle's whining stopped as soon as Paul opened the truck door. When they arrived at the mesa, Beadle jumped out with them.

They sat in silence, watching the colors change as the sun set. Yellow turning to pink, purple, orange, and red. Beadle nestled between them, snoring peacefully.

"So, talk," said Naomi, stroking Beadle's soft fur.

"I don't even know where to begin. And don't say start at the beginning, because I wouldn't know when that was, or even what it was." He poured each of them a glass of wine. "Sorry about the plastic glasses. It was all they had."

Naomi leaned against a mound of earth, waiting.

"Maybe it started with me thinking that I was too weird or different for a woman to be interested in me. I was six foot two when the next-tallest kid in eighth grade was a girl and she was maybe five foot six and, like me, skinny and friendless. In college, I was so grateful when Joanna showed an interest in me I promised myself I'd do anything to keep her in my life."

"I've made promises like that," said Naomi.

"I hope yours worked out better than mine."

"Don't bet on it," she replied.

"She left and I fell apart. Got myself together enough to get a PhD in public health administration and tried to tell myself that I could live a good enough life as a single person and uncle to my brother's two kids. Most of all, I would learn to stop wanting what it seemed I couldn't have. Which, as you might guess, was just about impossible. Meanwhile, I had trouble dealing with bouts of anger that periodically erupted, leaving devastation everywhere. The few women I met ran, fast."

He emptied his glass and poured another. Naomi wondered if he was an alcoholic. He saw her looking at him. "Sorry, I wasn't thinking. I'll slow down."

"I decided to get a dog. I'd always wanted one as a kid, but my mother refused to have one in the house. Too much mess, she said. Beadle was only a pup when I found him in the shelter. Or, to be more accurate, he found me. The folks there said he'd been rescued from a ditch, half-drowned and starving.

"I suppose it sounds stupid, but it felt like love at first sight. His eyes followed my every move while I was at the shelter but I didn't trust my feelings. When I got home, the woman at the shelter called to tell me he cried the moment I left and was inconsolable. She asked if I would consider adopting him. I would and I did, pleased and happy that someone, even if it was only a dog, wanted me in their life."

He stopped, embarrassed. "I apologize if it sounds like too much self-pity."

"I recognize the feeling. Go on."

He paused. "About a year after I got Beadle, I met Sarah, a biochemist, a few years younger than me, newly divorced, with two young girls.

I think they fell in love with me before their mother did, but pretty soon we were like a family. We even talked about buying a house together." Paul buried his face in Beadle's fur, then sat up and looked away from Naomi. "We had an arrangement. After work she picked up the older daughter. I drove the younger girl home from her after-school program."

He stood up and walked to the edge of the mesa. Naomi felt a moment of terror. Was he going to jump? She got up and went over to him.

He stared into the distance. "One day, I went to pick up Molly, a few minutes later than usual because a client had had an emergency. She wasn't there. The teacher said her uncle had picked up Molly earlier. I didn't know about any uncle, but then there was a lot I didn't know. When I got home, Sarah called to ask where Molly was. Even as I said her uncle picked her up, I felt a stab of fear."

" 'Isn't she home?' I asked. Turned out there was no uncle. Molly's body was found a few days later. I was blamed for being late, no matter that I was delayed by a client and that it was only fifteen minutes. No matter that the teacher should never have let Molly go with an unauthorized male. I tried calling Sarah, but she wouldn't answer the phone. When I went to her house, her sister wouldn't let me in. I tried to go to the funeral, but her mother told me I was not welcome, that Sarah never wanted to see me again. When I got home, Beadle ran to me, happy to see me I guess, but I didn't see him in time and tripped. I took my misery out on him. Even though I rushed him to the vet and apologized and hugged him and told him I'd never do it again, and I never did, when he hears the anger in my voice he wants nothing to do with me. I guess I can't blame him."

"I'm sorry," said Naomi, wishing she could think of something better to say.

Beadle whimpered, and Paul poured water into Naomi's cupped hands. The dog licked and splashed until the bottle was empty and the front of her skirt soaking wet. Paul brought a towel from his truck and mopped up what he could. "I apologize. I should have thought of this sooner. Even when he's slurping from his dish, he makes a mess."

Naomi shrugged. "It should be the worst thing that happens to either of us."

Paul heard the word "us" and something in him simultaneously relaxed and tightened. Talking about Molly's death and Sarah's reaction brought back his anger and frustration, his thoughts of suicide and feelings of hopelessness. Even now, face-to-face with the woman he thought stole Beadle, he felt disconnected, as if he were caught half in, half out of an unknown place inside himself.

Beadle licked his face, which helped a little, but he knew only too well his dog remained ready to run the minute Paul raised his voice in anger—a piece of himself over which he seemed to have little control. He nuzzled Beadle's face, then stood up.

"Don't know about you, but I'm feeling hungry."

Naomi nodded, still thinking about the horror of learning your child is dead, knowing there were other horrors that she didn't want to think about. "So, what are we going to do about Beadle? He wants both of us."

Paul shrugged. "Tell you what. I'll drive you to your car, and whichever car Beadle gets in is the person who has him during the week. The other person will get him on weekends."

Naomi laughed.

"What's so funny?"

"If I were a betting woman, I'd say he won't choose. He'll sit in the middle of the parking lot looking at both of us."

She was right.

Paul sighed. "Let's put him in my truck for now and get some dinner. Maybe we can toss a coin as to who gets him first."

Beadle sat, watching Paul get into his truck. Once again, only after Naomi got in and sat down in the passenger seat did the dog jump into the back seat.

"This is too weird," said Paul. "We don't even have a relationship and now we're talking about sharing a dog."

He found himself feeling strangely hopeful, especially when Naomi said she liked Indian and vegetarian food and was happy to try the new restaurant in the Solana shopping center.

Paul turned to Beadle. "We're going to get something to eat. We'll be back soon."

"Maybe you could get him something before we go in. That might convince him to settle down and wait for us."

Paul nodded, wondering why this strange woman seemed to be so concerned about his dog. Then he asked himself why he hadn't thought about feeding Beadle.

Paul came back with a plate of food. Beadle was hungry and ate it quickly. "Okay, dog," quipped Naomi. "Have a nap and we'll be back soon." Beadle looked at her, curled up on the backseat, and closed his eyes.

When Naomi ordered his favorite foods Paul allowed himself to feel a bit more hopeful, a feeling too quickly replaced by worries that his hopes might be misplaced. When the food came, he stared at it, waiting for Naomi to begin eating.

"Since we're sharing a dog, want to share what we've ordered?" asked Naomi.

"Sure," he said, trying to contain feelings he didn't trust. Given the quality of the time they had spent together, Paul was amazed at how easy it was to be with Naomi. He thought back to his feelings when Beadle left him and ran to her, licking her face, refusing to come when he called. I'm jealous, he thought. I want Beadle to love me more than anybody. Despite his embarrassment when he thought about how he had tackled Naomi on the trail, he knew he would do anything to keep Beadle to himself. So why hadn't he put his name and address on Beadle's tag? Why had he hurt an animal he loved? Why did his anger flare up so quickly? Too many whys.

14

"Paul, where are you?" asked Naomi.

He blushed. "I was thinking about our first, shall we say, meeting. If I were a scriptwriter, I'd be doing heavy-duty revision."

"Like what?"

"Well, for starters, I'd have gone up to you and your boyfriend and apologized for my dog's behavior. I'd have been thinking, even if I couldn't have said it, that he had great taste in women."

"He wasn't my boyfriend and I never saw him again. I always wondered what happened after I left."

"Nothing much. We glared at each other for bit and then he offered me a chocolate bar, which I took. We laughed at our foolishness and then I ran after you and Beadle. I never saw him again either. Were you together long?"

"About four hours. We met en route. His chocolate bars are irresistible. His priorities, in my not so humble opinion, leave a bit to be desired."

"I hope I have my priorities right this time," said Paul, amazed by his words, his eyes meeting Naomi's.

Embarrassed by the way Paul looked at her, Naomi changed the subject. "Good choice of restaurant. The food's great."

"Want a doggie bag?" asked Paul.

"I suppose it depends on who takes Beadle home," said Naomi. "We both seem to need his affection, but I don't know much about taking care of dogs. The only pet I ever had was a cat, which I had to help die last year. It's pretty clear you don't learn how to take care of a dog by having a cat."

"Well, no time like the present." He put his credit card in the folder with their bill. Naomi put hers in with his. Paul gave it back to her. "If it's okay with you, I'd like this to be my treat. Sort of an apology for being such a horse's ass."

"In a million years I couldn't have predicted us having an evening like this," admitted Naomi.

"I hope it won't be our last," said Paul, taking a chance on the feelings flying out past his determination not to let them show. "I'd like to see you again, no matter what we decide about Beadle."

Naomi surprised herself by saying, "Me too." There was an awkward silence. "I guess it's time to deal with Beadle."

Paul drove Naomi back to her car. Beadle refused to get into either vehicle. It was only when Naomi got into her car and Paul into his truck that Beadle jumped into Naomi's car. She got out, walked over to Paul, and said, "I'm sorry."

"Actually, I don't feel as bad about it as I would have a few hours ago. I can't blame Beadle. I have a problem with my anger and he knows it. What I did was inexcusable. At least now I can see him, and maybe in time I'll convince him he can trust me to be kind."

"How're you going to do that?"

Paul hesitated. "I'm . . . seeing a therapist . . . Anyway, I'll give you Beadle's collar and leash and his bed, which a friend made for him. I'd like to keep his water dish and food bowl, just in case . . ."

The next morning, as Naomi drove to meet the girls in the writing group, she debated whether to take Beadle in with her or leave him in the car.

"Dog, do I need you?" His lick answered her question. She stroked his soft fur, amazed at the love she felt for him. Deciding that working with the girls was more than enough to deal with, she poured water for Beadle, cranked open the car window, and left him with a hug and so many kisses he shook himself off before jumping into the backseat.

Just then her cell phone rang. Priscilla was obviously angry. "What happened between you and Ryerson?"

"It's so funny. Beadle can't choose between us."

"Nomi, this is no laughing matter. Just give him the damn dog and be done with him. Why ask for more problems?"

"Right now all I can think about are the girls I'm about to teach. I have to figure out a way to reach Martina. She's in big trouble."

"So are you. What you need to do—"

"Sorry to cut you off, Pris, but I need to get going. Talk to you later."

As she entered the building, Naomi vowed to find a way to get the girls writing but when she walked into the room, her spirits plummeted. Jeering voices were yelling, "Crybaby!" Martina and Juanita loomed over Nilda, cowering in a corner.

Not wanting to be the group's policeman or judge, Naomi asked, "Where are Carolina and Lupe?"

Martina ignored the question and punched Nilda in the stomach.

Naomi tried to control her exasperation. "Look, you're in this program because the court ordered you to come but that's not a good enough reason to be here. You have to want to write, and in order to do this, everyone has to feel safe."

"So how you gonna make that happen?" sneered Martina.

"I don't know," snapped Naomi, "but I do know I can't do it without your help."

"Well, if that's the case, you in deep shit," challenged Juanita. "All she knows is fists and fucks."

Naomi quickly separated Martina and Juanita. "You're behaving just like a lot of men. We're women. Can't we figure out something better?"

"You the teacher," snickered Juanita.

"Yes, but I'm only one person. We all have to help."

"Help with what?" asked Carolina, striding in, her shirt obviously shortened to reveal a bare navel pierced with two studs.

Lupe followed. "What's going on?"

"Put up or shut down time," snorted Martina. She glared at Naomi and in a falsely sweet voice begged, "Teacher, please tell us a special story, pretty please? Somethin' that's gonna warm our frozen hearts and melt our nasty thoughts so we can write stuff to please you and Señora Romero and Dr. Richey and Judge Cameron and God and—"

Naomi chose to ignore her sarcasm. "Maybe you'd be interested in a Tibetan folk tale I read when I was worried about losing my job at the university. I thought it would take me only a few minutes to find a story to use in class, but I got so engrossed in the stories I lost track of time and was stunned to realize I'd been reading for four hours. What was so amazing was that when I 'surfaced,' I realized I wasn't worried about losing my job anymore."

"All that from stories?" asked Lupe.

"One in particular. A pretty short story," laughed Naomi. Sensing the girls' interest, she said, "It's called 'The Little Parrot' and it goes like this—"

> Little Parrot loved the jungle. Every morning he flew over the greenery, looked at what lay below, and counted himself fortunate to live in such a marvelous place. Only when he was sure that all was well did he fly back to earth and eat his breakfast.
>
> But one morning when he soared over the jungle, he saw nothing but thick, dark smoke. The jungle was on fire! Little Parrot hurried to the river as fast as his tiny wings permitted, took a huge gulp of water, flew back to the fire, and spit out the water, trying to quench the flames. Back and forth he went, from the river to the fire, from the fire to the river, trying his best to put out the flames. He was small and could only take a few gulps each time. He soon became exhausted, but he kept on going; his beloved jungle was at risk.
>
> As he was flying for the umpteenth time to the river, worried that the jungle would burn up before he could put out the fire, he heard a loud laugh and then a cackling voice. "Silly parrot. How can a little bird like you hope to put out such a big fire?"
>
> Little Parrot looked up and saw Eagle, the largest bird in the

jungle. "I don't need advice. I need help," Little Parrot said quietly, continuing to fly to the river. The next thing Little Parrot knew, a huge stream of water poured from the skies, dousing part of the fire. Little Parrot did not stop to see who was helping him, he just kept flying to the river and back, hoping that with this new help the fire would soon be put out.

When there were no more flames, Little Parrot looked around to find the source of the help for which he was so grateful. When he saw that it was Eagle, although he was utterly depleted, Little Parrot flew to him and said, "Thank you. Were it not for your help, the fire would still be burning."

"No," said Eagle, "it is I who must thank you."

There was a moment of silence. Then Martina snorted and said, "A little bird gets help from a big bird. So what?"

"How many big birds helpin' you?" chided Juanita.

"Maybe it's 'cause the parrot said he didn't need advice, he needed help," suggested Nilda, her voice little more than a whisper. "Lotsa times I need help, but all I get is people tellin' me what to do."

"Plenty of people ready to do that," agreed Martina. "Too many in my opinion."

Naomi passed out clay and asked them to sculpt an image of *Me in relationship to Eagle* and *Me in relationship to Parrot*. Much to her surprise, they began sculpting without complaint or protest.

After a minute she said, "Time's up. Use whatever you have." She handed out small pieces of paper. "Look at your sculptures and write whatever comes to mind using 'I.' Write clearly and don't sign your writing. Whatever you write is what you need to write."

Once again they responded without a fuss. She collected their papers, mixed them up, then handed them out.

She was going to suggest that each girl read what was on the paper they had picked when Martina asked Carolina, "What you got?"

She read:

I ask for help.
I get hit.
There is no help for me.
I wish I had an eagle.

"Who wrote that?" asked Martina. 'It's good."

No one answered. Carolina asked Juanita to read what was on the paper she held.

I'm burning, just like the jungle.
Who cares?
In my world there are no parrots or eagles.
I'm afraid of the birds I see.
Who's gonna help me?

In quick succession the others read:

Parrot, you small like me.
Where you get your courage?
How you keep flying to the river?
Tell me your secret. Please?

I'm like the jungle, burning.
On fire.
I don't want the fire to be put out.
Just want it small enough to warm me.

Eagle, you big and powerful.
What made you help parrot?
It's okay.
I don't need help.
How can I find an eagle to help me?

"You gonna give these papers to Mrs. Romero?" challenged Martina. "I'd like to. With your permission."

"Unsigned, right?" asked Nilda.

"Absolutely." With more certainty than she felt, Naomi added, "What matters is that you're all writing."

"Only a couple of lines," muttered Martina.

"It's a beginning. Would you like to write more?"

Unexpectedly, Martina nodded, took a piece of paper from the table, and began writing. The others looked at her, then did the same. Naomi felt an urge to write to Parrot and Eagle.

> *Parrot, give me love and courage to keep going.*
> *Like you did.*
> *Knowing the odds were against you.*
>
> *Eagle, help me let go of the fear that I'm afraid of.*
> *Give me strength to choose a new path.*
> *Help me help myself.*

Driving home from class, with Beadle's head on her lap, Naomi smiled, remembering the look on Mrs. Romero's face when she handed her the girls' writing after she promised to return it the next session. At least for the moment, wasn't going to be fired.

"Good evening, Dr. Rosen."

He must have been hidden because when Naomi drove up to her house, she didn't see him. When she tried to get back into the car, he blocked her way. She was even more unnerved by Beadle's incessant barking. "I apologize for frightening you, but there was no other way since you refuse to talk or meet with me."

The man was tall, well-built, with graying hair, and dressed in the same dark blue suit he was wearing the first time he'd come to her house, with a lighter blue shirt and a blue patterned tie. She guessed he was in his late fifties. "Permit me to introduce myself. My name is André Solana. We need to talk, please." She detected a bit of an accent.

"No, we don't." Naomi opened her front door and tried to close the door on him but he was too strong. His gentle voice collided with her terror. "Beadle," she said, trying to calm herself and the dog, "it's okay." She stood up and said, "You're scaring my dog. Please leave. Now."

"I'm sorry to upset your dog, but we have to talk."

"I don't know who you are, but I'll give you a chance to leave before I call the police." She picked up the phone, ready to dial 911.

"Please, by all means, call the police. I am sure they will be interested in helping me."

The man sat down on the sofa, crossing his legs, looking as comfortable as if it were his house and Naomi the intruder. She was not ready or willing to ask what he wanted, and hoped he would leave if she refused to talk to him.

She went into the kitchen and made a cup of tea, drinking it while standing up, looking out the window into the darkness. Her nearest neighbors were away at their winter homes in Minneapolis and Tampa. She didn't feel comfortable calling Priscilla, especially with Pablo still there. Paul came to mind, but she didn't know him well enough. There was no one else. Dare she call his bluff and call 911?

"I'm prepared to stay as long as it takes," he said, entering the kitchen, his voice a curious mixture of seduction and resignation.

She kept staring out the dark window. Images of herself as a child, trying to become invisible, made her wish she'd learned how to do it.

"I want you to leave, now," she said, using her most professional voice.

"I would if it were up to me. Cloak and dagger interventions are not my style. I left before, thinking my presence would be enough to make you agree to talk with me, but obviously I was wrong." He paused, perhaps waiting for her to ask who he was and what he wanted, but she bit her tongue.

"I have a photograph. He wants to meet you. He's been looking for you for a very long time."

"Who?"

"Dr. Rosen, I was hoping we could avoid subterfuge and talk about what happened without pretense, but if you insist on pretending, I'll play your tedious game. However, I'd prefer to sit and talk if you don't mind."

"I do mind. I didn't invite you to come in, and I don't want to hear what you have to say. So, if you insist on talking, talk."

Naomi filled Beadle's dish with water and opened a can of dog food, studiously ignoring the man standing near her.

"You were in your early twenties when you went to Spain. Franco was in full power. The country was reeling from attacks by separatist Basques and anti-Franco guerillas. Franco's Guardia Civil were everywhere. Poorly paid, with powerful guns, they enjoyed a degree of power that was not in the best interests of the country or the people who experienced their terror."

"Mr. Solana, I don't know how you know all this, but it's late. I've been working hard. I'm hungry and I'm tired. I don't need a history lesson on Spanish politics."

"Dr. Rosen, your hostility is proof that you know exactly what I'm going to say, so I'll come to the point."

The phone rang. Saved by the bell, she thought.

"Hi, Naomi, it's Paul. How's Beadle doing?"

Naomi put the phone next to Beadle's ear. "Beadle, Paul wants to know how you're doing." Beadle slurped water.

"Dr. Rosen, please. I haven't got all day."

She talked away from the phone. "You mean 'night.' So, leave. I didn't invite you, and I don't care to have you stay."

"Naomi, are you all right?" She could hear the worry in Paul's voice.

"No, but I'll manage." She hung up the phone. *A man on the phone I hardly know. A man in my house I don't want to know. What's happening to me?*

"Dr. Rosen, how long I remain in your house as your uninvited guest is entirely up to you. Drop the pretense of not knowing why I'm here and we can finish our business in a few minutes."

"My life is my business, not yours."

"My client hired me to find you."

"Your client is your business, not mine."

"My client is your son."

Naomi reeled, holding onto the kitchen counter, unable to stop the dizziness.

André Solana waited.

"He's a grown man. Why does he want to meet me now?"

"He's been searching for you for most of his life. You're his mother, the only one who knows his birth father."

Naomi drank a glass of water and then knelt down, rubbing her face in Beadle's fur, trying to ignore the pain in her heart.

"I'm not the enemy, Dr. Rosen."

"How would you know?"

"Don't you want to know about your son?"

"No."

She walked into the living room, Beadle underfoot. Mr. Solana followed. "You're asking me to remember the most painful period of my life. The only way I've managed to keep sane, to make a life for myself, is to focus on the present. I've trained myself not to think about what happened, so you'll have to give me a very good reason to relive the past. Some man's curiosity about his genes isn't enough."

"He's not just some man! He's your son! Have you ever thought that perhaps this might be a way to heal the trauma of the past? For both of you?"

"He was given to kind and loving people."

"He remembers you."

"He can't. He was barely three when I left, and he knew them well. They weren't strangers. He loved them."

"He remembers you."

"What? What could he possibly remember?"

"He remembers you sitting in the bathtub with him, your arms around him, singing as you washed his hair. He remembers you telling him to lean his head back against you so the soap wouldn't get in his eyes."

"He can't. Someone must have told him."

Naomi collapsed against the sofa. Beadle jumped up and burrowed his body into hers. She tried to catch her breath.

Suddenly there was a loud knock on the door. Beadle ran to it, wagging his tail. Paul opened the door and followed Beadle into the living room.

"What's going on? Who are you?" he asked Mr. Solana.

"Dr. Rosen and I are having a friendly conversation."

"Doesn't look so friendly to me," he said, walking to a place between the two. "Naomi, are you all right?'

"No, but it isn't Mr. Solana's fault. He's only the messenger of news I never wanted to hear."

"Would it help if I stay?"

Naomi didn't answer. She couldn't make herself say yes or no.

Not sure whether to stay or go, Paul leaned against the wall, wondering if he should do something, not knowing what that something could be.

The lawyer looked as if he were waiting for Paul to leave.

Paul decided to stay.

"What does he want? This man you say is my son," asked Naomi, ignoring the looks that Mr. Solana directed at Paul.

"It is not what I say. He is your son. He wants to meet you. He wants to know who his father is. He wants to know about his father."

"So it's not about me. It's about his father. Go talk to him if you know so much."

Mr. Solana's voice was kind. "It's about you and his father."

"When?"

"The sooner the better."

"I need time to think about this."

"He's here, waiting."

"In Santa Fe?" gasped Naomi.

Mr. Solana nodded. "If he had had his way, he would have come with me."

"So he isn't concerned about how I think or what I feel," said Naomi bitterly. "Then again, why should he be? He couldn't possibly know what it took for me to give him up or how it made me feel. Children don't care about circumstances and they don't understand impossibility or coercion." She looked directly at the lawyer for the first time.

"I take it that when you leave here, you'll meet with him and give him your report." He nodded. "And what will you tell him?"

"I'm not sure. I was hoping you would say, 'Tell him to come.'"

"Why not say that his mother has no interest in him?"

"Because I don't believe that is the truth."

"And what, in your infinite wisdom, is the truth?"

The lawyer stood up and straightened his tie. "Sarcasm is not productive, only a way of hiding one's feelings. Perhaps I will tell him that his mother is an intelligent, caring woman who disconnected from herself when the pain of giving up her beloved son overwhelmed her. Perhaps I will say that her feelings for her son run so deep she still cannot bear to think about what she did. That her only comfort is the knowledge she gave him to loving people who couldn't have children of their own. That she was convinced he would have a good life with them."

Naomi doubled over with a pain in her stomach so powerful it took her breath away. Paul rushed over to her, then stopped, not sure if he had the right to comfort her.

He turned to Mr. Solana. "You've said what you came to say. I'll show you out."

"Dr. Rosen, I will call you tomorrow morning. I hope you'll be more receptive. Think about what it means to your son. And you."

Paul walked Mr. Solana to the door as Naomi muttered, "Excuse me," and rushed to the bathroom.

He watched helplessly as Beadle ran after her.

15

Naomi had no idea how she was going to make it through the night, much less the next day. She opened the bathroom drawer where she kept single-edged razor blades used to scrape paint off windows and pulled one out of its package. She held it, poised to cut, hoping she could do it, then, knowing she couldn't, put it back. She tried to ignore the knocking on the door and the worry in Paul's voice when he shouted, "Naomi, are you all right?" She heard Beadle whining, the frantic sound he made when he wanted to be let in.

Paul felt as if he were back in time, dealing with the aftermath of Molly's disappearance, being blamed for her death. In anger and frustration, he yelled, "Open the fucking door!" Beadle scratched the door as intently as Paul banged. Naomi wanted them to go away, to leave her alone, but their thumping and scratching grew louder and more insistent—impossible to ignore.

Questions assaulted her: What am I going to do? How can I face a child I gave away? If I can't forgive myself for what I did, how can he? What can I possibly say about my giving him to Russ and Shelly without telling him that they forced me to let them adopt him? She stood, paralyzed, barely able to breathe.

It was Paul's urgent pleading that got to her, the sound of a man pushed beyond his ability to cope. "Please, Naomi, open the door. I need you to open the door now."

Like an automaton, she unlocked the door, but couldn't will herself to open it. Paul heard the lock click and turned the knob, afraid of what he might see. Naomi stared at him, white faced, powerless, unable to respond to Beadle's pawing and whining. Paul took her limp hand and led her into the living room, helping her to sit. Beadle jumped onto her lap and licked her face, but Naomi was lost inside herself.

Paul looked for liquor but felt uncomfortable opening her cabinets, so he brewed tea. "Here, drink this," he said putting a mug in her hand. He pushed Beadle off her so he wouldn't knock against the mug, but the dog jumped back onto her lap, spilling the scalding liquid.

Naomi sat motionless, absorbing the pain, welcoming the punishment.

Paul felt like screaming at her. He wanted to grab her face and tell her to pay attention. He needed her to respond to his caring, to Beadle's loving, yet the words of his anger management counselor reverberated loudly: "If you feel an urge to hurt, back off, immediately! Do not act on your feelings." All Paul could think of was Molly's death. At least Naomi's son was alive. He wanted to see her. What could be so terrible?

Paul sat down next to her and forced himself to speak in a calm voice. "Naomi?"

"Go away."

"Please, let me help."

"There's nothing to help."

"I need—"

"You need to go. And take your dog with you, if he'll go."

Paul spit out his words. "What difference does it make what we do? You sure as hell don't care."

"You have no right to judge me," she snapped.

"That's true," he said. "But I'm not judging. I'm describing what I see. A woman so absorbed in her own misery she can't see anything beyond her own shit."

"Get out!"

"I'm going. But thanks for showing me what self-indulgence looks like. Not a pretty sight, that's for sure. I sure as hell hope I remember it the next time I'm wallowing in misery and self-pity."

As soon as the words were out of his mouth, he was sorry he'd spoken. Just what his therapist had warned him about: "You feel whatever you feel, but you choose how to express that feeling. Under no circumstances it is okay to use the energy of your anger against yourself or anyone else."

Well, here was the perfect opportunity to practice responding differently no matter how she reacted or what she said. He took a deep breath. "I'm sorry. I have no business talking to you like this. I apologize." He sank into a chair, embarrassed, wishing he could take back the words he'd spoken in anger.

He felt her hand touch his shoulder. Reaching up, without looking, he put his hand on top of hers. It was the best they could do.

"Thanks for coming," she said. "I owe you an apology as well. I guess from here on it can only get better."

Paul nodded. "Let's hope."

Everything in him yearned to stay, but he stood up. "I think I need to go."

Everything in Naomi yearned for him to ask to stay. "I'll walk you to the door."

Beadle followed, but at the last minute remained inside. "I guess he knows I need him more," she said, hoping her tone conveyed appreciation.

"I wouldn't bet on that," said Paul, "but at least I know where he is and that he's in good hands."

"Thanks, Paul. You're a good guy."

"Sometimes."

"That's better than some."

She closed the door, leaning on it for support, unable to move. When the doorbell rang, she jumped. Was it morning already?

"Naomi, it's me, Paul. My truck won't start. I think the battery's dead."

She tried to ignore the relief flooding through her body as she opened the door. "C'mon in. It's too late to call anyone. You can sleep on the sofa. It makes into a bed."

"Thanks. I wasn't looking forward to sleeping in my truck."

Naomi pulled out sheets from her bathroom closet and handed them to Paul. He helped her make the bed, feeling increasingly awkward and uncomfortable. What he wanted was to hold her. What she wanted, he didn't know and couldn't guess. She put the pillowcase on the pillow, turned off all the lights but one near the sofa bed, and said, "I'll see you in the morning. Sleep well."

He watched her walk resolutely to her bedroom, wishing he were there, knowing there wasn't a chance in hell that could happen. He wondered if she would be able to sleep. What was she going to say to the lawyer and her son? He sat down, deciding to take off only his shoes and socks. Anything more would leave him feeling too vulnerable, too close to acknowledging his desire.

In the bathroom, perhaps because she was trying not to look, Naomi saw herself in the mirror, gray faced, dead eyes, tight mouth. What will Pablo think when he sees me? Maybe his name isn't Pablo any more. Maybe Russ and Shelly—she couldn't bring herself to say "his parents"—changed it.

Naomi stared at the woman in the mirror, wishing she could disappear, knowing how hard she had worked to avoid what faced her in the morning. Why did he want to see her? She was sure Russ and Shelly had taken good care of him. There wasn't much she could tell him about his father. Should she lie and pretend they'd at least had a longer relationship? Did he have to know she'd slept with a man once, they'd made a child, and, despite all their feelings for one another, never saw each other again? "I tried," she said, defending herself. "When I was released from prison I was deported and had to leave Spain immediately. There was no way to contact Pablo or his sister or Manuela."

She could imagine her son asking, "Why did you give me up? Why didn't you find a way to keep me with you? Other women raised children alone, made up stories to protect themselves from the shame of being an unmarried woman with a child. And, if you decided to give me away, why did you wait until I was three? When I was old enough to remember?"

Naomi sloshed cold water over her face, hoping to stop the questions and the memories, but it was too late; the torrent was unstoppable. She walked into the living room on tiptoe, hoping Paul was asleep, but when she passed the bed to get to the liquor cabinet, he asked, "Having trouble sleeping?"

"Yes. I thought I'd pour myself some scotch. It helps sometimes."

"Want company?"

Yes. I want you to hold me and stroke my hair and tell me I can do this: I can meet my son. I can look into his eyes and remember his sweet baby smell. Remember the way his fingers touched my face. Remember having no food in the house, no money to pay for his medicine and the rent, no salary high enough for me to pay someone to take care of him. Not even able to keep satisfying men to pay the bills. Not wanting someone else to take care of him. The pressure to give him up.

"No," she said, afraid his comfort would undo her. That's okay, I'll manage. I'll just be a second."

Paul couldn't help himself. He walked over to where she was pouring herself a tumbler of scotch. "Are you sure you want to drink all that? You don't want to be hung over in the morning."

"No, I'd just like to be hung."

His head told him to go back to bed, to leave her alone, that he had no business interfering with her life. The words of his therapist reverberated: "You need to think before you act. Your feelings are energy. How you use them is up to you. You control them; they don't have to control you." Yet the urge was too strong. He took the drink out of her hand, put it on the counter, and placed his hands on her face.

"Naomi, no matter what you did, given that all your choices were bad, I'm sure you made the best choice you knew to make. That has to matter to your son."

"How can you be so sure?" She told herself she needed to take his hands off her face, to tell him to mind his own business.

"If you're anything like me, you've been running from yourself for most of your life. Maybe seeing your son will make it possible for you to stop."

"You don't know what I did."

"No, but Beadle chose you over me. He must know something."

"Yeah, that I didn't beat him when I was angry," she said wryly.

Paul tilted her face and lightly kissed her forehead. "That puts you ahead of me on the scale of moral measure."

"There are worse things than hitting a dog."

"Beadle would not agree." As if on cue, the dog settled between their legs, wagging his tail. "If you think it would help, I'm willing to listen."

"I don't even know you."

"So talk. We'll get to know each other."

"I can't." She moved away from him and took a long sip of scotch

"You mean you don't want to. Why not?"

She didn't answer.

"I have a confession to make."

"Maybe it's time for both of us to try to sleep."

"I lied. My battery isn't dead."

"What? Why . . ." She turned toward him.

"I'll go if you want me to, but I just didn't think it was right to leave you alone, even if you do have Beadle. I mean, he's great, but he's a dog. Sometimes you, I mean I, need human company."

"I couldn't even support my son as a whore."

"At least you tried."

"You could say that. Not much comfort though."

"I know what it's like to live with . . ." Unable to put his feelings into words, he walked over to her, yearning to take her in his arms, to help. "Naomi . . ."

She felt the warmth of his body through her back, the urgency of wanting to be held, to be forgiven. Instead she said, "It's late. You must be tired."

"Please, I know it's been crazy between us, and I have no right, but I need to hold you." He touched her shoulder. She didn't move. He stroked her neck. Then, taking the biggest chance he had taken in so long he couldn't remember, he put his arms around her, his need apparent to both of them. "Please," he whispered soundlessly.

She stood, motionless, wanting more than anything to turn around, to lose herself in the warmth of his body but memories she had stuffed down inside herself had been let loose. "I can't."

He dropped his arms.

She felt his disappointment.

"It's not about you." Unable to say more, she left the room.

Paul watched her go, Beadle following after. If it's not about me, who is it about? Feeling his old response welling up, wanting to yell and curse, he put on his socks and shoes and left.

When he discovered that his truck wouldn't start, that the battery really was dead, all he could do was laugh. "The moral of this story is," he said to the moon, "be careful of the lies you tell; they may come true."

Well, it wasn't the first time he'd slept in his truck. And, the way his life was going, it might not be the last.

16

In the morning, Naomi got out of bed, feeling anxiety hang over her like a tightly woven net. She noticed the pang she felt seeing Paul had gone, then put the kettle on and went out to get the paper. When she saw him in his truck, his head resting on the back of the seat, she knocked on the window. He opened his eyes and grinned.

"I guess the battery didn't want me to be a liar."

"It's dead?"

"Yup. AAA said they'd be here as soon as they could."

"How long you been waiting?"

"Almost an hour."

"Want a cup of coffee?"

"You can't imagine how good that sounds."

"Go on in, I'll be there in a minute. I'm just going to get the paper."

"What time do you think Solana and your son will be here?" asked Paul, grateful for the coffee and Naomi's friendly attitude.

"I don't know. I sure hope he calls before they come."

"How are you feeling?"

"Don't ask."

"At the risk of being totally presumptuous, want me to stay?"

"Don't you have to work?"

"What's that got to do with anything?"

Naomi smiled. "Thanks, but this is something I have to face by myself."

"Well, you know my number. Call anytime." He washed his mug and stood for a moment, wondering what to say, wanting to make himself feel better. "Guess I'll wait outside for the AAA truck. Can't be too much longer."

"Paul . . ."

"What?"

"Thanks."

"For what?"

"For being so caring. For hearing 'no' and not getting upset."

"Would it lessen your opinion of me if I told you I lied again, that I was upset?"

"What you do on your time doesn't count."

Now it was Paul who said thanks, and Naomi who said, "For what?"

"For being honest and making great coffee." He cocked his ear. "I do believe I hear a honk." Wanting to kiss her, but afraid to do so, he waved and left.

Unable to make herself eat breakfast, Naomi scrubbed the kitchen stove, wiped the refrigerator, mopped the floor, and was vacuuming the living room rug when the phone rang. She wanted more than anything to run, to keep running, until there was nothing to run from. Instead, she stared at the phone. At the last ring she picked it up. "Hello?"

"We will be at your place by ten o'clock."

"I thought the choice was mine, not yours."

"Very well, Dr. Rosen. What have you decided?"

There was no way she could push the river back to its origins. "I don't think I have much choice at this point. I just hope you know what you're doing." She hung up the phone and rushed into the bathroom, turning on the shower, wondering would help more, steaming hot or ice cold water. She tried both.

What do you wear to meet a son you haven't seen in almost forty years, she wondered. She tried on everything she could think of, then, glancing at her watch, settled for a dark green skirt she'd bought in Mexico and a light green hemp top—green for new beginnings. She put on a pair of jade earrings she'd found in the bargain bin of a store on the Plaza. In the past, the earrings had made her feel attractive. Did she want to feel attractive? Did she want to feel anything? She took them off and put turquoise studs in her ears. Not satisfied, she was about to take them out when she heard the car in the driveway. She reached the toilet in time to throw up.

Rinsing her mouth did nothing to take away the sour taste. The doorbell rang. She practiced the deep breathing her cranial sacral therapist had taught her as she walked to the door, her heart beating too fast to control.

Even though he stood behind Mr. Solana, she could see that he was tall, taller than her memory of his father. His dark hair was flecked with gray, but he had Pablo's eyes and way of looking.

When she opened the door, the word popped out, "*Bienvenidos!*"

Mr. Solana smiled. "*Muchas gracias*, Señora." He stepped aside to let the man behind him move forward. "Dr. Rosen . . . Pablo Rosen."

They hadn't changed his name? How was that possible?

Naomi decided to hold out her hand. A hug seemed intrusive.

Pablo made no effort to extend his hand for her to shake, nor did he speak.

"Shall we go inside?" asked Mr. Solana.

Naomi found her voice. "Of course." She led the two men into her living room. "Would you like coffee or tea or water?"

"Coffee would be nice. What about you, Pablo?"

"Nothing, thank you."

"I'll just be a minute," she said. Hurrying into the kitchen, questions pounded her brain: How do we break the silence? Do we break it? Is it right for me to ask what he wants? What if . . . What did Russ and Shelly tell him about me? Why now?

She put the coffee on a tray and brought it in, her hands visibly shaking. The two men stopped talking and looked at her. Naomi poured Mr. Solana a cup. "Would you like sugar or milk?"

"No, thank you, I take it black." He sat back against the sofa. Naomi poured herself a cup just to have something to do. After an interminable silence, Mr. Solana turned to Pablo, who was sitting next to him. "Pablo?" Pablo turned away. "Dr. Rosen?" Naomi studiously sipped her coffee. "Perhaps the two of you would like me to leave you alone." He stood up, taking his coffee with him, and walked outside.

Pablo looked at the woman who was his mother. Remembering all the years of looking for her, knowing she had not looked for him. Why had he needed to find her? Why had he thought that meeting her would dispel his anger and hurt? He tried to see her as he last remembered her, singing to him, stroking his back as she cradled him in her arms. But this woman, Dr. Rosen, bore no trace of her, not even her voice. He wished he had not allowed Mr. Solana to persuade him to come.

The silence was horrible. Was he supposed to break the ice? To say I'm happy to meet you after so many years? To ask her to tell him about his father? Maybe Russ and Shelly had been right about moving on and letting the past be. Well, he had tried, and the past wouldn't let him be. And now, here she was, the woman he'd been yearning to know for most of his life, a stranger.

Emotionally numb, Naomi decided she had to break the silence, but it took all her strength and courage to look at him as she spoke. "Leaving you with Russ and Shelly was the hardest, worst, most terrible time in my life. Not a day has gone by without my thinking about you and what I did."

Her son's stare unnerved her. "I don't expect forgiveness from you any more than I can forgive myself for what I did."

She waited for him to say something. He sat, mute.

Naomi allowed herself to say, "I must admit, I'm surprised they didn't change your name."

"They did. I found my birth certificate, and when I was twenty-one I petitioned the Boston court to restore my birth name. Tell me about my father."

"He risked his life to rescue me from Franco's Guardia Civil when I was in Spain. We spent the night together, hiding."

"Hiding? Was my father a revolutionary?"

"He and his friends were part of a group trying to overthrow Franco."

"What happened to my father?"

"I was questioned by the police, but knowing how dangerous the situation was, your father had made sure there was nothing I could tell them."

"But what happened to him?"

"I don't know. The police tried their best to get me to say what they wanted to hear." Naomi shuddered. Feeling Pablo's eyes boring into her, she continued. "I was finally released when I agreed to leave Spain immediately. Your father and I had no way to contact each other. But even if I did know how to find him, I wouldn't have tried. I knew the police were following every move I made, and I didn't want to put his life in danger."

"So it was a one-night stand."

"I knew your father for one night, that's true, but if it had been possible we would have found a way to be together."

"Are you sure it was his child?"

Naomi flinched.

"Yes, I'm sure." She sipped the cold coffee to give herself a moment's respite. "I didn't know I was pregnant until after I left Europe and returned home."

"Why didn't you have an abortion?"

"It was illegal in those days."

"Women found a way."

"Yes, but I didn't know a doctor who did them, and I didn't know anyone who knew one. Besides, I felt connected to your father in . . . some deep way."

"Why didn't you write to him, to tell him he was a father?"

"I had no address. Pablo Muñoz is a common name. I don't even know if that was his real name. It was the name the police used. I knew him only as Pablo."

"So you had me and we lived together for three years and then you gave me away." He paused. "Why did you wait so long? Why didn't you do it when I was a baby? When I wouldn't have had memories?"

"I thought I could earn enough money to take care of you. I was wrong."

"Now you're going to tell me you did the best you could?"

"I won't defend what I did, nor will I offer excuses."

Pablo stood up and turned away. "I've been looking for you ever since you left. Do you know what it's like for a child to keep looking for his mother, remembering her hugs and kisses? Remembering that one day she's loving you and the next day she's gone? Disappeared. No explanations. No warnings. Nothing. Just absence. Do you really think Russ and Shelly could make up for a mother who didn't love me enough to keep me?" He whirled around. "Do you?"

"What I thought was that they loved you. They weren't able to have children. They wanted to adopt you. They had money, a lovely house—"

"And you think that was a fair exchange?"

"No. I never thought that."

"What did you think?"

"I thought it was better to be brought up by respectable people than by a whore."

"Because you slept with my father?"

"No. I know I can't say I loved your father, but I loved how he treated me. The problem was that as soon as my pregnancy showed, I was fired from my job. Back then they didn't allow pregnant women to teach. I thought that after you were born I could get another teaching position, but word spread that I was an unwed mother, and no one would hire me. I did what I could to buy food and pay the rent, but even then it wasn't enough."

"So why didn't you leave? Move to another town?"

"Moving takes money. I had none."

"And I'm supposed to feel sorry for you?"

"No."

"Why didn't you come back for me after you started to earn money?

You have a PhD. You've published books. You live in a nice house."

Naomi decided to tell the truth, regardless of the consequences. "Russ and Shelly made me sign an agreement that I would never contact you. They were afraid you would leave them if I came back."

"You're lying. You're blaming them for your choice."

"I understood their fear. Losing the child you love is pain beyond measure."

"You didn't lose me. You gave me away."

"Yes. I did."

Naomi sat, unwilling to offer explanations. She understood his anger and heartbreak and pain. They were feelings she knew only too well. There was nothing she could say to make things better. Not to him. Not to her.

"So, you feel no need to offer explanations? No defense for what you did? No need to try to make me feel better?"

"There is no defense for desperation."

A huge boil inside her burst open, relieving pressure that had been building up ever since she realized she had to give her son to Russ and Shelly, that she couldn't take proper care of him, that she had failed him as his mother.

"Did you ever marry?"

"Yes, twice."

"How many children do you have?"

"None. I couldn't bear the thought of having another child."

He sneered. "Poor little woman, afraid to have another child she might love and then leave."

"I used my pain as best I could. After I got my PhD, I focused on helping children find their voices. I teach them how to express themselves in positive ways, to use their anger and frustration rather than to let it use them."

"So you think that's a fair exchange? My pain for your good work?"

"No."

"Didn't your husbands want children?"

"My first husband did."

"Did that break up your marriage?"

"I don't know. He wasn't good at talking about how he felt or what he wanted."

"Why did you marry him?"

"He asked no questions. I mistook his silence for wisdom."

"How is that possible?"

"I needed to feel safe."

"Did you?"

"No."

Naomi wondered if her son was married, if she was a grandmother.

She couldn't bear the tension any longer. Standing up, she said, "If you'll excuse me, I'll be right back."

"Where are you going?" His tone of voice sent shivers down her spine.

"I need to use the bathroom. If you need one, it's the second door on the left." Without waiting for his response, she left.

Pablo watched her leave, imagining himself as a child, saying good-night but not good-morning. He thought about leaving, going off with André without saying good-bye, just as she had left without saying good-bye. Yet he wanted something more from her. He just didn't know what that was.

Unable to wait for her to come back, he walked outside and found André coming toward him. "This is a wonderful place. You can't imagine the lovely walk I just took," said the lawyer, noticing the grim expression on Pablo's face.

"I can't say the same."

"How are you?"

"I don't know."

"Where's your mother?"

"Dr. Rosen went to the bathroom."

"What do you want from her, Pablo?"

"I don't know."

"What do you want to do?"

"Leave."

"Without saying good-bye?"

"Why not? This time I'll be the one who leaves without saying good-bye."

"Do you think this will help?"

Pablo shrugged. "History repeating itself, don't you think?"

"How do you know your mother didn't say good-bye to you?"

"What I know is that I've spent years looking for her. Now that I've finally met her, I can't imagine why it mattered so much. I guess fantasy trumps reality every time."

Pablo opened the car door and slumped into the passenger seat, closing the door behind him.

The lawyer opened the door. "Pablo, you and I have had many talks about this meeting." He paused, trying to find the exact words he wanted to use, not always possible for him when speaking English. "It is true that I do not have your experience, but I believe it is not a good idea to leave like this. You do not have—what do you say—closure. At the very least, I think you need to say good-bye."

"And if I can't or won't?"

The lawyer shrugged. "It is up to you."

"Pablo?" Naomi looked around, feeling increasingly anxious.

He left? Without saying good-bye? Well, why not? That's what he thinks I did to him. She took the coffee cups and pot to the kitchen and was about to wash them when she saw André Solana's car drive off. *If I had thought to look sooner, I might have seen them before they left. And if I had, so what? If he doesn't want to say good-bye, that's his choice, his notion of paying me back.*

Her stomach hurt. Her head ached. Her brain kept replaying the last time she'd seen her son, asleep in Russ and Shelly's house, in a bedroom he didn't know was his. Shelly had stood in the doorway as if to prevent Naomi from changing her mind and taking Pablo with her. Naomi remembered asking her to leave, just for a minute, so she could talk to Pablo alone, but Shelly had refused. "You said you wanted to kiss him good-bye, so do it." Naomi heard the fear in Shelly's voice. Why couldn't Shelly hear the pain in Naomi's plea to let her have a few more minutes with Pablo?

Naomi knew she had to get out of the house to release the hold that Pablo's words had on her. Knowing she had too much roiling energy inside her to weave or write, she called Priscilla. "Pris, I'll go crazy if I stay inside one more minute. I need to get out of here. How about hiking to Nambé Lake?"

"Okay, I'll meet you at the ski basin in half an hour."

Naomi put on her hiking boots, filled two bottles with water, and grabbed a bag of trail mix. As soon as she opened the door, Beadle ran out.

"Dammit, Beadle. I didn't invite you to come with me." Sighing, she looked around for the leash that Paul had given her, but when she couldn't find it, she realized she was in no mood to search for it. Grabbing the old leash, she hoped that it would restrain him should the occasion arise. She called to him, but the dog refused to come closer than about five feet. "All right, you can come with me, but you better mind." Hah, she thought, that's like asking a hurricane not to blow.

17

Naomi drove to the trailhead, hoping that walking up the steep path would absorb some of the chaotic feelings colliding inside her. She realized she was getting used to Beadle. He was good company, and his body cuddled against hers, was warm and comforting.

Priscilla was waiting for her. "You seem real upset. What's wrong?"

"Nothing much. Let's walk. I need the exercise."

"Just remember, I don't walk as fast as you do and I brought my camera. I plan to stop and take photos whenever I feel like it."

They started up the Winsor trail. Leading the way, Naomi was soon far ahead of Priscilla, walking up the steep incline, drinking water at regular intervals without slowing her pace, needing to walk off her anguish.

Beadle trotted slowly, keeping Priscilla company, stopping regularly at nearby streams, slurping up the cool water. When Naomi arrived at the fence separating the Pecos Wilderness from the Winsor Trail, she was surprised at how quickly she had arrived.

She heard Priscilla yell, "Nomi, stop. Beadle and I need a rest. You're walking like you're in a race with the devil."

Priscilla caught up with Naomi and sat down on a log, gasping for breath. Beadle collapsed next to her, panting.

"Sorry, Pris, I guess I got carried away."

"Where? You look like you're carrying the weight of the world."

"Oh . . . just thinking about the girls I teach. I'm finally getting them to write a little. But there's so much tension between Martina and Juanita, they keep the rest of the group on edge. It's hard to write when you don't feel safe."

"Maybe you could bring in one of the books you've written and tell them what it's like to be an author."

"What good would that do?"

"Show them what it means to be a successful woman."

"Yeah, right. I'm the poster girl for good decisions."

"Nomi, what's wrong?"

"I told you . . . C'mon, Beadle. Let's show this young'un what it means to boogie."

"Stop! I am not taking another step until you tell me what's going on."

There was no way Naomi could talk about her meeting with Pablo. "It's not just the tension between Martina and Juanita. Someone's beating Martina. Each time she comes to class, the bruises that I can see are worse than before. Even Juanita, her cousin, can't talk to her. What am I supposed to do? Ignore them like everyone else? Pris, looking at her makes me sick. She's smart and beautiful and talented, but she might as well be a piece of used toilet paper the way she treats herself. And then there's Lupe . . . her mother died when she was a baby. All she knows is 'Daddy's friends.' You can't imagine her misery."

"Maybe I can."

"What do you mean?"

"My mother died when I was ten. Pa didn't have 'friends,' but—"

"I didn't know. I'm sorry. What was it like?"

Priscilla shrugged. "It's hard to describe. Looking back, it was sort of like before she got sick and died the world was in color. Afterward it was gray."

"Oh, Pris."

"Well, that's the past." She stroked Beadle's fur. "Ready to roll, buddy?" The dog wagged his tail and ran to Naomi. "Let's go, I want to see this lake of yours," said Priscilla, feeling she had said too much, wondering why she'd said anything at all.

The two women began walking. After the steady uphill of the first part of the trail, it was a relief to go downhill for a little while and their pace quickened. Walking in the vast wilderness gave Naomi a sense of being one with nature. At first, the intensity of her emotions fueled her pace, but as she walked deeper into the forest she slowed down, the sounds of the birds, the dappled sunlight coming through the tops of the trees, and the abundance of wildflowers soothing her jangled nerves. Beadle's constant loping next to her was a gift. She turned around to Priscilla. "I'm so glad you came with me."

"Thank you for asking. This place feels like it has healing powers."

"I hope so. I can use all the healing I can find."

"That makes two of us." Priscilla took a few more photos, then stood up.

Naomi gave Priscilla an inquiring look. Priscilla gave her a hug. "I've never hiked here before. It's beautiful."

"Wait until you see the lake. You'll think you're in Switzerland."

When Naomi heard the rushing sounds of the stream, she ran to greet it, taking great pleasure in dipping her hands into the cool water, washing her sweaty face. Beadle jumped in without checking the power of the current, and the two women had to rescue him. He thanked them by shaking himself out all over them. Given the heat, the shower felt good. Then, he jumped in again.

"Dog, what does it take for you to learn?" Naomi realized she could as well have asked herself the same question. Once more she fished him out. This time he ventured close enough to drink but not far enough in to be swept downstream.

Priscilla bent down to take a photo of a clump of pink flowers growing from a patch of earth in the middle of the stream and noticed Naomi kneeling beside the stream, crumbling a chunk of a power bar. "What are you doing?"

"Sending my worries down the water on bits of my lunch."

"Does it help?" asked Priscilla.

"Can it hurt?" shrugged Naomi.

"Good point."

The two women silently watched the current take the crumbs downstream.

"What did you send down the stream?" asked Priscilla.

"It's bad luck to tell," said Naomi, not knowing if this was true. "We still have a ways to go. Are you ready?"

Priscilla nodded, and the two women and Beadle began to climb up along the stream. The trail, such as it was, was steep, narrow, and often hard to follow. Naomi watched Beadle, hoping the incline wouldn't be too much for him. They walked more slowly, sliding on loose pebbles and sand. She took comfort from the sounds of the water and the profusion of wildflowers in color combinations she would never use in her weaving, yet delighted her in nature.

The sight of the lake as they emerged from the woods, surrounded by high stony peaks, some still snow covered, filled them with delight and awe.

"Oh, Nomi . . ." Priscilla had no words to express what she was feeling.

Naomi squeezed Priscilla's hand, grateful she had a friend with whom to share the view. Priscilla squeezed her hand back. The two women stood quietly until Priscilla's stomach grumbled. "Guess we need to find a place to sit. I'm hungry."

Looking around, they found a cluster of rounded rocks that provided a comfortable place to rest and munch. Beadle laid his head in Naomi's lap, his snores providing comic relief from thoughts of her son. She wondered what his life was like and how he felt about their visit. She wished he were sitting next to her, sharing the beauty, allowing their proximity to silently speak. She had no idea what he wanted from their visit or why he'd felt the need to meet with her now, or if he'd gotten what he came for. Had something fomented his search?

The hike back seemed to take less time, although Priscilla still huffed and puffed as she walked up the long hill to the gate dividing the Pecos Wilderness and the Winsor Trail.

"Not tomorrow," laughed Priscilla, "but I'd sure like to do this again.

I can't believe we have such beauty so close to town, and I've never hiked this trail in all the time I've lived in Santa Fe."

"When I was a kid, I spent a lot of time walking in the woods," said Naomi, "and there's something about feeling the dappled light of the sun coming through the trees that relaxes parts of me I don't even know are tense."

"How 'bout us trying to do a hike once a week?" suggested Priscilla.

"Sounds good to me. Let me know what day is good for you," said Naomi, putting her gear and Beadle into the car.

Beadle was still asleep when Naomi drove up to her house, so she left the car door open. Tired from the hike, she felt calmer, able to ignore the blinking light on her answering machine. While taking an unusually long shower, letting the hot water soothe her tired muscles, she heard the phone ringing, but refused to rush to answer it. Whoever wanted her would have to wait until she felt ready to deal with the world.

Feeling much better after her shower, Naomi walked into the living room, walked past her answering machine, which now had seven messages on it, and went to the car to check on Beadle. She tried waking him up, but he didn't respond. Had the walk been too much for him? She rushed into the house and dialed Paul's number. He gave her his vet's name and directions. "I'll call and tell him it's an emergency," said Paul. "If I can cancel my next appointment, I'll meet you there."

As she drove, Naomi had to force herself to concentrate on the road. Worries that she'd inadvertently done something to hurt Beadle made her feel sick to her stomach. At least Paul had sounded sympathetic on the phone, rather than accusatory.

She was grateful that Beadle stirred when she opened the car door. At least he was still alive. Just as she was trying to lift him out of the car, Paul drove up. The two of them carried the limp dog into the office where the vet's assistant was waiting to take him into an examining room.

It was a long wait. "For two people who've never even been on a date, we seem to be spending a lot of time dealing with crises," said Paul.

"I'm ready for a pleasantly boring week."

"How did the visit with your son go?" he asked.

"Do you want the short or long version?"

"Long. I'm not going anywhere."

"He came. He yelled. He left."

"If that's the long version, what's the short one?"

"He came. He left."

"How are you?"

"I hiked to Nambé Lake and hardly noticed the uphills."

Paul whistled. "That's a hell of a lot better way to get rid of your feelings than what I did. Way to go."

"Maybe the hike was too much for Beadle."

"Knowing him, you didn't ask. He hates to be left behind. Besides, as we've both learned, he has a mind of his own."

"Thanks, Paul. I needed that."

He put his arm around her, and she rested against his shoulder. He leaned his head against hers and held her hand as they waited for the vet. "Naomi, no matter what happens, you know Beadle loved you from the first moment he saw you lying in the grass. And if—"

When the vet came into the waiting room, Paul saw the look in his eyes and knew. He choked out the words. "How?"

"His heart. Died in his sleep. Would you like to see him?"

Grief stricken, Paul and Naomi nodded, following the vet to where Beadle lay, his body still warm. Naomi bent down, leaning her cheek against his body, and silently said good-bye. Paul stroked Beadle's head, wishing he could cry.

The vet's assistant came in to ask what they wanted to do with the body.

Paul said, "If you don't mind, Naomi, I'd like to bury him in the woods, near my house. He used to love chasing squirrels there." She nodded, unable to talk. Paul carried Beadle out and laid him on the backseat. "Let's go in my truck. I'll drive you back afterward, if that's okay."

She nodded, hardly able to believe Beadle was dead. "If you don't mind, I'd like to wrap him in the blanket I have in my car. Silently, Paul and Naomi took turns digging the hole. When it was deep enough, they carried Beadle's body from the truck and lowered him into the earth. Feeling like she had to perform some kind of ritual, Naomi found a few pebbles and placed them on the mound of earth covering his body. She and Paul knelt down, grieving, thinking what they could not speak, each remembering how Beadle had lived and loved.

As they walked back to Paul's house, Naomi was surprised to notice they were holding hands. The day felt years old, yet she still had to pick up her car and drive home. "I guess I'm ready for a ride back to the vet's," she said dispiritedly.

"It's late and I'm sure you're exhausted. Come in. I'll make dinner for you."

Naomi said, "I'm so tired, if I sit down, I might never get up."

"You're welcome to stay as long as you like. Go lie down; I'll call you when supper's ready."

Sinking into the softness of the couch, she didn't hear Paul calling her to come eat. She didn't feel him kiss her tenderly on her cheek, nor was she aware of him putting a light blanket over her. What she felt was a sense of comfort.

When she awoke, it was morning. He had gone to work, leaving her a note.

Dearest Slumberbug,

I didn't have the heart to wake you, so I hope I'm not messing up any plans you might have. There are clean towels in the bathroom. Help yourself to whatever you want for breakfast. The coffee beans are in the freezer, the grinder is next to the fridge. If you can wait until lunch, I'll come get you. If not, give me a call and I'll try to get away earlier.
P.S. In case you're interested, you don't snore.

Paul

Naomi wasn't even sure what day it was, much less what she was supposed to be doing. She took a leisurely shower, refusing to feel guilty about wasting water. As she was making coffee, she realized she hadn't eaten since munching trail mix at lunch the day before, when Beadle was still alive. Neither Paul nor the vet had held her accountable for the dog's death, yet she couldn't help feeling the hike had been too much for him. Well, he was dead and there was nothing she could do to change this. And there was nothing she could do about her son's coming and leaving. And there was nothing she could do about the parts of her past she wanted to erase.

Naomi took her coffee, eggs, toast, jam, and newspaper outside, to a tree-sheltered portal just off the kitchen, appreciating Paul's neatness, his spare sense of space, and the muted colors of the walls and furnishings. He might have problems with anger, but his house radiated calm, something she desperately needed. She was not ready to leave when she heard his truck.

He looked approvingly at the remains of her breakfast. "Glad you found what you needed."

"It's lovely out here. I'll just wash my dishes and we can go."

He grinned. "You don't have to leave on my account. Feel free to stay for as long as you like."

"It's tempting. More than you can imagine. But I guess the vet would prefer I stop using his limited parking space." She took her dishes into the kitchen.

"Naomi?"

"Yes?"

"I don't know how to say this . . ."

Naomi didn't know what he wanted to say, but she was sure she didn't want to hear it. The morning had been like a respite from the real world—which was waiting, as always—and the longer it took her to re-enter, the harder it would be.

"Would it be all right with you if we talk later? I need to face the unanswered messages on my answering machine."

"How about dinner?"

"How about I call you when I know what's going on?" Naomi turned away from the look of disappointment in his eyes. She saw his hand ball into a fist and felt his anger.

Paul fought the impulse to shake her, to remind her how well he'd treated her, how he hadn't blamed her for Beadle's death even though he believed Beadle would still be alive if she hadn't taken him on such a long hike. Fighting the urge to let her know how angry he was, he said, "Sure," then walked away. "I'll be back in a minute."

In his bedroom, he kept smashing his fist into his pillow as hard as he could, trying to work through the intensity of his feeling. Where did this need to hurt come from? Why would he want to harm a woman he liked? Then again, why had he hit Beadle? His only solace was that this time he'd taken out his feelings on a pillow and not himself or anyone else.

He went into his bathroom and looked at himself in the mirror, not liking what he saw—a tense man with unfriendly eyes. He kept staring at himself until his face relaxed enough for him to rejoin Naomi.

"Ready?" he asked.

A dozen replies occurred to Naomi. "Yup. Are you?"

A dozen replies occurred to Paul. "Let's go."

Naomi opened the note from Priscilla, pasted onto her front door.

> *Where are you? Why aren't you answering your phone? Call me the minute you get home. Pablo and I are worried about you. If I don't hear from you soon I'm notifying the police. It's not like you to just go off without letting me know where you're going. I'm afraid Ryerson did something to you.*

She crumpled the note, annoyed at Priscilla. Staring at the answering machine, the seven messages now twelve, didn't improve her mood. She wished she could delete them without listening, but she knew Priscilla had no qualms about contacting the police. She called her first. Relieved to get her answering machine, she left a reassuring message.

After making a cup of tea, Naomi decided she wanted something stronger. The alcohol warmed her and, despite not liking to attribute to liquor any improvement in her ability to act, she felt more ready to deal with what awaited her.

There were four messages from Priscilla, increasingly irate and worried; one from Mrs. Romero asking Naomi to stop by before the next class began; two from people asking for help with election registration; one from the Democratic Party asking if she would volunteer to make phone calls; and one from Paul asking how she was doing.

More troubling were the two from André Solana and one from Russ asking her to please return their phone calls. She decided to call Russ first even though he was no one she wanted to talk to. Why was he suddenly contacting her after repeatedly telling her, even making her sign a contract, that under no circumstances was she ever to have contact with him, Shelly, or Pablo? Her hand shook as she dialed his number. What was the worst that could happen? She hadn't violated their agreement. The line was busy. She decided not to call him again. If he wanted to talk with her, he could call back. She had no need to talk to him.

She then tried Mr. Solana. The secretary was pleasant but offered no information about the lawyer's call. He would return her call as soon as his meeting ended. Naomi felt like saying, "So, I'm just supposed to sit and wait until he decides to call me?" but instead she thanked the woman and hung up.

Knowing work was her best antidote to deal with anxiety and depression, Naomi began reading stories to prepare for her next session with the girls. When the phone rang, she picked it up, thinking it was Mr. Solana, unprepared for the raging voice that screamed at her.

"What the fuck are you doing? You promised to have no contact with Pablo. You signed a legal document agreeing to stay out of his life. We've spent years trying to make him feel loved, but you, as always, don't care about anyone but yourself. We're ready to sue you for breach of contract. You're nothing—"

Naomi felt assaulted but tried to stay calm as she interrupted his diatribe. "Hello, Russ. If you want to talk, fine. If you're going to keep yelling, I'm hanging up. It's your choice."

"Where's Pablo?"

"I don't know. The visit was arranged by his lawyer."

"I don't believe you. Why now?"

"According to Mr. Solana, he's been looking for me for a long time."

"You're making this up."

"Why would I do that?"

"You've been seeing him all along. That's why he's become so weird."

"Good-bye, Russ." Naomi hung up.

Hearing his voice brought back too many memories. What did he mean by weird? Was Pablo in trouble? She resorted to her usual response to stress: cleaning, washing, and preparing a box for the thrift store. Despite two hours of scrubbing and tidying, she was still too tense to work, and it was too late to hike. Walking near her house would not help.

When the phone rang, she made herself let the answering machine take the call. After hearing Russ's curses, she pressed delete, wishing she could do that with every problem. She felt in limbo, wondering if her son would contact her again and, if so, under what circumstances.

Thinking about Paul didn't help. Despite all her effort to avoid acknowledging it, she reluctantly admitted to herself that she was attracted to Paul, yet she was put off by his anger and her wariness. Normally, she would have called Priscilla and asked if she wanted to have dinner, but her Pablo was still there and Naomi didn't feel comfortable talking with Priscilla while he was around.

Time passed slowly, with four more phone calls from Russ but no word from Mr. Solana or Pablo. She sensed Paul was waiting for her to call him, but she could not make herself do so. Feeling tense and unsettled, she packed her paints and clay into a bag and headed for her session with the girls, stopping first to see Mrs. Romero.

She knocked several times before the door opened. Mrs. Romero looked as if she'd been crying. "Is something wrong?" asked Naomi?

"Martina's in the hospital, in intensive care, on life support. We don't know if she's going to make it."

"What happened?"

"Her so-called boyfriend . . . I tell you, if it was up to me, I'd cut off his *cajones*." Naomi didn't need a translation.

"What do you want me to do?"

"Actually, this is not the reason I left the message for you. I showed the girls' poems to the psychologist. She wanted me to tell you she thinks you're making good progress with them. But now, who knows what will happen?"

Any animosity Naomi felt toward Mrs. Romero disappeared. She hadn't realized how much the woman cared about the girls. "I was going to work with an African story about saying "no" to people who don't care about you. What do you think? Should I go ahead and use it?"

"Sounds like a story I need to hear."

"You're welcome to join us."

"I don't know if Juanita will come. She kicked the nurse when she wouldn't let her see Martina." Mrs. Romero sighed. "Those two—can't live with each other, can't live without each other."

"How is Juanita now?"

"I persuaded the nurse not to press charges, and got her caseworker to talk with her, but I haven't heard anything since." Mrs. Romero looked intently at Naomi. "I just don't understand why someone as smart and pretty as Martina would put up with a man who beat her."

"I'm not sure smart and pretty matter much if she thinks she deserves to be treated badly."

"That's one of the reasons I'm hoping this writing project will continue," said Mrs. Romero. "These girls need a safe place to talk about their lives. They also need a smart, successful woman to act as a role model."

Naomi resisted the impulse to argue that she wasn't a role model for anyone; she had survived and, in some ways, prevailed. Maybe that was good enough.

The two women walked to the classroom in companionable silence, arranged the chairs in a circle, and waited. Juanita arrived, looking as if she'd been forced to attend, which turned out to be the case. When she saw Mrs. Romero sitting in a chair, she motioned for Naomi to come to the door.

"What's she doin' here?"

"She wants to hear the story I planned for today."

"How come?"

"Because she's upset about Martina and doesn't know how to make it better."

"She's not the only one. Stupid bitch."

"Mrs. Romero?"

"No. Martina. I kept tellin' her to throw José out, but she kept sayin' she loved him, that he told her he was sorry, that I don't understand. I'll find his sorry ass and tell him what I understand." Juanita's Spanish curses increased in intensity, worrying Naomi.

"He's not worth it. You'll just get in trouble."

"You mean more trouble."

"I heard. I'm sorry. I wish I could help."

"Yeah, well it's too late for help."

"Maybe not."

"What, you got a special arrangement with God?" challenged Juanita.

"No, but there might be something we could do that would make a difference."

"Yeah, like what?"

"When I was sick, a woman I knew organized a vigil. People stood at the foot of my bed, not saying anything, but it felt as if they were keeping me from dying."

"Did you want to die?"

"Yes."

"Why?"

"I guess you could say I found dying easier than living." Juanita stared at Naomi, who wished she'd kept her mouth shut. "Anyway, that's enough about me. I'm here to help you."

"Well, for starters, ask Mrs. Romero to leave. She don't belong here."

Juanita's thoughts were echoed by the girls straggling in, glaring at Mrs. Romero when they saw her sitting in their circle. Naomi hoped the woman would leave after noticing the girls' reaction, but the supervisor remained seated, a friendly smile on her face. The silence grew increasingly tense. Juanita's mocking smile let Naomi know she had to decide whose needs were most important.

"Mrs. Romero, could we go to your office? I'd like to talk with you for a minute." Naomi walked to the door hoping she would follow.

"Let's do it after the story."

Juanita's glare told Naomi this was not good enough. "I think we need to talk now." Mrs. Romero did not look pleased. Naomi was annoyed at Juanita for being so intransigent and at her supervisor for being so obtuse. "Careful," Naomi muttered to herself as the two women walked to the office, "you don't want to say something you'll be sorry for."

"What couldn't wait?" asked Mrs. Romero as she opened the door.

Naomi hesitated, trying to find the right words. "I think you may have noticed that the girls are upset."

"As well they should be."

"I think, under the circumstances, it might be better if I met with them alone. It's hard for them to trust someone who has authority over them."

"I have a right to be there, to see what you do with them. I hired you, remember?"

Naomi cursed under her breath, feeling a dam break inside her. "It's not about rights, it's about what's good for the girls."

Naomi's camaraderie with Mrs. Romero disappeared. *If the supervisor wants to fire me, let it be for protecting the girls.*

"I'll make a copy of the story for you," Naomi said. Pasting a smile on her face, she left, careful not to slam the door.

18

Juanita stood up, arms folded against her chest. "What's the plan?"

Naomi had none, but the accusatory look in Juanita's eyes demanded a response. "As long as Martina's in ICU, visitors are limited and her family has preference."

Juanita snorted. "Family? You got to be kiddin'."

"You know Martina better than anyone. What do you want me to do?"

Juanita turned away, not wanting anyone to see her tears. "I don't know."

"Sometimes it helps to hear a story. May I tell one?"

The girls nodded. Without Martina, they seemed more open, less afraid to show their feelings. Naomi wondered if Martina's sarcasm and hard-edged comments were her defense against pain, a fortress keeping everyone from knowing what was happening to her. A barrier that no one knew how to cross.

The girls leaned in toward Naomi as she began the story.

> There was once a village that enjoyed many years of prosperity. The rains came regularly. The crops flourished. In time, the grain bins were so full one of them collapsed and the grain scattered. However, people had stored as much as they could and left the grain where it was.
>
> Soon, birds found the grain and decided the village was a good place to live. They flew down and began eating. The next morning, when people saw how much grain the birds had devoured, they worried that the birds would find a way to eat their stored grain. So, the people tried to chase them away with noise. When this didn't work,

they shot arrows into the air but this too failed to stop the birds.

The villagers called a meeting to discuss how to get rid of the birds. No one wanted to be the first to mention the Old Man, yet he was on everyone's mind. One villager finally had the courage to tell the Headman, "We will starve if we do not rid our village of the birds. Nothing we have tried has worked. Perhaps the Old Man will once again help us."

Everyone was silent, each remembering how the village had banished the Old Man after he had helped them.

The Headman said, "It is true we chased away the Old Man because we were afraid of his magic, but he is our only hope. I will go to him. Perhaps he will take pity on us and agree to return to help us."

The next morning the Headman went in search of the Old Man. He found him dressed in worn clothes, with little in the way of goods. The Old Man was not pleased to see the Headman, nor did he want to return to the village. But when the Headman told him the children would starve if he didn't help them, the Old Man agreed to return.

Before going back to the village, the Old Man collected roots and plants to make a powder. That evening, after the villagers thanked him for coming, he showed them how to dip their arrows into the powder and how best to use them.

The leader of the birds saw the people with their bows and arrows, but he was not afraid and continued to eat the grain. When the Old Man quietly said, "Now!" the villagers shot their arrows into the leader of the birds and killed him. Seeing this, the other birds flew away in fear.

The villagers held a great feast to honor the Old Man. For a time, all was well. Then whispers began. People said, "If he has magic to kill the birds, he can kill us. We must tell him to go." The whispers grew into a loud chorus, and soon the villagers forced the Old Man to leave.

In time, the birds returned. The villagers watched helplessly as their grain disappeared. Once again they tried to get rid of the birds and once again they failed. They worried that with winter coming they would starve. The villagers decided there was nothing to do but to ask the Old Man to come back to help them.

The Headman went to the Old Man and told him about the village's troubles and how sorry they were they had asked him to leave. The Old Man listened carefully.

He said, "No!"

The girls were silent as Naomi passed out paper, paints, and clay. "Let's paint an image of *No* on the left side of the paper and write words that come to mind. While they were still writing, she said, "On the right side of the paper, paint an image of *Yes* and write words that come to mind."

When it was Juanita's turn to share her paintings and words, she covered her paper with her hands. "I don't want to show you what I did."

"What do you want?" asked Naomi.

"I wanna see Martina."

"You're not allowed in the hospital."

"I need to see her."

"You could take us," said Carolina. "They'll let you in."

Naomi tried to think of a plan, but it was Nilda who came up with an idea. "We could write her a story and make her pictures. Maybe they would let us read the story to her. We could tell the doctor it would make her feel better."

The unexpected look of gratitude on Juanita's face made Naomi realize how desperate she was to see Martina, especially when she politely asked, "Will you, Dr. Rosen? Will you talk to the doctor for us?"

There was nothing in Naomi's contract to prevent her from taking the girls on a field trip, and the hospital wasn't far away, but she had no prior authorization. She thought she could get away with it as long as she brought them back in good time but would the girls listen to her? Would Juanita behave?

Naomi was exhausted. First the visit from Pablo, then Beadle dying, and now Martina in intensive care . . .

"*Por favor*, Dr. Rosen." Juanita's tears left Naomi no choice.

"Okay, we'll write a story, the five of us, and then we'll make a cover. I have a folder in my car we can put it in. But I need you to promise there will be no scenes. If the hospital staff says no, we go without a fuss." She looked at each of them in turn, waiting for Juanita to respond.

"Martina needs me. They don't know what it's like, the two of us. She's gonna die if I don't see her."

"She might die even if you do see her," said Naomi, cursing herself as she said it.

"No, she won't. I know her. I'm all she got."

Not willing to argue, Naomi asked, "Who wants to start the story?"

"I do," said Juanita, glaring at the group. "Here's the first sentence: 'She had a big mouth, but she never learned to say no.'"

"She had a big heart," added Nilda, "but she hid it so no one could hurt her anymore." She stole a look at Juanita, who nodded.

"I think we should make it more like the stories Dr. Rosen's been telling us," said Carolina. "Like 'Once upon a time there was a princess who was so beautiful her mother couldn't stand to look at her, so when she was four she took her into a big forest and left her there.'"

"That's good," agreed Lupe, "but if she was so little, who took care of her? Maybe we could say that her mother was mean to her and jealous, so she told her daughter she was ugly and stupid."

"Yeah," said Juanita, showing more enthusiasm than Naomi had ever seen. "Maybe she ran into the forest because she felt so bad, but she didn't know how to live in the forest and she was hungry and tired and cold—"

Carolina interrupted. "A hunter found her and gave her some food and she was so grateful she—"

"Let him treat her like shit," said Juanita, "just because he fed her and gave her a place to stay."

"Martina's in the hospital. We need to have a happy ending," said Lupe.

"Maybe some animals find her and rescue her," suggested Nilda.

"Yeah, they eat the hunter and steal his guns so they can protect her," sneered Juanita. She stood up and walked to the window, tears pouring down her face.

Naomi walked over to her. "Would you like to forget about writing a story and just go?" Juanita nodded, unable to stop crying. Naomi gave her a tissue, which Juanita took without speaking. Naomi was surprised when, after patting her shoulder, Juanita briefly rested against Naomi before returning to the other girls, who were watching anxiously.

"I'm wondering if you would be willing for us to try visiting Martina now, and then write something for her before we meet next time. Or, if you write a poem or story and want her to have it sooner"—she hesitated, realizing this would mean giving out her home phone number—"give me a call and I'll arrange to pick it up and take it to her. What do you think is best?"

Nilda looked at Juanita's tears and said, "I think we should visit now and write after." The three nodded and stood up, ready to go.

"Thanks, guys," said Juanita, helping Nilda pick up papers that had fallen on the floor.

Naomi left a note for Mrs. Romero—she didn't ask for permission, not wanting to be told she couldn't drive the girls to the hospital.

Juanita sat in the front seat, quiet except to give directions. She hated and loved Martina with equal ferocity. With no one else was she herself. When the bruises first appeared, she had fought with Martina, begging her to leave José, but Martina's accusations that Juanita was jealous stopped her—until she saw Martina with a cast on her arm.

"Dr. Rosen, why did Martina stay with a man who beat her up?" asked Juanita.

"Good question. You know her better than I do, what do you think?"

"I asked her lotsa times and she always said she loved him. What kinda love is that?" Juanita wiped the tears that ran down her face. "If that fucker killed her—"

"Juanita, you have to promise me, no matter what happens, you will stay calm. He's not worth your spending one minute in jail. We have to use the law—to make sure he's arrested and stands trial."

"Who's gonna pay for it?"

"If he's charged, it's his problem."

"He better be arrested."

"Juanita!" Naomi's voice was sharp and anxious.

"I'll try. But I can't promise."

Naomi pulled to the curb, stopped the car, and waited, a grim expression on her face.

"Why you stopped?" asked Juanita. "We got three blocks to go."

"You tell me."

"You want me to lie?"

"No. I want you to promise me you won't get into a fight. You lead with your fists and you'll end up in prison or worse. Is that what you want?"

"I been takin' care of myself all my life. Nothin's changed."

"Oh yes it has. You have the law on your side."

"Where was the fuckin' law when my father—"

"Juanita, I can't change the past. But I think I can help now, if you'll let me."

"Shit." She turned away from Naomi. "Will you start the fuckin' car? Martina could be dyin' while we're crappin' around."

Naomi stared at Juanita's back, waiting, worrying that Juanita would open the door and run to the hospital, and if she wasn't allowed to see Martina, she'd turn her wrath on anyone who stood in her way.

Carolina touched the back of Juanita's neck. "*Por favo*r, Juana, *prométele*."

Juanita's rage was palpable. "Okay, but—"

"There can't be any buts," said Naomi. "Not for you or for Martina."

"Let's go." Juanita spit out the words. "I promise."

The nurse behind the desk raised her eyebrows as the four girls and Naomi walked toward them.

"We're friends and family of Martina Sanchez," said Naomi. "We'd like to see her."

"She's not allowed visitors."

Using her most professorial voice, Naomi hoped it would convey the authority she didn't feel. "ICU permits family visitors to see their loved ones for five minutes. We believe Martina's recovery depends upon her seeing us. I request permission for a visit. If you won't give it, I'll speak to the doctor in charge."

Naomi felt Juanita's tension and held her hand. "This is her sister and I'm her aunt, Dr. Rosen," lied Naomi, hoping to stare the nurse into submission. "I can assure you we will not disturb the patient. All we wish to do is enter her room and send her loving thoughts." Sensing the woman's hesitation, she added, "You're welcome to monitor our behavior."

"I assume you have proof of your relationship?"

"If you and I were sisters, could you prove it?" asked Naomi. Not wanting to start an adversarial relationship, she softened her tone. "Martina may not make it. We know this. Please, let us see her. We promise to be quiet and to leave immediately when you say it's time."

"You know we've had problems with visitors—"

"Surely you can tell we're not here to cause trouble." Naomi gave her what she hoped was a kind, caring, reassuring smile.

Naomi could feel Juanita's rage and knew she had to convince the nurse to let them see Martina. She gave the woman her most compassionate look. "Perhaps her sister, you, and I could stand at the foot of her bed for a few minutes. We'll do whatever we can to show you we have Martina's best interests at heart."

Naomi took one look at Juanita and realized that one way or another, Juanita was not going to leave without seeing Martina. The group huddled around Juanita, who seemed to welcome their connection. Naomi didn't know what she would do if the nurse refused to allow them into Martina's room.

Nilda, standing with Carolina and Lupe, behind Naomi and Juanita, spoke. "We're writing a story for our cousin, Martina, and then we're gonna paint pictures and make it into a book. Want to hear what we already wrote?" Lupe tried not to smile. Carolina hid her face in her hands. The silence felt like forever.

The nurse looked at the group, feeling Naomi's pressure, Juanita's desperation, the concern of the three girls. "All right. Two of you can visit, one at a time, but—"

"Thank you," said Naomi. "I'm sure you'll find that we're respecting all your rules and the needs of the patient." She turned to the three behind her. "Why don't you work on the story we started while Juanita and I visit." She put her arm around Juanita and said to the nurse, "We're ready."

The nurse led Naomi into Martina's room while Juanita paced outside it. Naomi stifled her impulse to scream when she saw Martina, connected to tubes, swathed in bandages. What was left of her face was unrecognizable. She stood next to Martina's bed, trying to send her strength and courage, to let her know that people cared about her.

"Martina," she whispered, "I'll do what I can to keep you safe. Please, find the energy to live. Please know we love you. Please know we miss you. Please . . ."

Unable to say any more, Naomi walked outside to tell Juanita that she could go in, but before Juanita could move, Naomi whispered, "It's bad. Worse than I imagined. Don't let Martina feel your anger. We'll find a way to use it. We can't let it use us."

Naomi hoped Juanita would hear the "us" and not feel so alone when she saw what José had done. Not for the first time, Naomi wondered how a man could hurt a woman he said he loved. What fueled a rage so great it killed?

Juanita steeled herself as she opened the door, yet Dr. Rosen's words did nothing to prepare her for the inert white mass of bandages and tubes that used to be Martina. She tried breathing the way Dr. Rosen showed her, but it didn't touch her rage and fear. How would she manage without Martina? She tried to tell herself that Martina was tough, that she would survive and live to testify against José, but at the moment this seemed impossible.

When the nurse told her it was time for her to leave, Juanita asked if she could kiss her sister's hand, the only part of her that seemed whole enough to bear the pressure of her lips. The nurse hesitated and then nodded. Juanita bent down, whispering, "I'm here, *Chica*. I'll come as often as they let me. *Te quiero mucho*."

Juanita lightly kissed Martina's hand and thought she saw her eyelid flicker. "*Te quiero mucho*," she repeated, kissing Martina's hand once more before she forced herself walk to the door.

Outside, she turned to the nurse and said, "Thank you for letting us see her. How often can we visit? Even if I only stand near her bed and give her a kiss when I leave, it makes me feel like we're helping her fight."

"She's not really allowed to have visitors," said the nurse, "but I think it would be all right if you come once in the morning and once in the afternoon. Her vital signs seem a bit stronger now, so you obviously did no harm."

Yeah, but did we do any good? "Thank you. I'll be back tomorrow morning," said Juanita, determined to do what she could to help Martina live.

Holding Juanita's hand, Naomi said to the nurse, "Thank you so much. We appreciate your help. Here's my card. Please call me anytime. I'll come as soon as I can."

"Rosen doesn't sound Hispanic."

"No, it was my husband's name. My maiden name is Sanchez, the same as Martina's," lied Naomi, hoping there was no way for the nurse to check.

In spite of her pain, Juanita maaged a bit of a smile.

The three girls were waiting for them, looking anxiously at Juanita.

"Here's the story we wrote for Martina," said Lupe. You can change whatever you want."

Juanita's face clouded as she took the three pieces of paper. She didn't want to say she thought Martina would never live long enough to hear it, much less read it herself.

"We need to get going," said Naomi. "I want us to be in the room before the end of the session."

"You gonna get in trouble for taking us here?" asked Carolina.

Naomi grinned. "Someone has to know, first."

"No problem then," said Lupe. "We can lie just as good as you."

Mrs. Romero knocked at the door, opened it, and found the room empty. Puzzled, she looked outside, just as the four girls were emerging from Dr. Rosen's car. She walked outside to meet them.

Juanita caught Mrs. Romero off guard. "Thank you so much for allowing Dr. Rosen to take us to see Martina. They let me and Dr. Rosen in while the others wrote a story for her. It isn't finished, but you can see what we have if you want. We're gonna make some paintings to go with it, and the nurse said she'd read it to Martina."

The three girls nodded in support, knowing much of what she said wasn't true, at least not yet.

"How is she?" asked Mrs. Romero.

"Bad," said Juanita. "Real bad. I don't think she's gonna make it."

"Maybe she'll surprise you."

Mrs. Romero turned to Naomi and said, "Come to my office when you're finished, and bring the story. I'd like to see it."

The girls watched the door close, waiting to speak until they heard her footsteps fade.

"What's gonna happen?" asked Juanita.

"The worst she can do is fire me."

"For what? Helpin' us see Martina?"

"Don't worry. No matter what happens, I'll keep working with you. If not here, we'll find a place. If that's okay with you, that is."

The girls nodded. Carolina and Lupe put their arms around Juanita and walked her to the classroom. Nilda put her hand in Carolina's, needing to be part of the group. Carolina held it.

19

Naomi walked to Mrs. Romero's office, so pleased the girls wanted to keep working with her that Mrs. Romero's stern look didn't bother her as much as it might have.

"Sit down, Dr. Rosen. We need to talk."

"If it's all the same, I'd prefer to stand," said Naomi, bracing herself for what was to come, already thinking about places where she could meet the girls.

"Martina's dead."

"What?"

Naomi slumped down into the chair.

"I got the call a few minutes ago. I'm worried about Juanita. You know how close they were."

"Who's going to tell her?"

"You. I've arranged for the girls to stay longer than usual. You can tell them their ride was delayed. They need to be told by someone they know cares about them."

"You care about them. Why don't you tell them?"

"They respect me, I think, I hope, but they like you."

Naomi blushed.

"I don't fool myself, Dr. Rosen, no matter how it makes me feel." Mrs. Romero looked away. "I was furious when I read your note, that you'd taken the girls to the hospital without my permission, but now I'm relieved. I don't know what Juanita would have done if she hadn't seen Martina."

Naomi thoughts whirled, too fast and too many to think clearly, but she managed to ask, "Does Juanita's caseworker know?"

"I've notified her, but, like most of them, she has too many clients and too little time. We need to do something to help Juanita now."

"What's her home situation like?"

"Bad." Naomi waited for her to say more. Mrs. Romero got up from her desk, went to her file cabinet, and pulled out a thick file. "This is Juanita's."

"I thought you said you didn't want me to read the girls' files."

"I know, but this is different. Juanita's in trouble. She needs to be with someone she knows cares about her. I realize that my request is more than irregular, but would you let Juanita stay with you for a few days, until she calms down? She seems to listen to you. There's no one else I can think of to ask."

Naomi felt torn and flattered. "I can't possibly be the only one."

"I know we can count on you."

"Who's the 'we'?" asked Naomi.

Mrs. Romero flushed.

After Beadle's death and her son's dismissal of her, Naomi needed to be wanted but in her heart, she also knew this was not the answer, despite anything anyone said. Not for Juanita. Not for her. She forced herself to be truthful. "I'm sorry, but I can't."

"How will you feel if she gets into more trouble?"

Naomi felt angry and guilty. Where was her social conscience now? No matter how she tried, she couldn't bring herself to say yes.

"The girls are waiting. I'd better go tell them." Naomi handed Mrs. Romero the story she had told the girls. "Funny, isn't it? Telling the girls a story about saying no, and then me having to say no to you?"

"Think about it. You could be saving her life."

As soon as Naomi walked into the room, she felt their tension. Nilda, wide eyed, was watching Juanita pace the room like a caged tiger. Carolina stared out the window. Lupe was doodling without looking at the paper. They crowded around her, plying her with questions about the delay of their pickup.

"Let's sit," said Naomi, wishing she knew a good way to tell them. "I don't know how else to tell you so I'll just say it straight. A few minutes after we left the hospital, Martina died."

Juanita howled in pain. The others stared in shock. Naomi gathered them into a group hug, hoping the contact would be comforting. She argued with herself about saying no to Mrs. Romero's request. Maybe if she were a better person, less selfish, she would say yes, but right now she was too tired. And what if her son called and said he wanted to see her?

The driver arrived, heard Juanita's howling, and returned to the van. Mrs. Romero carefully opened the door, watched, then, not knowing what else to do, retreated to her office. Naomi held Juanita until her howls turned to sobs and then to gasps, as if she couldn't breathe. "Juanita, we're here for you. Tell us how we can help."

Carolina and Lupe spoke to Juanita in Spanish. Tears streamed down Nilda's face, her hands gently patting Juanita's back. "I'll get a glass of water for you."

Naomi knew Juanita's grief could not be assuaged in days or weeks. What she hoped was that Juanita would get enough help so that she wouldn't hurt herself or anyone else. Naomi put her arm around Juanita and led her to a chair. "Where will you go when you leave here?"

"Don't know."

"Can you go home?"

"No."

"Is there someone we can call?"

"No."

Naomi felt her heart lurch.

"Who's gonna pay for the funeral? She's gotta have a funeral. Can't just bury her like she was a nobody." Without waiting for an answer, Juanita put her head on the armrest and sobbed.

Mrs. Romero stood in the doorway and beckoned Naomi to come to her. She spoke softly, trying not to let Juanita hear. "Please. Can't you let her stay with you until I find someplace where she'll have someone to take care of her? Her home situation is so chaotic, I'm afraid she'll . . ." She stopped mid-sentence, not wanting to think about what might happen.

Trying to ignore her sense of guilt and pain, Naomi shook her head no.

Naomi saw herself kissing her son for the last time as Shelly watched.

"How long will it take you to pack and leave?" Shelly asked.

"I don't know."

"Russ is buying you a used car. You need to be out of here tonight. We need to start giving Pablo the care he should be having. That you can't give him."

Naomi whispered, afraid Juanita might hear them talk. "Mrs. Romero, I want to help Juanita, you know that. But I can't do what you're asking me to do. I can't take Juanita home with me."

As they were talking, Juanita ran out of the room. The two women ran after her yelling, "Juanita, wait," but she paid no attention and kept running.

Naomi got in her car and drove until she caught up with her. Stopping the car, she screamed, "Juanita!"

"Leave me alone. You don't care about me. I heard what you said to Mrs. Romero. Once a week is enough for you."

"Please, get in the car so we can talk."

"There's nuthin' to talk about."

"Yes there is. Get in!"

Taken aback by the authority in Naomi's voice, Juanita obeyed, slumping against the car door.

Naomi took a deep breath. "I do care about you. What I said to Mrs. Romero has to do with me, not you."

"Yeah, right," muttered Juanita.

"If I tell you something, can it remain between us?"

Juanita mumbled, "I guess."

"Does that mean yes?"

Juanita nodded.

"When I was in my early twenties, I got pregnant. It wasn't possible for me to marry the father, and abortions were illegal. In the school system where I was teaching, pregnant women weren't allowed to teach, so I was fired. After the baby was born, when word got out that I was an unwed mother, no principal would hire me. I couldn't find a job and still look after the baby."

"What's this got to do with me?" Juanita had her hand on the door handle, ready to run.

Naomi wondered what she could say that would help Juanita understand why she couldn't let her stay with her without revealing what had happened. The girl's cold stare made Naomi realize that if she wanted to help Juanita, she had to tell her the truth. "I was renting a room from a couple, and the wife said she would take care of my baby while I worked. I didn't feel good about her offer, but I couldn't afford to hire anyone, so I finally said yes."

Naomi looked out the window, wondering how much more to say. Judging from Juanita's stony face, she'd have to say a lot more than she felt comfortable telling.

"Then what happened?" asked Juanita, taking her hand off the door handle.

"The woman couldn't have children. She and her husband wanted to adopt my child. She kept reminding me they could take better care of him than I could.

"I always said no, but one day he got sick. I had no money to take him to the doctor. The woman found out and said they were calling the authorities to file charges of parental neglect against me unless I immediately agreed to the adoption."

"Nice woman," sneered Juanita.

"She was desperate. I was exhausted."

"So you let her and her husband adopt him?"

"Yes."

"What's this got to do with me?"

"When Mrs. Romero asked to let you stay with me, all I could think of was, if it didn't work out, you'd leave, and I'd feel like a miserable failure all over again."

Juanita closed her eyes and leaned against the seat.

"Please, Juanita, I do care about you, and I'll do what I can to help you. It's just that right now it's not possible for me to have you stay with me."

Juanita opened her eyes and turned to Naomi. "If I tell you somethin', can it stay between us?"

"Of course."

"I think I know how you feel. I got pregnant when I was thirteen. My father beat the shit out of me and said he was gonna kill the boy so I ran away. A lady helped me find a place I could stay until the baby was born, but I had to promise to give it up. They wouldn't let me see it. Don't even know if it was a boy or girl."

Her eyes met Naomi's. "I think about that baby every day. I don't know what I'd do if I had to take care of another baby right now."

"Oh, Juanita." Naomi reached over and gave her a hug, trying unsuccessfully to find the wherewithal to tell Juanita she had changed her mind.

Juanita squirmed but allowed herself to be hugged.

"I guess we better be goin'. That driver's gonna be mad at me for keepin' him waitin'."

"I think Mrs. Romero will be so happy to see you, she'll take care of his grumps."

By the time Naomi arrived home, it was all she could do to fall into bed but once there, she was too tired to sleep. She kept replaying Juanita's despair and longing, wondering how Juanita was going to live without Martina. Disgusted with herself for not being able to agree to take Juanita home with her, she got up and made a cup of tea and toasted half a bagel. When sleep continued to evade her, she dressed and walked outside into the cool night air, wishing Beadle were alive to accompany her.

Despite the beauty of the moonlit night, she felt torn and guilty and bad. A few weeks ago she hadn't known Juanita and Martina existed, yet here she was, feeling a kind of responsibility for Juanita and a need to make Martina's life mean something despite the way it ended. And then there was her son. In the past, Naomi's thoughts about him had been limited to the first three years of his life, but now she kept seeing his adult image, replaying his words, feeling worse about herself than she had in years. As for her relationship with Paul . . . who knew where that was going, if anywhere.

She remembered the many times she'd considered suicide, when her heart was breaking and she could see no way out. Now she wondered if fatigue was a reasonable enough excuse.

She walked toward a grove of trees and stopped. At first, she wasn't sure what she was seeing, so she took a few slow steps, hardly daring to breathe. A doe was licking what looked like a newborn fawn as it nuzzled its mother's flank, their fur glistening in the moonlight. Naomi had never been so close to wild creatures before, and she stood transfixed with delight. It was only after they loped away that she dared to stretch her arms upward, stiff from holding herself so still. Filled with a quiet joy, she walked back to her house, watching dawn emerge from the night's darkness, feeling as if she had witnessed a miracle.

Three days later, after a frantic call from Juanita, Naomi was sitting on a park bench waiting for her. She was more than a little surprised when the whole group appeared.

Juanita howled out her words. "They arrested José and he told them I did it so the police came and got me. I was at the police station for five hours before they finally let me go."

"What? Why would you beat up Martina? Everyone knows how much you two loved each other."

"He says I did it 'cause I was jealous he was takin' her away from me."

"José is counting on you getting into trouble so he can say, 'See, I told you,' " said Naomi. "Please be careful, Juanita. Take up boxing if you have to . . ."

"I told the police about our writin' class and you takin' me to see Martina."

"Did you tell them about the bruises Martina had when she came to class and how she didn't want us to notice them or make any comments?"

"No, but I told them he broke her arm a few months ago and I made her go to the hospital and she told the nurse her boyfriend did it but it was an accident."

"Some accident."

Naomi gave Juanita a heavy plastic bag. "Here's the clay I bought for you. You'll have to throw it against something hard like a thick board until it's soft enough to use. You'll also have to keep it wet while you're working it. When you make anything you want to keep, let me know. A friend offered to fire it for you. If you're interested, she said she'd show you how to glaze it."

Naomi noticed the other girls looking at Juanita cradling the clay. "I didn't know all of you were coming, but if you like, I'll get you some clay as well."

"Could I have fingerpaints?" asked Nilda. Naomi was surprised at the strength of her voice. Where had the whispers gone? "I like to paint. It makes me feel good."

"Sure. I have paints in my car; I'll get them for you." Now that Nilda's voice was stronger, Naomi hoped that one day she would look less anxious.

"What about the two of you?" she asked Lupe and Carolina. They shrugged.

"I was hoping you'd tell us another story," said Carolina. "I been thinking about the old man who said no. Did he keep living by himself?"

"What do you think?" asked Naomi.

"Don't know," said Carolina. "You're the storyteller."

"We're all storytellers. What do you think he did?"

Lupe grinned. "He got himself a new life and never looked back."

Not to be outdone, Carolina added, "Yeah, and he sent postcards to the village telling them the next time they get help, they should know a good thing when they see it."

Naomi arrived early for Martina's funeral and was surprised to be told that a seat in front had been reserved for her. She hugged Juanita, a shadow of her former self—pale, thin, and exuding pain. Carolina, Lupe, and Nilda followed close behind, forming a protective flank around her.

When José's brother appeared, Juanita glared at him.

"What the fuck is he doin' here?" she muttered.

Naomi put her hand on Juanita's shoulder.

Carolina strode toward him. "Get outta here, you muthafucka."

When he paid no attention and kept walking toward an empty seat, two burly males escorted him out of the church.

"Sonofabitch," said Carolina. "Probly came to tell us it wasn't his brother's fault. Some people got shit for brains."

The closed casket, draped with flowers, was a stark reminder of Martina's violent death. As Naomi touched the plain wood casket, she was joined by Mrs. Romero, the psychologist, and the driver, who all mourned Martina's death.

"We need to do something to help girls like Martina," said Naomi to Mrs. Romero. "Her death has to matter. I can't bear the thought that her need for love was so great she was willing to endure whatever José did to her just because he said he loved her."

"Were you thinking about anything in particular?" asked Mrs. Romero.

"Sort of. Martina wanted to be a writer. Maybe we could establish a fund in her name to provide money for girls who want to write or do something in the arts. . . . What do you think?"

"It's an idea worth pursuing. Martina wasn't the easiest young woman to deal with, but if she'd had more of a chance, maybe she wouldn't have been so frustrated. Maybe she would have been able to say no to José. Maybe she'd still be alive." Mrs. Romero wiped tears that continued to roll down her cheeks.

Naomi winced with pain. Mrs. Romero patted her shoulder. When an usher showed Naomi to her front-row seat, Mrs. Romero said nothing as she was shown a seat in the back.

The priest, who'd baptized Martina, began the service by talking about Martina as a young child, full of joy and promise, hoping to be an author when she grew up. He urged the congregation to extend their hearts and hands to young people, to help them grow into caring, responsible adults.

Then, to Naomi's astonishment, he asked her to speak a few words. This time it was Juanita who patted Naomi's shoulder as she stood up to walk to the pulpit, wondering what she could say. Naomi saw the grins on the faces of Carolina, Lupe, and Nilda and knew they had planned this. Well, Carolina said she was a storyteller. If ever there was a time to tell a story, it was now.

As Naomi started walking up to the pulpit, she heard Juanita whisper, "Tell Panther and Hummingbird. Martina loved it."

Surprised, Naomi nodded, relieved to be able to do something for Juanita that would honor the life of Martina. As she told the story, feeling Hummingbird's willingness to act in spite of her fear, she felt a little better and ended with a brief comment. "Like Hummingbird, Martina knew there was more to life than being drab, that there were possibilities beyond her current knowing. Unlike Hummingbird, Martina was eaten by her panther. Today, we come together to celebrate the life of a young woman who yearned to be more than she was, who knew there was a better way to live life but didn't know how to find it. Let us fulfill Martina's dream by making choices that will help our dreams come true."

The service ended with music performed by a small group of musicians who had known Martina. Only the thought that her death might achieve some benefit to young women like Martina kept Naomi going through the burial and reception, hosted by Mrs. Romero and the psychologist when they realized no one from Martina's family was able to pay for one.

Outside, after the funeral, Naomi walked over to where Juanita was standing, alone. "Juanita—"

"Don't worry. I decided the muthafucker's not worth my time."

Naomi felt a bit reassured as she watched Lupe, Carolina, and Nilda catch up with Juanita, walking with her to where Mrs. Romero was waiting.

A few days later Naomi could feel something beginning to shift inside her. She resisted the idea that Martina's death had energized her, lifting her out of her sense of hopelessness and personal futility, yet she no longer feared the answering machine's blinking. When she saw that none of the messages was from Mr. Solana, she called him.

"What, if anything, have you heard from Pablo?"

"What would you like to know?"

"Right! I'm sorry I called." She hung up, feeling foolish. Might as well make one more call, she thought, dialing Paul at work. He at least seemed happy to hear from her.

"Want to take a walk after work?" she asked.

"Sure. Meet you at St. John's at five-thirty. How about dinner afterward?"

"Great. See you then." She was surprised by how happy she felt.

Juanita's call, asking her to meet at a coffee shop, was not a request Naomi could turn down. She was sitting in a booth to give them privacy when Juanita appeared. Naomi hardly recognized Juanita who seemed to keep shrinking.

"Thank you for comin'." Juanita's voice was a whisper of what it had been.

"How are you doing?" asked Naomi, not knowing what else to say.

"Fine," answered Juanita, sitting opposite Naomi.

"Liar."

"Takes one to know one," countered Juanita.

"So, liar to liar, what's going on?"

"I wish it had been me."

"I think I know the feeling."

"How could you?" barked Juanita.

She felt her anger surge. What did this old white woman know about pain? So she gave up a son, so what? What did she know about watching Martina disappear into a shadow of herself before she died? What did she know about not being able to save the life of the person Juanita loved most in the world? What did she know about feeling useless? Or worse?

Naomi saw Juanita's fury building and tried to diffuse it. "What's in the folder?"

"I found some of Martina's writin' when I was packin' up her stuff. Maybe you could read it when you have time."

Juanita couldn't bring herself to read it. Just looking at Martina's handwriting made her feel sick to her stomach. Losing her cousin was like losing her self. There was no one else who understood her. When she heard that José had been charged with murder, and that he hadn't been able to raise bail, she felt relieved. In spite of what she had told Dr. Rosen, she wasn't sure she could meet José on the street and let him keep walking. Just thinking about how her social worker was pressuring her to go to something called anger management class made her even more angry. She didn't want her anger managed. She wanted José dead and Martina alive. When Mrs. Romero asked Juanita if she'd help with the project to raise money for battered women, she'd said she would, but she didn't really care. Martina was dead. Nothing could change that. There was no way she could tell anyone that Martina was pregnant, that José had taken two lives.

Naomi wondered if it would help if she told Juanita a little about her experience. She decided it was worth taking the risk.

"Shall I tell you how I know?"

Startled, Juanita nodded.

Naomi hesitated before speaking, carefully choosing her words. "I think it's hard to look at someone who seems successful and imagine that they've ever been anything else, but how I look now isn't how I've always been."

Juanita asked, "So how did you used to look?"

Naomi forced herself to speak the words out loud. "I was once a battered woman, just like Martina, only I also had a child to protect."

"But you're smart. You got an education!"

"Education isn't everything. If you don't feel good about yourself, you tend to think everything is your fault, that you deserve to be punished. I told myself that if I tried hard enough to be good and kind, he would be nice to me. The problem was, I couldn't figure out how to do this."

"But you're a doctor."

"I didn't have a PhD then, but even so, a woman, no matter how well educated, has to have healthy self-esteem. She has to believe she deserves to be treated right. Even then, plenty of women realize they need to get out of a bad situation, but don't have the resources or a place to go. Some don't leave because they're too afraid."

"So how did you get out of it?" asked Juanita.

"Not easily and not quickly, I'm ashamed to say."

"You don't need to feel no shame 'round me."

"It's a feeling that never goes away. At least it doesn't for me."

"Is that why you been teachin' our class?"

"I wouldn't want anyone to go through what I did."

"Didn't help Martina."

"I am painfully aware of that."

"Do you think the thing Mrs. Romero is settin' up is gonna help?"

"I hope so. At least it's a possibility. Are you going to work with her?"

"Don't much feel like it."

"What do you feel like doing?"

"Nuthin.' "

Juanita stood up. "Thanks for comin' . . . . We havin' class this week?"

"As far as I know. I'm certainly planning to come."

Juanita nodded and walked away. Naomi wanted to call to her back, to stay and talk, but she didn't know how to break through Juanita's emotional wall. Suddenly Naomi felt too exhausted to move. She ordered a cup of coffee and a toasted bran muffin, hoping the comfort food would make her feel better. While she was waiting for her order, a voice intruded on her thoughts.

Juanita was standing next to the table. "Dr. Rosen?"

Naomi looked up. "Juanita!"

Juanita blushed. "I . . . I . . ."

"Would you like to join me? How about a sandwich?"

Juanita shrugged and shook her head. "Thanks, but I'm not hungry." She twisted the ring on her finger. "I just wanted to say . . . I know . . . I know you're tryin' to help me."

Before Naomi could respond, Juanita rushed away.

20

As soon as she got home, Naomi read Martina's work, stunned by the power of her yearning to live a different life. The first page hit her especially hard.

> I am so tired of feeling like shit. I want to be strong. I want to be treated nice. I want to be someone I can be proud of. I wish I could be the person I think I am deep down. I wish I could put what I feel into words. I wish I could paint what I see in my head. I wish I wish I wish. How do wishes come true?

Naomi tried not to think about what might have happened if Martina had found a way to talk about the abuse and ask for help, or if she had shown Naomi her writing. She was deep in thought when Priscilla, who did not take kindly to being ignored, called to complain about Naomi's silence.

To ward off the inevitable scolding, Naomi asked, "How's life? Is Pablo still there?"

"Where've you been? I've been calling and calling and calling. If you hadn't phoned today, I was going to call the hospital. Why didn't you answer my messages? Really, Naomi, you are so irresponsible at times. You could have just called to say you were okay and would get back to me when you had time."

Naomi listened without her customary defensive interruption, waiting until Priscilla finished.

"I didn't have the energy. Martina died from Jose's beating."

"Oh, Nomi . . ."

"Yeah, and that's just the beginning. My boss, Mrs. Romero, wants me to take in Martina's cousin Juanita, who's hanging on by a fingernail, as well as help her start a foundation for battered teenage women, and and and . . ."

"Come for dinner. We'll sit in the hot tub and drink a great bottle of wine I just bought. Pablo's still here and he'd love to see you."

"Thanks, I appreciate the offer, but I'm meeting Paul for a hike in a few minutes."

"Paul? You mean Ryerson? The guy who Beadle ran away from!"

"That's not exactly a fair description."

"Naomi!"

"Gotta go. I'll be late. Love you."

"Call me tomorrow! Love you too."

The parking lot at St. John's was full of people and dogs preparing to walk. Paul was waiting for her, a large brown dog by his side. He grinned as she approached.

"I hope you don't mind sharing my attention with Sadie. Couldn't bear to be without a dog, and she, it seems, couldn't bear to see me leave the shelter without her."

Paul saw Naomi looking approvingly at the collar that had the dog's name and Paul's name, telephone numbers, and address.

"I took your advice. Seems you can teach an old dog new tricks."

"She sure is well behaved. Why would anyone give up such a nice dog?"

"The wife had to put her husband in an assisted living facility, and she moved into an apartment nearby that didn't allow pets."

"Not even cats?" Paul shook his head. "That's so mean-spirited. All the research shows people do better when they have pets to hug."

"Do they do even better when they have people to hug?" he asked, moving close enough to hold Naomi's face in his hands.

Naomi felt the tingle up and down her body.

"I hope you'll have dinner with me at my house after our walk."

She nodded, uncomfortably aware of wanting more than dinner.

Even after years of living in New Mexico, the pink light bathing the mountains at dusk filled Naomi with awe. She walked ahead of Paul, who was training Sadie to stay by his side. When Naomi stopped to look at a small purple flower she had never seen before, Paul came up behind her and put his arms around her, pressing her tenderly to him. She felt his desire and wondered if he felt hers.

There are always levels and layers of wanting, she thought as they started walking again. No matter how lucky I am, how blessed I feel, despite this wondrous environment, enough money, good health, an amazing place to live, there's always something that's just out of reach—a battered woman who lives, a son who forgives . . .

Naomi knew she had spent most of her adult life trying not to want or feel, with little success. For a time, struggling to earn enough money to subsist and then working to get her PhD and succeed at the university took all her energy. Teaching and writing were so demanding that at night she was generally too tired to think or feel much beyond what was required by her job.

Now, no matter how busy she was, no matter how tired she felt, she could not stop her thoughts and feelings. It was as if the steel curtain she had created between her mind and body had become porous—the barriers, once so rigid, permeable. She knew only too well she could have been Martina, stuck in an abusive situation with no money and no safe place to go.

Looking back, she still wasn't sure what had finally given her the strength to take her infant son and run away from Jesse whose charming demeanor hid a murderous rage. She still didn't understand why she had chosen to go to a place where she had no job and no friends or family to help. Was this why it felt safe? Had she chosen differently, would she have been able to keep Pablo? This thought was too painful to think. She reminded herself that there was no point in looking back. There were no second chances. No changing your mind. No rewriting history.

Lost in thought, Naomi stopped paying attention to the path, slipped on pebbles, and fell. Sadie ran to her, licking her face. "Oh, no, dog. Not again." She laughed in spite of the pain.

This time Paul came to her and helped her sit up, smiling as Sadie hovered. "I don't know what it is about my dogs, but they certainly do love you."

"Shows what exquisite taste they have," she quipped, gently moving her foot. "I don't think anything's broken." At least not on my foot.

With Paul's help, she stood up and put a bit of weight on it. She ignored the pain. "I think I'm okay. Let's keep walking. I've been looking forward to the view from the top."

"How 'bout we wait for another day to see the view? It's not going anywhere."

Without waiting for her response, he put his arm around her, and they started walking down.

"You don't need to help me, I can walk," she protested.

"I like helping you. Are you going to deprive me of a chance to feel good?"

"What if helping you feel good makes me feel bad?"

"Then we have a problem, which I don't think we have. Look, I know you can walk as fast and as long as I can, or longer, so helping you doesn't mean anything other than I'm helping you. Next time it might be you helping me."

Naomi remembered what Paul had told her about being shut out of his girlfriend's life after her daughter was murdered. And, maybe, if she'd been able to ask for help when Pablo was an infant, she could have kept her son. What had kept her from asking for help? Why did she feel so utterly powerless and unbearably vulnerable when she allowed someone to help her?

"Amazing how something simple like asking for help can feel so dangerous and complicated," she said. Even saying it made her feel anxious.

"Maybe that's because we're taught that it's better to give than receive. But all giving and no receiving is like all talking and no listening. So, let me give you a little help, and then I promise to receive what you have to give."

His exaggeratedly lascivious leer made her laugh.

"I hope that's a promise," she teased.

"You better believe it," he said, taking her arm, helping her down the steep incline.

They were in no hurry. Sadie, freed from her leash, romped around them, chasing whatever moved, always coming back to check in. Naomi felt herself begin to relax, and hoped she could find the wherewithal to trust Paul enough to keep letting go.

She grimaced as she thought about her meeting with Stan at the conference. Their encounter had left such a bad taste in her mouth it would not dissolve no matter how often she brushed her teeth or rinsed her mouth with mouthwash.

Paul mistook the grimace for pain and tightened his hold on her. "Slow down, we're not in a rush. Dinner will wait. It's only a salad that needs to be assembled, and some goodies from the market."

Naomi admitted to herself that Paul's arm around her waist felt good. Then she thought about lying naked next to him and her anxiety level skyrocketed. She told herself over and over again: Paul is not Jesse. Paul is not Stan. Paul is Paul. Paul is Paul.

When they got back to the parking lot, Naomi tried to start her car, but her foot was too painful. "Paul, the clutch seems to be too much for me. Would you mind if I drove your truck and you drove my car? I can manage an automatic."

"Sure, but you'll have to put up with Sadie."

"That is my idea of not a problem."

Paul and Naomi exchanged keys. Paul rubbed Sadie's nose as he helped her hop into the back. "See you soon, girls."

Naomi shook her head, teasing. "You're treading on dangerous ground, my dear, calling me a girl. But, for the moment, you get a pass."

Paul's response was a wave and a grin.

"How about ice for your foot and a glass of wine for your spirits?" asked Paul after helping Naomi settle on the couch.

"Sounds like just what the doctor ordered," grinned Naomi.

"In that case, the doctor has a few other prescriptions," he said, putting a pillow under her knees and a plastic bag with ice cubes on her foot. He gently caressed the top of her foot.

"Maybe we should take one at a time," she said, in what she hoped was a joking tone of voice, trying to ignore the tension building up in her stomach.

"White or red?"

"White."

He handed her a glass of wine. "To you, to me, to Sadie, and to the memory of Beadle, who made this moment possible."

They drank in silence, thinking about the role Beadle had played in their lives.

Paul shivered, remembering how he had taken out his rage and anguish on Beadle, and yet the dog had continued to love him even as he remained wary of Paul's moods. The memory of the jealousy he felt when Beadle seemed to love Naomi more than him was strong enough to make him wish he could be sure that his anger was under control, that he would never, ever hurt anyone or anything again. Was he ready to love another woman, particularly one who gave him such mixed signals? When he thought about his initial responses to Naomi, which weren't exactly loving, caring, or kind, he could hardly blame her if she never wanted to see him again. He hoped Beadle's loving nature had worked itself into him and that what was happening was Beadle's legacy and gift. He found himself wishing this with a fervor that astonished him.

Sitting down next to Naomi, he adjusted the ice bag, tenderly stroking her swollen foot. She watched his hand move from her ankle to her knee and then, tentatively, to her thigh. She moved nearer to him, wanting the closeness, hoping he wouldn't speak, wanting their bodies to do all the talking.

Suddenly, Sadie jumped onto the couch, knocking off the ice bag. Paul cursed.

Naomi laughed.

Paul thought about pushing Sadie away, but memories of Beadle stopped him. Instead, he sat up.

Naomi hugged him.

He let himself be hugged.

"Paul, I have an idea," said Naomi, searching for the right words. "I like you. The more I know you, the better I like you, so I guess what I'm saying, and I can't believe I'm saying it, is that I'd like us to love each other before we go to bed." Embarrassed, she looked away from him.

Paul took her face in his hands and kissed her lips so softly he barely touched them. "You're a remarkable woman, Naomi. I treasure knowing you."

Naomi laughed again. "Treasure?"

"Treasure," he said, looking at her, smiling.

Sadie, who had moved to the end of the couch, watching them, suddenly decided she'd been ignored too long and nuzzled her way between Paul and Naomi, nosing Paul.

He laughed. "I think she's hungry."

"I think I am too," said Naomi.

"Well, then, let's eat."

After dinner, Paul insisted that Naomi lie on the couch while he cleaned up. When he went to ask if she wanted an after-dinner drink, he found her asleep. Not wanting to wake her, he put a blanket over her and a pillow under her head. Maybe she was right about wanting to wait. Maybe he needed time to get used to loving and being loved. What he knew was that right now he was happier than he had been in a very long time.

Paul awoke first and walked into his kitchen feeling joyful. He made coffee and brought two cups into the living room. Naomi woke, stretched like a contented cat, and smiled. "Am I dreaming or do I smell coffee?"

"This time, reality is better than any dream I could ever have." He handed her a cup and looked at her swollen ankle. "I think you'll need to stay off your foot for a few days. You're welcome to stay here." As if to underscore Paul's offer, Sadie rested her head on Naomi's lap. "But before you decide, let me make some breakfast. I don't know about you but I'm starved."

Naomi laughed. "Me too."

"Otherwise, how are you?"

"I'm fine, Paul. Finer than I've been in . . . who knows how long? What about you?"

Watching how she would react, he took the chance and said what he felt. "Ready to cook for my lady love. How about breakfast in couch?"

"Sounds delicious."

After breakfast, Paul realized he didn't want Naomi to leave. "Why not stay here for a few days. I've got leave time coming to me, so I can be back by two."

"I really can't. I'm in the middle of stuff that needs taking care of. But my ankle is still too sore to drive a shift. Do you have time before you go to work to drive my car to my house while I drive your truck?

Paul's disappointment was palpable. "Okay, but I'll have to call the office and make sure my first appointment isn't until ten."

Naomi recognized his look. "I'm not making up an excuse to leave. Being with you has been wonderful—is more than wonderful." He smiled ruefully. "If you can, come for supper. I should be able to put something together."

"Sounds great. I'll get some takeout so you don't have to bother."

"Are you asking or telling me?"

"Oops. Have I hit a nerve?" asked Paul.

"Yup, a big one," answered Naomi, trying to keep from showing how a small, kind offer triggered such a big response.

"Okay, I'll try again. How about me bringing some takeout for supper?"

"Thanks. Takeout would be lovely. I'll make a salad."

It felt weird to be driving Paul's truck while he followed her home, but his "see you tonight" kiss before he drove off left her hopeful and energized. She was still feeling the afterglow when Priscilla called, worried and upset.

"You spent the night with the guy who threatened to call the cops on you, whose dog ran away from him?"

"He's not like that. He owns his anger."

"Spare me the psychobabble. Come over and tell me what's going on."

"First of all, I hurt my ankle so I can't drive. Second, I'm always coming to your place. It's time for you to visit me."

"And third?" mocked Priscilla.

"Not that I need one, but third is I don't feel like dealing with Pablo. He's your friend, not mine."

"He'd like to be yours, but you don't give him a chance. You never even thanked him for helping you out with the dog owner," she snapped.

"I'm home. I'd like to see you," said Naomi, not wanting to start an argument. "Come anytime."

"What's going on? Sleeping with a guy who's threatened to hurt you doesn't make sense to me."

"Pris, you don't know what you're talking about. If you want to come and talk, I'll be happy to see you."

"And if not?"

Naomi suddenly wondered about her relationship with Priscilla. She had the uncomfortable feeling it had begun because she admired her and felt that if Priscilla liked her she must be worth knowing. Had the bargain been if you'll be my friend, I'll do whatever it takes to keep your friendship? When had she ever said no to Priscilla? Her discomfort grew. She needed to get off the phone. "I have to go. I've got a grant proposal to finish. See you soon, I hope."

It was as if doors she thought had been bolted shut were quietly opening, allowing her to look at what she had been avoiding since giving up her son. Trying to hide from herself had ended up compounding her loss. It seemed, in ways she couldn't fathom, having Paul know the worst about her, and still want to be with her, had given her a strength she didn't know she needed—a feeling of being centered that felt new and strange, almost as if stones, mute for eons, had found a way to speak.

Naomi felt a strong urge to write a letter to her son, yet she was unable to begin writing. Every decision she had to make was difficult. Should she write it by hand or type it? Plain paper, letterhead, or note card? Simple is best, she thought, sitting in front of her computer staring at the screen. She wrote and rewrote so many versions that it took most of the morning to compose the letter. Deciding how to sign it was just as difficult. She tried all the variations of "mother" she could think of, feeling uncomfortable with all of them. Disgusted with herself, she settled for simply signing her name, hoping this would not seem cold or unfeeling.

Dear Pablo,

I am guessing that our visit was difficult for you, as it was for me. I understand that my choice to allow you to be adopted may preclude further communication, but should you decide to contact me, I would welcome this.

I appreciate the courage and energy it took for you to find me.

Love,
Naomi

She had an equally difficult time writing the cover letter to Mr. Solana.

Dear Mr. Solana,

I hope you will forward the enclosed letter to my son. I am aware that my previous behavior toward you was neither welcoming nor helpful. I hope you will accept my apology.

I am cognizant of the effort you made on behalf of Pablo. I hope that whatever the result, he is more able to live life as he chooses.

I recognize that my choice to give him up for adoption, and the agreement I signed, while seeming to be in his best interest at the time, were made in the midst of great personal turmoil when I felt I had no other choice. If I could live this part of my life over, with the advantage of hindsight, I would not make the same choice. But, I cannot change the past. I accept full responsibility for the consequences of my action.

I thank you for your help.

Cordially,
Naomi Rosen

She hobbled out to the mailbox hoping the mail had not yet come. Having written the letters, she needed to send them as quickly as possible.

Back in the house, Naomi felt restless. She called Sam.

"How are you doing?" she asked.

"Working on amnesia. What about you?"

"Are you and Rebecca talking about divorce?"

"I filed the papers yesterday."

"How do you feel?"

"Crappy but lighter. I've done a lot of thinking about the whole mess, and I remember that you once told me about the bargain you sometimes made—you know, I'll do or be whatever you want as long as you love me? Well, now I recognize that that's what I did with Rebecca. Gave her all my power. So why am I surprised that she used it?"

"I guess we just couldn't believe someone would like or love us as we are," said Naomi, "but for me, I've decided it's a bad bargain and can only end badly."

"You sound different. What's happening?"

"I guess you could say I ran out of run," said Naomi.

"What does that mean?"

"For one thing, I'm having a problem with Priscilla and I don't know how to deal with it, and I can't just forget about it."

"Wow! I can't believe that. According to you, she's perfection itself."

"Sam!"

"So, I'm wrong. I'm just a guy. Forgive me."

"You're not just a guy, you're my oldest and dearest friend."

"What happened between you and Priscilla?"

"I'm not sure. It feels like she's more interested in being my judge than my friend, but maybe it's my imagination."

"Stop it. Every time you have a problem with someone, you either think it's your fault or your imagination. If you feel Priscilla isn't treating you right, she probably isn't."

"So what do I do about it?"

"I'm hardly the one to tell you what to do about a relationship problem, but I think you need to tell Priscilla how you feel. If she's really your friend, she'll listen. If she isn't, she won't. I'll tell you what you've told me so many times—not talking about how you feel isn't a solution."

"You're right, but it's a whole lot easier telling you to do this than doing it myself. I don't even know why I'm so scared."

"Maybe it's because you've never confronted her before. You said you ran out of run. I see this as a good thing. You're taking your power back." Sam paused and then said, "Talk to her and let me know how it goes. I wish we could talk longer, but I have a client waiting so I have to go. I'll call you in a few days. In the meantime, I'm sending courage to do whatever you need to do."

"I miss you, Sam. Talking on the phone isn't good enough. Why don't you come visit? A change of scenery might do you good, and it's been ages since we last saw each other. You'll love Santa Fe."

"Sounds good. I'll let you know if I can arrange it."

"I want to hear when, not if," said Naomi.

"Okay, 'when' it is. Gotta go. Love you."

"Same here. And Sam, you deserve better than Rebecca, so don't settle."

"I hear you. I hope you hear you."

Naomi hung up the phone, knowing Sam was right. She did need to talk to Priscilla. She also had to figure out why she was so afraid. Why couldn't she just tell Priscilla how she felt, calmly and quietly, describing rather than judging or blaming? Was she just worried that if she talked honestly about her feelings, afterward Priscilla wouldn't want to be her friend? Or was there something else?

Feeling like she'd hit a wall, Naomi sat down at her loom and started to unweave a portion she'd been weaving and unweaving for days. Nothing she tried pleased her. Her difficulty finding a satisfying weaving solution mirrored the discombobulation she felt when she thought about what she might say to Priscilla.

Naomi stood up, staring at what was left of what she'd woven. The muted earth tones seemed cowardly and boring, yet she was unable to decide what yarn might work. After looking at the myriad colors, textures, and thicknesses of yarns in baskets around her loom, she picked up a bright burgundy, thickly spun, with tails every few inches. Grimly, she began to weave, determined to move through the impasse. By the time she'd woven a few inches in one area of the weaving, she felt better, less tangled. Encouraged.

21

Naomi made herself a cup of tea and was about to go to her desk to try to get some work done when the phone rang. Picking it up, she was delighted to hear Daniel's voice.

"Hey, Cuz, how you doing? Long time no hear."

Naomi laughed. "Last time I looked, the phone lines ran in both directions. What's up?"

"Got the feeling I needed to call. Your voice sounds different. What's going on?"

"Too much for one conversation."

"Is that good or bad?"

"Like everything else, blessings and curses."

"Start with the blessings. You're overdue for good times."

Naomi told him about meeting Paul through Beadle and how their relationship had changed. Then, before he could comment, she told him about her work with the girls, Martina's death, and her connection with Juanita. She did not feel ready to mention her meeting with her son.

"Wow. You weren't kidding when you said blessings and curses. How are you doing with all of this?"

"It's hard to describe. If I weren't sixty-seven, I'd say I feel like a newborn chick that's cracked open the egg and is looking at the world for the first time."

"Given how you grew up, maybe part of you is a newborn chick. If so, the birth is long overdue. Enjoy! You deserve all the happiness you can find. I hope you and Paul stay together long enough for me to meet him."

"You think it's just a passing fancy?"

"Nomi, what's wrong?"

"I'm scared. I feel too vulnerable. And I think I just had a fight with Priscilla."

"That could be a good thing. The way you talk about her, she walks on water."

"I do not," she said, irritated that she sounded so defensive.

"Sorry, love, but you do. I never said anything before because you seemed so happy knowing her. Every time we talk, you compare yourself to her, and she's the most and you're the least."

Naomi gasped. "So what's new with you?"

Daniel chuckled. "Nomi, when it comes to changing the subject, you are the best. But if you don't want to talk about it, I'll tell you my news. You probably won't believe this, but Elizabeth and I have decided we want to be married."

"Really?" Naomi bit her tongue to keep from asking why.

"I know, I'm fifty-nine years old and we've been happy living in separate homes, so why rock the boat. Right?"

"You said it, not me," she laughed.

He laughed too, but then his tone changed. "I like coming home to her."

"Wow, that's different. You always said the best part of a relationship was being able to go home and unwind. What happened?"

"It's hard to describe, but it's like she doesn't take my space and she doesn't use up my air. When I was with Andrea, after a while I felt like I was being sucked dry, all giving and no getting. Elizabeth is easy to be with. We seem to know how to balance our separate lives and the one we share."

"Almost sounds too good to be true."

"I know, but it's not that we always agree. It's just that when we have a disagreement, we talk about it pretty reasonably. Like you, I'm allergic to people who deny, blame, judge, and attack."

"Tell me about the wedding."

"That's one of the reasons I called. We want you to be part of the ceremony."

"But Elizabeth doesn't know me."

"She feels she does since I talk about you a lot, and she thinks it's great that we're so close. She's an only child and has no living relatives except her son and daughter-in-law, and she's not close to them."

"How come?"

"They have different values. She drives a Honda Civic. They each have BMWs. She recycles everything; they don't even think about it. Her ex-husband drives a Mercedes and uses a Hummer to travel to his cabin."

"Her son and daughter-in-law will come to the wedding, won't they?"

"I hope so, but she says, 'Don't count on it until they're there.'"

"That's awful."

"You never had a child, so you wouldn't know, but watching a child you love grow up to be someone you don't know is unbelievably painful."

Naomi recoiled. Part of her felt like telling him the truth but the habit of silence was too strong. Even though Paul knew, and she trusted Daniel to be kind, she still couldn't find the wherewithal to talk about giving up her son for adoption. What was the point of telling him?

"Nomi, are you there?"

"I'm happy for you, Daniel. I look forward to meeting Elizabeth."

"I'm so glad you're coming. If you were a man I'd ask you to be my best man."

"I accept. You're not going to let a little thing like gender stop you, are you?"

Daniel laughed so hard he could hardly get the words out. "Nomi, you are absolutely the best!"

She hung up, feeling energized by Daniel's caring, acutely aware of how much he didn't know about her. But then he was much younger, barely in his teens when she'd felt forced to allow Russ and Shelly to adopt her son. Her closeness with Daniel as an adult began a few years after the adoption, when she was visiting his mother—her aunt Lillian— helping to prepare for the party her aunt was giving for a famous artist living nearby. Not the best of cooks, her aunt was having the affair catered but still felt the need to prepare snacks in case the caterers were late.

Daniel, his brother Cody, and Naomi had been raking leaves, cleaning up the garden. When the pile was hip high, Naomi couldn't resist diving into it, scooping up handfuls and throwing them at her cousins. They retaliated, and soon the three were rolling around in the leaves, pushing armfuls at whoever was closest.

Their laughter came to an abrupt halt when they heard Lillian yell, "Whore!" The two brothers looked at Naomi. Their mother's voice boomed again, "Whore!"

Like a deflated balloon, the three shook off the leaves and quietly stuffed them into bags. Only after raking up the remaining leaves was Cody, four years older than Daniel, able to speak. "I'm sorry, Nomi. She's such a bitch."

Naomi ran out of the garden and onto the road, running until the pain in her side forced her to stop. Daniel found her sitting by the side of a stream, numb. He got out of his car and sat down beside her. "Cody told her she was an ungrateful asshole, and she smacked him. He was so mad he smacked her back. I didn't know my mother knew so many curse words."

Naomi sat, unable to stop hearing "whore."

"What she'll expect you to do is play her game. Go back, change your clothes, smile, and pretend nothing happened." Naomi looked at him uncomprehendingly. "I'm telling you, that's the way she is. When she sees you all dressed, she'll probably say, 'You look lovely, darling.' C'mon, get in the car." He gave her a hug and said, "You'll see, she'll be so nice you'll think you imagined what happened."

Swallowing her misery, Naomi did as he suggested, not even cringing when her aunt introduced her as "my darling niece." All evening Naomi emptied ashtrays, served trays of delicate tidbits, replenished wineglasses, smiled, and numbly accepted compliments.

After the last guest had left, Naomi started to go downstairs to the bedroom Daniel had vacated so she could have her own room.

"Where are you going?" hissed her aunt.

"Downstairs. I'm tired."

"Just make sure you don't fuck my sons. You can't fool me. I see the way you look at them."

Holding onto the banister so she wouldn't fall, Naomi just about made it to the bathroom. When the retching stopped, Daniel and Cody knocked on the door and then pushed it open. Naomi, her face deadly white, was leaning against the toilet bowl. Daniel poured cold water on a washcloth and gave it to her.

"Wash your face, you'll feel better."

"Why didn't you tell the bitch to go fuck herself?" asked Cody.

"What's the use? I'm supposed to leave on the two o'clock train tomorrow but I want to leave before she gets up. Can you drive me to the station? The earlier the better. I don't care how long I have to wait for a train."

Shortly afterward, her aunt had sent her an expensive blouse from a Fifth Avenue boutique. Naomi threw it in the garbage, then thought better of it, fished it out, and cleaned it up. She gave it to her next-door neighbor, a struggling actress, who couldn't imagine being given such an expensive gift, especially for no reason.

The next time she saw her aunt, at Cody's wedding, her aunt had acted as if Naomi was the dearest person in the world. Naomi had struggled to keep from feeling as if her aunt's actions had been a figment of her imagination. She decided that what turned a bad action into evil was the denial and coverup of the original act.

After Daniel's phone call, Naomi felt exhausted and thought she'd lie down for a few minutes. Three hours later the doorbell woke her up. Hobbling to the door, she couldn't hide her surprise when Priscilla and Pablo walked in.

"Hi! We're here to rescue you from whatever's ailing you. Pablo made a dinner reservation for us, so we need to get going."

"Thanks, but I already have dinner plans."

Priscilla's mouth tightened. "With whom?"

The smell of barbecue announced Paul's arrival.

"Who are you?" asked Priscilla as Paul walked toward them.

"This is Paul. He's bringing dinner, "said Naomi, hobbling to meet Paul.

Paul stopped walking when he recognized Pablo as the man who'd passed himself off as Naomi's fiancé. He wondered who the woman was. The last thing he wanted was trouble. When Pablo was about a foot away, Paul said to him, "I've got more food in the truck. Would you take this into the kitchen?"

"Why don't you take your food where it's wanted," retorted Pablo.

Naomi limped between the two men. "Pablo! Paul's my guest. He was kind enough to bring dinner." She took the food from Paul and whispered, "Please, don't leave. I want you to stay no matter what."

Paul nodded, grim faced, hoping he could control his rapidly rising temper. Who the fuck were these people anyway, he wondered as he walked back to his truck to get the rest of the packages. He tried to practice the breathing that his therapist had shown him, but the urge to knock the proprietary expression off Pablo's face grew stronger every minute.

"Priscilla, why don't you and Pablo go inside," said Naomi, wanting to reassure Paul. "There's a bottle of wine on the counter that needs to be opened."

"It's clear we're interrupting. We'd better go," said Priscilla.

"Who says?" asked Naomi.

"Paul wasn't expecting us, and it seems you weren't either."

Naomi exploded. "Priscilla! How long have we known each other? How many times have I come to your house for dinner? When have you ever told me I was interrupting, even when I arrived without an invitation?"

Naomi told herself to cool it, with no success. "You call yourself my friend. Yet the minute you can't control what's happening, you run off in a huff with your current bedwarmer and feel virtuous because you haven't interrupted. That's not my idea of friendship. If you want to be my friend, get your ass inside and join us for dinner."

"How do you know there's enough?" asked Priscilla, shocked by Naomi's outburst. "We weren't invited."

"There's enough," said Paul, standing behind Naomi, trying to quiet himself.

Sensing Priscilla's wavering, Naomi changed her tone of voice. "I really hope you and Pablo will stay for dinner."

"We have a dinner reservation, Priscilla," said Pablo. "We need to go."

Naomi looked at Priscilla. *Whose friend are you?* Priscilla could not meet Naomi's gaze, and started to walk toward her car.

"Priscilla, wait!"

Paul saw the self-righteous look on Pablo's face, and his anger rose so quickly his fists clenched. He knew that if he hit Pablo, Naomi would not give him a second chance. Silently he repeated the instructions he had memorized: If you get into a situation where you feel your anger is about to get out of control, leave immediately. Do not act on your feelings.

"Naomi, why don't I go since I seem to be the cause of the problem? There's plenty of food. I'll call you tomorrow and see how you're doing."

Without waiting for her to agree, he thrust the rest of the food into her arms and turned to walk toward his truck.

Naomi hobbled after him as fast as she could. "Paul, wait. Don't leave."

He stopped, knowing she couldn't run.

"It seems I'm learning, rather painfully, who's a friend and who isn't," said Naomi. "If they don't want to stay, that's their decision, but please don't leave because of them. I want you to stay."

"I'm not leaving because of them. I'm leaving because I don't want to lose control and do something I'll be sorry for. Seems to be the sensible thing to do."

"Anger management?"

"An attempt to manage my anger."

"I don't want you to do something you'll be sorry for, but . . . but, please, stay. Pablo and Priscilla can stay or go. Why should we suffer?"

Paul heard the "we" and felt something inside him release. She wanted him. She wanted him to stay. Unable to stop himself, he put his arms around her and held her, brushing her hair with his face. "Thank you. You have no idea how much your saying 'we' means to me."

"Let's go inside. The food's getting cold."

"How's your foot?"

"It hurts. I think I twisted it again."

Paul took the food from her and helped her into the house. They found Priscilla checking the temperature of the oven while eating stuffed grape leaves. Pablo was nowhere to be seen.

"Tastes good," said Priscilla. "Where shall I set the table?"

Naomi limped over to Priscilla. "Where's Pablo?"

"He decided to eat at the restaurant. I asked him to pick me up in a couple of hours. But if he doesn't, can I borrow your car?"

Naomi nodded.

"I'll be happy to give you a ride when you want to leave," said Paul.

Priscilla forced herself to speak. "Thank you."

There was an awkward silence while Naomi put the food in the oven. She looked at Priscilla, who was glaring at Paul, and said, "I'll open the wine. When the food's ready, I'll put it on the counter. We can eat buffet style." She poured them each a glass.

Paul offered a toast. "To friends."

Priscilla's questions came out with the force of carbonated water released from a warm bottle. "So, how did the two of you go from being mortal enemies to friends or lovers or whatever you are?"

"We discovered Beadle couldn't choose between us," said Naomi, "so we figured out a way to share him. He died on my watch. Paul was kind enough not to blame me."

"Why should he blame you after the dog kept running away from him?"

Paul tried to defuse his rage. "Priscilla, if you have a problem with me, talk to me. I'm here, in this room."

"If you don't mind, I was talking to Naomi."

"I do mind. You were talking about me."

"You are not my friend."

"No, but I'm not your enemy either."

"That remains to be seen."

"My stomach is hurting." Naomi limped out of the kitchen.

"Hey, you haven't eaten anything," said Paul.

"I lost my appetite."

"Can't face the music?" mocked Priscilla, following Naomi into the living room.

Naomi turned around, glaring at Priscilla. "I don't know who died and left you judge, but I am not accountable to you. Besides, you're a fine one to talk about running." Naomi remembered hearing about Priscilla leaving a fellow researcher in the jungle when there was room for only one in the boat. "What about Chico?"

Priscilla shrieked. "Naomi! You have no right—"

"No? Well neither do you."

"I think I should leave," said Paul, not wanting to witness their private argument.

"Good idea," agreed Priscilla.

"No, don't go, Paul. You're my guest. I invited you."

"I thought you invited me," mocked Priscilla.

"I invited both of you. And I invite both of you to listen to Bach and drink a glass of wine in peace."

"Are you sure?" asked Paul, trying not to show how much he wanted to stay. "I'd understand if you said it was better for you that I leave."

"Easier? Maybe. Better? Definitely not." She filled his glass and hers and turned to Priscilla. "Shall I fill yours?"

While waiting for her answer, Naomi looked Priscilla in the eye, feeling a spasm of fear, afraid she was going to lose the woman who had been her friend for so many years. Yet something in their friendship had always been missing if she'd never trusted Priscilla enough to tell her about having a son.

"Well?" asked Naomi, realizing that she was no longer willing to do whatever she had to do to keep their friendship. If Priscilla wanted to leave, Naomi decided she would have to let her go.

The silence was palpable.

"I think I'll take a walk," said Paul. "See you in a little while."

He took his wineglass and left. Neither woman made an effort to stop him.

Priscilla stared at Naomi, wondering what had happened to the woman who had always followed her lead. She felt like leaving, yet their years of friendship were undeniably important to her, necessary even. Pablo was a passing fancy and she knew it, just like all the other men she had known after her husband died. Maybe Naomi was right. Maybe it was time to renegotiate their friendship, even though Priscilla would have preferred to do it on her own terms, without Paul around. Apparently this was not her choice to make. She realized she felt jealous—something she would never admit to Naomi. Was Paul more important to Naomi than she was? Didn't Naomi value their friendship? Priscilla did not like what was happening. Not to her. Not to them.

A thought occurred to Priscilla that made her knees buckle. Could she have been the one keeping Naomi at arms' length? Had she been the one to control the parameters of their friendship? She'd never told Naomi about growing up motherless, about serving as wife and mother to her father and brothers, about her determination to keep control of her life no matter what. The word control kept haunting her. Paul's presence in Naomi's life was opening up events that Priscilla didn't want to look at, that she thought were finished simply by being in her past. Priscilla felt weak in the knees and leaned against the wall, sensing Naomi's eyes on her, unable to stop the rush of emotions threatening to undermine her. Talking honestly about her feelings meant breaking a very old habit. Priscilla wasn't sure she could do it. Still, the alternative was worse.

Taking a deep breath, Priscilla handed her glass to Naomi. "Fill 'er up."

Naomi's hug felt unaccountably good.

"What do you see in Paul?" asked Priscilla, trying to hide her jealousy.

"Paul's been a friend in need," said Naomi.

"And I haven't?" asked Priscilla, unable to stop the edge in her voice.

"What does my friendship with Paul have to do with ours?"

"I don't know. It feels like there's been a change in you—since he's come into your life, you don't have time for me anymore." Priscilla could not believe she had given voice to her fears.

Naomi started to deny the charge, then reconsidered. "Maybe our friendship was based on an old pattern that wasn't so healthy, at least for me."

The look on Priscilla's face frightened Naomi. Had she said too much?

Naomi thought she would explode if she didn't move so she motioned for Priscilla to follow her into the kitchen.

"Paul?" Naomi looked around and called again. "Paul?" She peered out the window and saw his truck. Her body relaxed. Once again he had kept his word.

"You think he got tired of waiting?" asked Priscilla.

"No, I think he's giving us space to talk."

"Sensitive soul, isn't he?"

Naomi stared at Priscilla. "Are you jealous of Paul?"

Priscilla did not hesitate. "No, of course not."

"I think you are."

"Think what you like. I know what I feel."

"Tell me."

There was no way Priscilla could admit to feeling jealous, so she attacked. "Ever since I met you, you've been running away from something. Now you're running to Paul. But as soon as he wants to go beneath the surface, you'll be off again. I hold you accountable, so you run from me. That's what you always do."

Naomi realized that even if she had been inclined to run, there would be no place to run to, much less hide. Paul knew the worst and still wanted to know her.

"What you're saying makes me feel you'd rather be my judge than my friend. Are you my friend?"

Priscilla stared at her. Her anger was so great she couldn't speak.

Naomi felt herself slipping into a familiar numbness and fought the urge to act on the old bargain: I'll do anything you want as long as you'll be my friend.

She knew she had to say something, but fear kept her silent.

Paul looked in the window and saw the two women staring at each other. He thought to himself, they need more time to talk. Knowing that Naomi wanted him to stay made all the difference in how he felt about leaving. Now he was choosing to go, in his own time, for his own reasons. She hadn't said he wasn't wanted. He wasn't being kicked out.

As he walked into the house, he was startled to realize that when he was with Naomi, he felt known for the first time in his adult life, and it was a good feeling. Entering the kitchen, where the silence was so thick and the two women looked so unhappy, he felt like taking them both in his arms and comforting them.

Instead, he said, "I'm going to take off."

Naomi searched his face. "Are you sure? You're welcome to stay."

"Thanks, but I think you two need time alone. I'll call you in the morning."

He turned to Priscilla. "If you need a ride, give me a call. I'll be glad to drive you home."

Paul gave Naomi a warm hug. She whispered in his ear. He grinned. Then he waved good-bye to Priscilla and left.

Naomi waited for Priscilla to say something, growing increasingly more tense. "I need to sit down." She walked into the living room without waiting to see if Priscilla followed.

Standing in the doorway, Priscilla watched Naomi limp into the living room. She was unable to speak—too many words were colliding. Still, Priscilla couldn't help recognize how much she'd grown to be like her father, always having to be in control, always determining the roles people played in her life. She flashed on the memory of a time when she'd been denied a huge grant that had been given to a man much less qualified than she was, and how Naomi, irate at the injustice done to her friend, had drafted the letter to the board, doing what she could to give Priscilla the energy to fight for what should have been hers, calling, offering to come and see her. She recalled other times when Naomi's support had made the difference between her giving up and going on. They'd never closed the door on each other, no matter what.

Priscilla walked into the living room and looked at Naomi as if seeing her for the first time. "Nomi," she said slowly, each word a new experience, a break with habit, "I think we both have a lot we need to talk about."

"I'm willing to try," said Naomi, hesitating. "Are you?"

"It won't be easy," admitted Priscilla.

"So much has happened in the last few days—I can't take it in. Seems like the past caught up to me and smacked me in the face."

"Will you tell me about it?" asked Priscilla, afraid the answer would be no.

"Only if the talking goes both ways," said Naomi.

"It will. I promise," responded Priscilla, feeling strangely relieved.

Naomi mused, "Maybe it's good that Paul left so we can talk. I don't like what seems to be happening between us. Are you my friend?"

"What a crazy thing to ask."

"Maybe. Maybe not."

"It's not that I don't want to be your friend, I do . . ." She sat down next to Naomi and slowly sipped her wine, needing time to find the right words. "Sometimes I have the sense that the me you see isn't really me. I know you think my life is great—my work is going well and I have no problem meeting interesting men—but I'm beginning to realize that I'm in danger of turning into the same kind of person as my father."

"What do you mean? What does that have to do with our friendship?"

"After Ma died, Pa was like a different man. Had to be in control, kept us kids at a distance. No hugs. No closeness. I guess he never got over her death. I know I didn't. I was angry at her for dying and angry at

Pa for becoming so cold and remote. It's odd that you should say I seem to be your judge, not your friend, because that's the way I felt about Pa. I guess he and I both closed down emotionally."

"I think I know something about how you felt."

"You do? How could you?"

Naomi stared at Priscilla. Could she tell Priscilla what happened? She decided to take the chance. "After the Spanish authorities deported me, I came back to the States and discovered I was pregnant. I lost my teaching job, and after that, no matter what I tried, I couldn't support my son. When he was three, I was bullied into giving him up for adoption. Had to sign an agreement saying I'd never see him again."

"Oh, Nomi."

"His lawyer found me. He brought my son, Pablo, to my house."

"Pablo?"

Naomi looked away.

"And you hadn't seen him since he was three?"

The kindness in Priscilla's voice encouraged Naomi. "No. In a way, I think part of me died the day I said good-bye to him."

"What was it like, seeing him again?"

"Horrible. He was very angry. I don't know what he wanted or why he came. It got so bad I thought I was going to collapse."

"Oh, Nomi, I'm so sorry. I wish I'd known about your son."

"And I wish I'd known about your mother."

"Why has it taken us so long to really talk to each other?" asked Priscilla.

"I don't know. Maybe the hurting places inside us took up so much space there wasn't room to let anyone in."

Naomi's hand shook as Priscilla poured each of them another glass of wine.

"Well, that's definitely changing," said Priscilla. I propose a toast—to our friendship."

"To us. To healing old wounds so we can make new lives," added Naomi.

It was as if a tightly coiled bud inside her began to open, despite not knowing whether her son would contact her again, or how the battered women's program would go, or if she could help Juanita move beyond violence as her habitual way of dealing with the world. Naomi certainly didn't know what would happen between her and Paul. What Naomi did know was that she felt stronger and clearer, more ready to deal with whatever life presented.

Priscilla stood up and reached out for Naomi, helping her to stand up. She put her arm around Naomi's waist. Slowly, the two women walked outside.

Awed by the brilliance of the night sky, and the relief of sharing what she had worked so hard to keep secret, Naomi leaned against Priscilla.

For the first time in forty years Naomi allowed herself to cry.

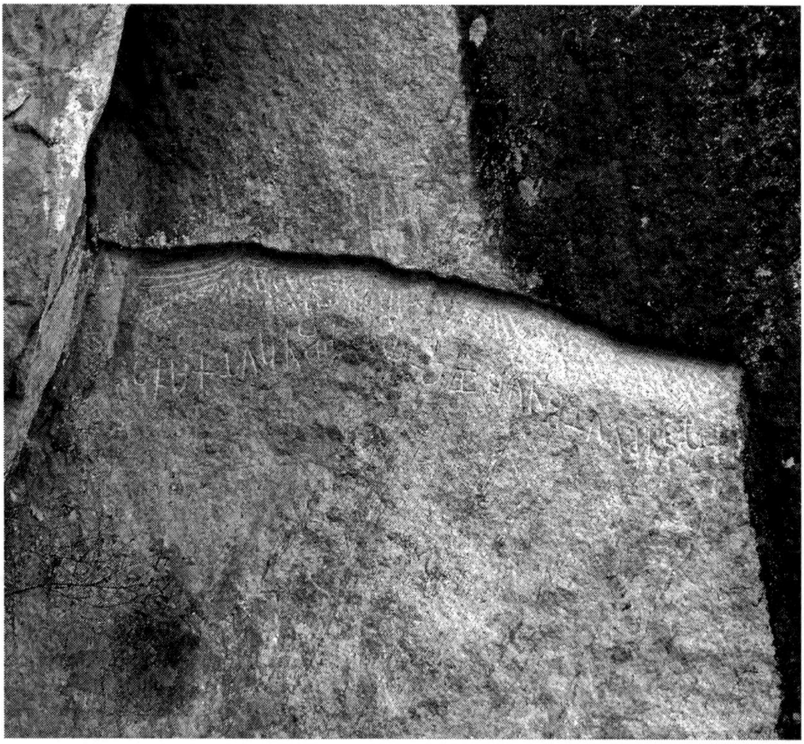

ACKNOWLEDGMENTS

I wish to thank Andrew Adelman and Suzan Hall for their editing expertise, stimulating conversation, and emotional support as I worked through difficult issues.

I am grateful to Barbara Roth for her caring and careful copyediting.

I am blessed to have friends like Claudia Reder, Diana Wolff, Vinette Davies, and Anita Grunbaum, who are willing to read drafts and offer suggestions that help me find and hone my voice.